FORCE OF FIRE

TOUJOURS A VOUS

Praise for Ali Vali

Beauty and the Boss

"The story gripped me from the first page, both the relationship between the two main characters, as well as the drama of the issues that threaten to bring down the business…Vali's writing style is lovely—it's clean, sharp, no wasted words, and it flows beautifully as a result. Highly recommended!"
—*Rainbow Book Reviews*

Balance of Forces: Toujours Ici

"A stunning addition to the vampire legend, *Balance of Forces: Toujour Ici* is one that stands apart from the rest."
—*Bibliophilic Book Blog*

Calling the Dead

"So many writers set stories in New Orleans, but Ali Vali's mystery novels have the authenticity that only a real Big Easy resident could bring…makes for a classic lesbian murder yarn."
—*Curve Magazine*

Blue Skies

"Vali is skilled at building sexual tension, and the sex in this novel flies as high as Berkley's jets. Look for this fast-paced read."—*Just About Write*

Carly's Sound

"Vali paints vivid pictures with her words…*Carly's Sound* is a great romance, with some wonderfully hot sex."—*Midwest Book Review*

"It's no surprise that passion is indeed possible a second time around."—*Q Syndicate*

Acclaim for the Casey Cain Saga

The Devil Inside

"Vali's fluid writing style quickly puts the reader at ease, which makes the story and its characters equally easy to get to know and care about. When you find yourself talking out loud to the characters in a book, you know the work is polished and professional, as well as entertaining."—*Family and Friends Magazine*

"Not only is *The Devil Inside* a ripping mystery, it's also an intimate character study."—*L-Word Literature*

"*The Devil Inside* is the first of what promises to be a very exciting series…While telling an exciting story that grips the reader, Vali has also fully fleshed out her heroes and villains. *The Devil Inside* is that rarity: a fascinating crime novel which includes a tender love story and leaves the reader with a cliffhanger ending."—*MegaScene*

The Devil Unleashed

"Fast-paced action scenes, intriguing character revelations, and a refreshing approach to the romance thriller genre all make for an enjoyable reading experience in the Big Easy…*The Devil Unleashed* is an engrossing reading experience."—*Midwest Book Review*

Deal with the Devil

"Ali Vali has given her fans another thick, rich thriller…*Deal With the Devil* has wonderful love stories, great sex, and an ample supply of humor. It is an exciting, page-turning read that leaves her readers eagerly awaiting the next book in the series."—*Just About Write*

The Devil Be Damned

"Ali Vali excels at creating strong, romantic characters along with her fast-paced, sophisticated plots. Her setting, New Orleans, provides just the right blend of immigrants from Mexico, South America, and Cuba, along with a city steeped in traditions."—*Just About Write*

By the Author

Carly's Sound

Second Season

Calling the Dead

Blue Skies

Love Match

The Dragon Tree Legacy

The Romance Vote

Girls with Guns

Beneath the Waves

Beauty and the Boss

Forces Series

Balance of Forces: Toujours Ici

Battle of Forces: Sera Toujours

Force of Fire: Toujours a Vous

The Cain Casey Saga

The Devil Inside

The Devil Unleashed

Deal with the Devil

The Devil Be Damned

The Devil's Orchard

The Devil's Due

Heart of the Devil

Visit us at www.boldstrokesbooks.com

FORCE OF FIRE
TOUJOURS A VOUS

by
Ali Vali

2018

FORCE OF FIRE: TOUJOURS A VOUS

ISBN 13: 978-1-63555-047-4

This Trade Paperback Original Is Published By
Bold Strokes Books, Inc.
P.O. Box 249
Valley Falls, NY 12185

First Edition: July 2018

CREDITS
EDITOR: SHELLEY THRASHER
PRODUCTION DESIGN: STACIA SEAMAN
COVER DESIGN BY SHERI (HINDSIGHTGRAPHICS@GMAIL.COM)

Acknowledgments

It's always nice when writing a book is like revisiting old friends—old friends who have interesting friends of their own, like vampires and werewolves. Thank you to Radclyffe for your support, for the opportunity to let my imagination run rampant, and for the opportunity to be a part of the BSB family. Thank you as well to Sandy Lowe for all you do to make every project a success, and for answering all those questions.

Thank you to my editor, Shelley Thrasher, as we complete our twenty-first book. Every book starts as a solitary exercise, but I appreciate the input and dedication of my beta readers Kim Rieff, Cris Perez-Soria, and VK Powell. You guys were great.

Thank you to each and every reader. You're the best part of this whole process, and meeting you along the way certainly gives me the encouragement I need to keep writing. Every word is written with you in mind.

Curiosity and imagination are things every writer needs to create worlds in which characters like vampires exist, but I think they're important tools in life was well. They're the two things I hope my great-niece inherits from our family along with the curly hair and mischievous streak. Your grandfather certainly possessed plenty of both, along with that very wide mischievous streak. Fly high, my girl, and never stop asking the why of everything.

And to C, thank you for the fun times. *Verdad!*

For Olivia
Always dream big, and above all else, be happy

For C

CHAPTER ONE

"Ah...damn," Piper Marmande said as she squeezed her partner Kendal Richoux's hand. She'd been in labor for a couple of hours, and while she wasn't tired, she was in pain.

"A couple more big pushes, my lady, and you should be done," the Genesis Clan's healer said as she smiled up at her.

"That's what you said about a half an hour and fifteen pushes ago, so your assessment doesn't mean—"

"It's not wrong this time." Kendal interrupted her before her pain overtook her mouth and senses. "You're doing great, my love, so just a couple more."

"Don't try to sweet-talk me, you big ox," she said, squeezing Kendal's hand again as the pain of another contraction started. "It won't make me forget that you got me pregnant, and with my luck, this kid will be as big as you."

"Not right away, my lady," the healer said, and Piper figured she was either trying to be helpful or entertain Kendal when her love tried and failed to suppress her chuckle.

"Ah, shit...shit, this hurts." She sat up a little, and Kendal moved with her so she used Kendal as a backrest and pushed with all her strength. She felt a sudden rush of sensation, and then the pain stopped.

"It's a girl," the healer said loudly, followed by a baby's cry.

"And she's as beautiful as her mother," Kendal said as the healer held her up. From the obvious emotion in Kendal's voice, Piper knew she'd fallen instantly in love with their child as much as she had.

"You're sweet, since I doubt I look anything remotely resembling beautiful right now," Piper said as she watched Kendal's gazing face soften.

"Don't argue with me when it comes to that, my love," Kendal said, kissing the side of her neck. "You've been nothing but beautiful from the day we decided on this child. I'd take ten more if Aphrodite sees fit to bless us again."

"Bite your tongue, for a few months anyway. I'd like to see my feet again before I even think of letting you anywhere near me with any glowing orbs," she said and laughed.

After she and Kendal had worked to keep the only weapon Aphrodite had ever forged from her brother Ares, the goddess had fulfilled a long-kept promise to two souls who'd sacrificed themselves in her honor. So instead of releasing the power of Ares into the world, the Sea Serpent Sword had served another purpose, and she and Kendal as well as their closest friends Morgaine and Lenore had accepted her gift. The goddess had given her word that the babies she and Lenore carried held the essence of those two long-ago lovers, but only an essence.

When they accepted her offer, Aphrodite had made the baby possible through the power of the sword with the promise that it was as much Kendal's as it was hers. So they'd made love, and that one night had resulted in the child that the healer very lovingly cleaned up before handing her over. It had been an interesting nine months, but like their time after Kendal had mixed the elixir of life for her, Kendal had taken a break from her duties as a slayer for the Genesis Clan so she could spoil Piper as the pregnancy progressed.

"For as long as I've been alive, I've enjoyed the gift of immortality because I've witnessed the world changing and evolving," Kendal said as she moved to allow the healers to finish. "I've been a silent witness to all the wonders of man through the ages, but you and our daughter are the closest things to miracles I've ever been given."

Kendal and the group of elder immortals who were thousands of years old had served silently through time to keep mankind safe from the monsters they believed existed only in fairy tales. Kendal was their greatest slayer and had battled vampires and every other evil Piper had no clue existed, but as her partner she was devoted and kind.

"You are the same to me, warrior mine." She watched the healer hand the baby to Kendal, who kissed her forehead before handing her to Piper. The healers left the room, so Kendal lowered the sheet covering her upper body and placed the baby on her naked chest.

Kendal smiled as she held the baby's hand and nodded. "We've come a long way, haven't we?"

"We have, and I love you more each day."

Piper had never imagined herself as a wife and mother, but her life had certainly changed when Kendal came into it under the pretext of buying their family business against her and her grandfather's wishes. She'd despised Kendal at first, but the relationship that had started out as adversarial had turned into the greatest treasure she could've imagined.

The Genesis Clan's greatest slayer had begun her life as Asra of the house of Raad and had lived many lifetimes before meeting her true mate. Piper was young by comparison, but her time as an immortal had been foretold far before Kendal found her. The elixir of life that had granted them all immortality had failed to change Piper's eyes to the pale blue all the immortals created by the Genesis Clan shared.

Piper's had stayed the vibrant green of her birth, but the elixir had awoken her sight that could see far into the future. She was still working to perfect that gift, but she'd already been graced with the picture of Kendal holding their baby with a wide, proud smile. Kendal, or Asra, as she thought of her now, had certainly left the path of solitude with the new family she surrounded herself with. They had both been somewhat broken when they met, but together they'd healed.

"So what will we call you?" Piper asked as she lifted the baby to count her fingers and toes, making the baby shiver but not cry. "Have any ideas, my warrior?"

"We narrowed it down to a few, but now that I see her, none of them fit." Kendal sat next to her and laid her hand on the baby's back. The small beauty had yet to open her eyes, but she saw a little of Kendal and her own features in the baby's face. She followed the healer's instructions and cradled her and placed her nipple in her mouth.

"In honor of Aphrodite, how about something Greek?" She tickled the baby's cheek and smiled when she latched on to her nipple.

"Considering where this little one has waited, how about Hali? It's Greek and means the sea."

"Hali Richoux, welcome to our lives," she said, and the baby finally opened her eyes, which were the same pale blue as Kendal's.

"Wow," Kendal said, making the baby let go and look up at her.

"Does this mean she's like us?"

"I honestly don't know. This is my first baby," Kendal said, seemingly delighted with the infant. "I don't think the goddess would've gifted us with this beauty if she didn't envision a multitude of happy years."

"Is that your way of telling me not to worry about it?"

"She's gorgeous, my love, and she's ours—yours and mine. All we can do is love her for as long as we can before she flexes her wings and flies out of our nest."

"I love you, and you're right."

"I believe I've mentioned that before," Kendal said, and she pinched her for the jibe.

"Okay, know-it-all. Go get my grandparents so they can start spoiling."

❖

"*Cuidado*," Oscar Petchel yelled as his workers moved a large stone where the ground-penetrating radar had showed a void. He'd warned everyone to be careful to try to preserve the stone filled with what looked like Mayan hieroglyphics.

Oscar had done a masterful job of hiding the dig from the Costa Rican government and the university where he headed the archeology department. He'd gone deep into the rain forest out of Monte Verde, not really expecting to find anything since he'd been responsible for all the major digs in Costa Rica for the last twenty years. After meeting with Alejandro Garza at his father, Sebastian's, request, he'd traveled to the site on the map Alejandro had provided, surprised to find a rather large complex.

His father, from Oscar's earliest memories, had one foot in the past, and he'd preached that's what had made him good at his job. Sebastian had a doctorate in Mesoamerican studies, but like all his male descendants, he was brought up to be a faithful believer of the Order of Fuego. Oscar had been the first to break the chain of following blindly something he considered preposterous.

"Slowly put it down," his assistant Pauline Chevalier said in a very accented Spanish. French was her first language, but she knew enough Spanish for the workers and students to understand her. Pauline had moved from France to study with him and had become a quick convert to the Order of Fuego after a dinner with his father and Alejandro.

The ground under the stone was moist, but that wasn't surprising since they were in the middle of the jungle during the rainy season. Trying to get into the void would be tricky, so he waved the workers away. They backed up gladly, considering they'd already lost five workers provided by Alejandro's Order after they'd gotten into the first chamber they'd discovered.

"Where do you think the trigger is?" Pauline asked.

"Last time, it was located just where we entered the empty chamber. I'm beginning to think this place has been picked clean, but that doesn't explain the deadly booby traps. Why go to all that trouble to protect an empty room?"

"Maybe they're not empty." Pauline glanced back at what they'd already dug up.

"When a room has four walls and nothing in it, that defines empty." He knew that was true, but this place—it had a different feel to it. The Mayans had a certain fingerprint, as it were, and this site was almost perfect—almost.

He walked back to the first room they'd uncovered. "Let's see if we missed something. Tell one of those guys to bring the small radar."

"We've already checked every wall."

"Did you do the floor?" He climbed down the ladder one of the men had built, already knowing the answer.

That's what didn't fit here. The Mayans weren't really deep diggers. They mined obsidian glass and jade, they buried their dead, but mostly they were builders. Their traditions were to touch their sky gods, not dwell in the earth.

"You think it goes lower than this?" Pauline climbed down and stood next to him.

He studied the stone walls for anything he might've missed, but that was unlikely considering how much he prided himself on his thoroughness. Just then, the worker came down with the equipment that was the size of the backpack and broke the silence.

"Start in the middle and see if you can find anything to justify bringing the bigger one down."

"*Sí, señor.*"

It took forty minutes for the worker to methodically scan the floor of a space that made no sense to him. Nothing in it gave a hint as to why it was there at all. That also made him wonder if this wasn't Mayan or Incan. The Maya were storytellers. Blank walls weren't their norm.

"Come back once you have the results." He dismissed the short man of Mayan descent, wanting to be alone with his thoughts.

"We're already pretty deep, so why would you think there's anything lower than this?" Pauline asked.

He understood her need to know, but she hadn't learned how to keep her mouth shut when he was trying to concentrate. "You've been with me long enough to be able to look at the glyphs and decipher the Mayan language. We're at the southern region of Mesoamerica but still in Mayan territory."

"We haven't found any glyphs in here."

"We found some outside."

"We did," she said, sitting next to him.

He nodded before lowering himself to the stone floor. "So tell me a story, then."

"Even you can't read the tablets covering these rooms. None of them are even close to the known Mayan written language."

"Exactly." He pointed to each wall and the ceiling. "The Mayan kings were fanatical about recording their history. They wouldn't have left all this blank space."

"So someone from that time period replicated an entire city as a hoax?" She laughed, as if knowing, like he did, that would be entirely far-fetched.

"It's the whole chicken-and-egg debate." As soon as he finished they heard a scream, followed by total commotion outside. The men had to have set off another trap by rushing. If they lost any more men, the others probably wouldn't stick around much longer.

"What's happening?" Pauline jumped up and headed for the stairs.

"Perhaps we need some more answers before we continue." Alejandro would have to show more cards than he had, because the other mystery was how his men were dying. The bodies they'd had to dispose of on the old altar at Alejandro's direction showed no signs of any trauma, but each and every one's frozen expression showed abject terror. No one else would venture inside until he and Pauline had descended the ladder carefully, but even then, he saw no sign of anything deadly enough to kill five men.

"Señor Petchel," one of the men yelled.

He reached the top of the steps in time to watch a large number of snakes come out of the dirt where they'd just removed the stone. They were the biggest pythons he'd ever seen and appeared to be coming from the chamber he knew in his gut was there.

"*Dios mio*," he said, genuflecting like the nuns had taught him as a small boy in school. "What the hell is this?"

CHAPTER TWO

Congratulations, old friend," Kendal said to Morgaine after she'd left Piper to watch the baby take a nap. It wasn't until Piper had given birth that they'd been told that Lenore had also gone into labor and given birth to another girl.

"I don't think either of us was planning for this," Morgaine said, though she was smiling like she couldn't contain her joy. "But this should be fun."

"What name did you two decide on?"

"Lenore thought it should be Greek, so we went with Anastasia."

She laughed and hugged Morgaine. They'd been friends and sporadic lovers, but their fight with the traitorous elder Julius had made Morgaine realize that Lenore was her true mate. Morgaine had been truly surprised that the woman who'd made her whole was someone who'd been in her life for thousands of years. Aphrodite had blessed that love by giving them one of the souls trapped in the Sea Serpent Sword.

"Great minds must think alike, so Anastasia and Hali will share a birthday."

"Two girls?" Morgaine asked, pulling a little away from her and shaking her head. "Are we ready for this?"

"Not really, since I've been alive forever but have very little experience with children, much less babies."

"You'll find that it's a lot like all those battle strategies you're so good at," Bruik, the Genesis Clan's most senior seer, said as he joined them. "Your life will be very regimented for a while, but enjoy it. I'm ancient as well, but I was able to experience fatherhood before the elixir."

Bruik had traveled back with them to help Piper with her newfound ability to see into the future. It had been Bruik who'd foreseen her finding Piper and awakening that part of her mind she'd never experienced before. With his patient tutelage, Piper's vision was becoming clearer and easier to access.

"Will you stay on?" Kendal asked, grasping his offered arm for the greeting she would've given one of her fellow soldiers when she served in the pharaoh's forces. Like her, that's the region Bruik was from, but he had already lived many lifetimes before her birth.

"Rolla requested I stay, but that's what I wanted, especially when Piper told me we were returning to New Orleans. I've read of your time here and was looking forward to seeing your history come to life with Charlie as my guide. He's never ventured far and had done a masterful job of writing your history."

Charlie had started his life with Kendal after she'd bought him from the slave auction blocks, but his chains had come off once he'd reached her home, only then Charlie had known her as Jacques St. Louis. Kendal had given him the elixir so he could avenge his family after her brother Henri had slaughtered them.

It had taken years, but Charlie had used her father's sword to kill Henri and give them both the justice they sought.

"Charlie would love nothing better, and you're welcome to stay as long as you please. Piper would appreciate you staying close."

"Piper, as you know, is hard to say no to, so I accept your invitation." When he smiled, he, in a way, reminded her of her father. "But now, Asra, you need to welcome the sun with your mate. You too, Morgaine. Don't keep them waiting."

"Have you seen the babies?" Morgaine asked him.

"Don't worry yet." He took Morgaine's hand and shook it. "Time will only tell what those eyes will bring."

His answer saved Kendal from asking the same thing. She was well aware of how they were able to bring these children to life but was wary of their futures. Gifts from the gods weren't commonplace, but Aphrodite had told them to have faith, so she would do just that.

"Have you seen them as adults?" she asked out of curiosity.

"They'll be beautiful and accomplished women, Asra. Each will have a mind, heart, and spirit of her own. Those who gave their lives to the goddess will be only an echo in their essence, but a very faint echo. They might grow up to love each other, but they might not. No one deserves the burden of someone's past from birth."

"Thank you for your honesty, but I have a date with a beautiful woman and our daughter."

❖

"Did you read it?" Lowe Carey asked her pack leader, Convel Lupo. They'd settled outside of New Orleans and had managed to stay out of the sight of the Genesis Clan, even though their most talented slayer lived less than five miles from them.

Convel got some kind of thrill from hunting on Kendal's property. Lowe thought it was risky, especially when Kendal had returned, but Oakgrove had gone dark for a while, though now it was definitely populated with a full staff that liked to patrol every bit of the acreage Kendal owned. That had cut the thrill, so Convel had thought of moving them, but Lowe feared what could come from settling somewhere more populated.

"Not yet," Convel said as she stared out the window. "I'm trying to figure out how he knew we were here."

The scroll one of their pack delivered from the great Rolla himself had made her shiver when her pack mate had handed it over, but she tried not to show fear. His seal was for Convel to break, but Lowe figured she would've forgiven her for reading it. "Do you think it could've been Kendal?"

"She wasn't here long enough to figure it out." Convel spoke sharply and rubbed the top of her right hand. The scar would never disappear or fade, and it was a constant reminder of Kendal's skills. The battle had been fierce, she'd heard, and Convel had never forgiven Kendal for marking her.

"Please, love, read it. If you need to move us, we have to start planning." She pressed against Convel's back and put her arms around her waist. The greatest honor of her life was when Convel had picked her as her mate—only death would sever the bond.

"Go on and open it. Let's see what the bastard wants. They usually can't be bothered with the rabble."

"The seal is yours to break." She reached for the scroll and handed it over.

"You're as superstitious as you are beautiful." Convel kissed her forehead but did what she asked and broke the seal, then dropped into her desk chair and unrolled it.

"Do you want me to read it?"

"Come sit with me." Convel pushed back some and invited her to sit on her lap.

She readily joined Convel and kissed her. The act would help her steady herself if the news was bad. "You are my life, and I'll destroy anyone who tries to harm you."

"Rolla very seldom starts with that kind of threat, love." Convel held the scroll up so they could read it together.

Greetings to Convel Lupo and her family.

I extend a hand of peace to you and your pack. Asra recently informed me of your presence, so I'd like to request that you stay now that Asra has returned. Her family will be settling back in the city, so we need to set a meeting.

You may pick the location, but Charlie says you are quite familiar with the grounds of Oakgrove. Perhaps you will consider coming to her home under a banner of truce—a truce that could extend for as long as both sides honor it.

Rolla

Convel held it up long enough for both of them to reread it three times. "This is good, don't you think?"

The scroll fell from Convel's fingers, and she closed her eyes. "This is strange is what it is. Rolla commands killers who do just that. Peace offerings aren't his style at all."

"Then why this?"

"The old codes are still honored. If he invited us, then he can't destroy our family without consequences."

"If they know we're here, couldn't he have ordered that already?" She asked because she was tired of living with old fears. "Maybe we should at least hear what he has in mind."

"Maybe we'll get some answers as to what happened at Oakgrove all those months ago before Kendal disappeared for a time. We both witnessed it, but I still haven't figured it out."

"Let's accept only if Onai, Sepf, Varg, and Zaylz agree. They're our family, and they believe in you."

"Don't worry so much, love, and we'll go. Write a response and send it with Varg. Have him go back to wherever Rolla's lackey found him."

"Are you sure you want to send Varg? He's still young and doesn't yet control his hunger very well, especially now."

"Who do you suggest then?"

"Let me go for you, or better yet, we could go together." She kissed Convel again and finished by nipping gently at her bottom lip.

"We'll go together, but not now," Convel said as she slipped her hand in her jeans. "Now all I want is you."

Lowe felt alive when Convel touched her like this, and she gladly gave herself over to the passion between them. "You have all of me."

Those were the last words they shared for the rest of the afternoon after Convel laid her down on the desk. Rolla's truce was important, but not as important as this.

❖

Kendal carried Piper outside to the spot where they'd shared lunch under the large oaks months before. They'd made love under the trees at Oakgrove like they had that first night in Napa, when they'd brought legend to fulfillment after Piper made the tattoo she'd been given by Aphrodite hundreds of years before reappear on her skin. Piper had said seeing the stars above them reminded her of the night she knew without a doubt that she belonged to Kendal as much as Kendal belonged to her.

She remembered Piper's hesitation that night before putting her hand on her lower abdomen, because if the dragon tattoo had stayed dormant, Kendal wasn't her true mate. That same hesitancy hadn't occurred to her after she knew who Piper was to her. The mate to her mark had appeared on Piper's chest, proving her right. Their reward was the baby the healer carried out for them.

"Thank you," Piper said when the young woman handed her the baby. She waited until they were alone before she leaned back against her and exposed the baby's face to the warm predawn air. "Are you as deliriously happy as I am?"

"Every day I've spent with you has made me feel that way. Our road will be long, and we'll enjoy each step because we'll walk it together." She kissed the side of Piper's neck and sensed the first ray of light break across the horizon.

"If anyone I know deserves a child to carry on her blood, baby, it's you."

The sky was pink, so she kissed Piper again and reached into her pocket for the old amulet that had been hers as a child. It was one of the only things she'd taken with her that night she'd followed Morgaine out of the bloodbath her brother had made of their father's house. She'd kept it because her father had placed it on her while he was alive, then asked the gods to bless her with a long and happy life. Now she'd ask the same for her and Piper's child.

She stood and unwrapped the blanket, placed the amulet on Hali's chest, and lifted her over her head. The baby shivered a bit but didn't cry.

"I am Asra of the house of Raad," she said in her native tongue. "Bless our child and have the gods watch over her so her days will be filled with love, joy, and peace. Father, carry my words into the heavens and make it so. Hali is of your blood, your line, and your courage. Guide her as you have me."

She carefully wrapped Hali up again and gave her back to Piper so she could hold both of them. Piper glanced back at her with tears in her eyes, but they didn't need to say anything else. Once the sun was up, Piper closed her eyes and took a few deep breaths.

"This is the first time I've ever had to test these healing powers, so I have to say they're pretty amazing." She stood up and stretched.

"I've never had a complaint about them," she said, taking Hali back so Piper could raise her arms toward the sun. "If you've finished your sun worship for the moment, let's join everyone for breakfast."

The baby woke up as if understanding the word, so they sat back down so Piper could feed her. "What now, my warrior?"

"Our battles are done for now, my love, so we get on with the business of building boats."

"Pops will be thrilled."

"We might get years of peace since I made that truce with Vadoma. Hopefully she'll keep her minions in line, but even so it'll be years before she gains anywhere as much power as Ora."

"I don't see Vadoma as a problem going forward," Piper said as the baby latched onto her nipple and suckled enthusiastically. "She might be something right out of my nightmares, but she'll keep her word and your truce."

"Then what do you see as a problem?"

"I'm not sure about that yet, but Rolla will probably tell us when he arrives tomorrow." Piper handed Hali over for her to burp after she explained that was what she was supposed to be doing. "I thought you read those books I gave you?"

"I did, but having her here has short-circuited my brain, so be patient with me, my love." Hali let out a burp that belied her size. "Why do you think Rolla is coming? There's usually a bit of fanfare before he graces anyone with his company."

"You're going to have to trust me. He's coming, and it's not a social call." She took the baby back and finished feeding her. "Something's not right in the world, though I can't quite figure out what that is."

"Believe me, there's always something not right in the world, but we don't necessarily always have to be the ones who fix it."

"That I can agree with, but he wants to talk to you, and I don't sense that urge is negotiable."

Kendal cradled her and Hali and sighed. "It never is."

CHAPTER THREE

Rolla stood in the window of a high-end hotel, the Piquant, in New Orleans, and stared down at the streetcar rumbling by. He didn't come to the United States often, but the young country had intrigued him enough that he'd been present when George Washington was sworn in as the first president.

Those had been trying times, not because of a revolution that had given birth to a nation, but because so many of those they'd tried to keep a rein on had found a new frontier to try to conquer. A great number of people who had lain dead on the battlefield had lost their lives not to British aggression, but to the hunger or rage of some beast with very little or no soul.

"Have you sent word we're coming?" Rawney Lumas asked. Her dark skin and hair really set off her pale-blue eyes. Rawney was a distant relative of Vadoma, the new queen of the vampires, and they both had learned the craft of magic from the Gypsy women who'd raised them. Granted, Rawney was much older than Vadoma, so the power of her spells and potions would take Vadoma many more years to perfect, but she still respected Vadoma's talents.

"Convel had been put on notice, but I wanted to give Asra and Piper some more time, considering the baby has just arrived." He joined her at the dining table in his suite and accepted the cup of tea she'd brewed for him. "I never did ask you what you thought about the child brought forth by the sword."

She glanced at him and smiled. "The gods of old were so important at one time, but it's good to know they're still perched on their mountain looking down on us. That they showed Asra favor doesn't surprise me, but I would've thought it would've been the god of war who tried to seduce her."

"Do you think she would've been swayed?" The tea was bitter but not excessively so, so he sipped it slowly and felt his mind relax. Only Rawney had the ability to alter the mind of a Genesis Clan immortal, but never for evil intent.

"I've met Asra on only a few occasions, but Morgaine chose well. Asra has a true spirit, so the only way a dark force could sway her would be to save someone she loves. Julius didn't understand that, and it cost him his life," she said of the traitorous elder who'd tried to unleash the Sea Serpent Sword's dark half.

"The other thing I didn't think possible was her truce with Vadoma. Do you think it'll hold?"

"Vadoma is no fool, and nothing like Ora. The first queen was partially mad before the sickness, and immortality didn't improve her state of mind. Knowing that, it should be easy to guess the truce will hold."

"How do you know for sure?" He drank the last of his tea and his entire body felt heavy.

"My job is to wield what power I have to do your bidding. The spells I cast are for protection and to bury things that shouldn't be found." Rawney's voice wove around him like smoke from a fire, and his eyelids were suddenly too heavy to stay open. "Relax your mind, Rolla, so you may see and remember."

Rawney spoke softly and caught Rolla's cup before it fell to the floor. He'd asked for the state he was in, but he responded better when he didn't see it coming. She signaled for the young man guarding their leader to carry him to the bedroom and lay him down.

"Is he all right, ma'am?" the guard asked.

"He's perfectly fine. Bring Bruik in when he arrives." She unbuttoned Rolla's shirt, took a few things out of her bag, and started applying three different infused oils in a swirl pattern to his chest as she uttered the incantations softly.

Once Bruik arrived and laid his hands on Rolla's head, they would both share the seer's gift. Bruik would have to take him back, before they could go forward into an unknown future.

The world was so different than it'd been in the early years of her life, and it still amazed her that man went searching for things better off buried. Not everything could be controlled, no matter how much you wished it or how much power it could bring you.

"Are we ready to begin?" Bruik asked when he came in.

"Not really, but we must, old friend."

"We found it close to the property line, sire," one of the men Rolla had sent told Kendal after he and some of the others had driven her out to the mutilated carcass of a deer.

From the scraps and the bloating of the head it was only a few days old. The wounds and how it was killed concerned her because very few things were able to rip something so savagely, and the outskirts of New Orleans weren't known for active lion packs or wolves. At least not the kind of wolves found in nature.

"Have you found any others?" Kendal removed the new, very plain Sea Serpent Sword and twirled it from hand to hand for a few minutes to help her think.

"I have the men looking now, but we might have an active pack in the area," the man said.

"Call the house and make sure everyone is vigilant. If you're right it'll be my turn to go hunting, and I'll be happy to get a new pelt to wipe my feet on once I find these fools." Werewolves, like vampires, usually hunted and lived in groups, but the weres were after more than their victim's blood. She didn't want any of that near her family.

"Yes, sire."

She nodded and poured gasoline over the deer, then lit it on fire to do away with the scent. "I'll walk back, so let me know if you find anything else."

The trees and brush had reclaimed what had once been the tobacco fields she loved working in and growing along with the vegetables that fed the residents of Oakgrove. She wished her old friend Lola had lived to see the baby and thought about how badly Lola would've spoiled Hali.

"Problems?" Charlie asked. He rode up on one of the horses from the stables and had Kendal's favorite, Ruda, following behind.

"Have you seen any strange kills on the property? Any animal that appeared mauled?"

"Nothing like that, but I usually stick to the trails when I'm exercising the horses." Charlie glanced back at the spot burning and sat up straighter in his saddle. "What do you think did that?"

"It's not something we've ever seen here before, but unless I'm wrong, we've got some new and different kind of neighbors." She mounted Ruda and led them to the fence line that surrounded the property.

"I thought vampires weren't into animals." Charlie rode next to her while the trail was wide enough.

"It's time for you to venture out, my friend," she said as she dismounted when they reached the fence line and started walking alongside it. There had to be some sign of how they'd gotten in. "If you choose, I'll start training you to be a slayer. You can eventually work on your own, or you can serve with me and Morgaine."

"She and Lenore won't eventually leave?" His riding pants and form-fitting shirt made him appear as if he were waiting to do a photo shoot for the cover of a fashion magazine.

"Not for years, since we've made a pact to keep the babies together for as long as everyone is agreeable. They're unique in how they got here, so I think it'll help to have someone who understands that position better than any of us." She stopped and put her hands on his shoulder. "You did well in the fight against my brother, but this isn't something someone can force you into."

"The only reason I drank from your cup, Asra, was to avenge my family."

"We have that in common."

"That I know, and I'm sorry you had to wait much longer than me to rid the world of your father's killers. You gave me my freedom all those years ago, along with my dignity, and I loved you like a brother for it." He moved closer and hugged her. "I never thought I'd ever sense the kind of belonging I had when I was a boy growing up with my parents, but you proved me wrong and encouraged my relationship with Celia."

"I know you miss her still," she said, guessing that Charlie was planning to refuse her offer.

"I have for a very long time, and my misery is what's kept me locked up here. Driving your father's sword through Henri's rotten heart finally brought me peace, and even though you aren't my brother," he said, making air quotes, "you're my family. I want to serve with you and venture outside these gates at your side."

"Thank you, Charlie, and I've always considered you the brother I never had."

"Everyone you brought here loved you, Asra. You have no idea how much we feared the unknown when we finally got off those pits of hell we sailed in, only to be dragged toward you with our heads full of the stories those men who worked the blocks told us. When they led me to that platform, I wished and prayed to die like those who didn't make the crossing. You and Lola were waiting, and all I felt was hate."

"No one could blame you for that, my friend, and I wish I could say it was the only time in my life I'd seen that kind of brutality, but I'd be lying. The world's changed, according to the scholars, but we know better." She sighed and continued their walk. "There's always someone willing to put us all in chains if we give them the opportunity. I am so sorry all that happened to you. Words aren't much, but I did the best I could."

"Jacques," he said with his perfect French and smiled. "Like I said, I don't think you ever realized how much everyone you saved loved and respected you. None of them were blind or deaf as to what happened to those not lucky enough to stand on those blocks the days you weren't there. We loved you because we wanted to, not because we were forced to."

"Until Piper came into my life, this is where I felt the most at home. You and your family, along with Lola and the others, made me happy."

"You're still my family now, so tell me, brother, what killed that deer?"

"There," she said, finding a part of the fence cut away. The hole was low to the ground and had a few strands of fur along the top. "We've got a family of werewolves close by, and they've got to know whose land they're hunting on."

"Seriously?" Charlie said, rubbing the strands between his fingers. "I need to read more books from the list Lenore gave me."

She chuckled and called for a crew to ride the fence and make repairs. "She'd love to hear you say that."

"So how do we kill them?"

"Not everything deserves killing, so let's see who they are before we call the taxidermist."

Oscar jumped down from the helicopter to the opulent grounds of the Garza estate. Alejandro was the current heir since his father had disappeared eight years earlier on a dig somewhere in Asia. His father had told him the story, but he hadn't paid attention, not as fascinated with the Garza legacy as Sebastian was.

He smoothed his shirt down and followed the servant who'd stood by to meet him. "*Bienvenido*, Dr. Petchel," the man said, leading him toward the back of the house.

The view of the mountains was spectacular, but he figured that on particularly cloudy days the coffee plants and everything else that lined the mountainside wouldn't be visible since they were so high up. The house was magnificent, but it was also remote. Alejandro and his family obviously valued their privacy.

"Señor Garza is waiting for you on the deck on the edge."

Alejandro was standing on a wooden platform with no sides, wearing a thick leather glove that stopped just short of his elbow. He whistled loudly, and a hawk flew up from the slope below him. Standing so far out along the edge was probably an attempt to show Oscar how fearless he was.

"There's something special about these birds in flight, don't you think?" Alejandro asked, handing his pet to one of the handlers. "This is one of the offspring of my father's favorite hunter."

"They don't hunt anymore except to take the meat from your hand. The only freedom they have left is flight, but they'll never venture too far, or they'll get no more steak from their master." Oscar was tired of playing these games, and he wasn't in the mood to fawn like everyone else in Alejandro's life did. The second stone had been removed, and the pythons had killed another six of his crew.

"You know I tolerate your disrespect only because of your father, but tread carefully unless you can fly like my hawk." The glove came off a finger at a time, and Alejandro walked away as if he expected to be followed.

"Either you give me more information or you can find someone else to dig for you, and you can forget that it'll be my father. We lost more men today to the most bizarre thing I've ever witnessed." He waved the servant off, along with the drink he offered. "The first five died for nothing because that's exactly what we found—nothing."

"The information you gathered is what's important to me. Our search will end only when we find what we've been after for centuries, and you'll be leading that search, Dr. Petchel." Alejandro spoke softly and drained whatever liquor was in his glass. "We've come too far to allow anyone to jeopardize our ultimate goal. Either you keep digging, or—"

"What, you'll kill me?" he asked and laughed. It was like Alejandro had watched too many movies.

"You don't think many have died in our pursuit? Those men gladly gave their lives to the order, and plenty more are waiting to take their place. Honor your commitments, or I won't kill just you. I'll have your entire family killed, along with the French slut who's dying to get you into bed." Alejandro accepted another drink and appeared as calm as if they were talking about baseball scores. "Don't try my patience or my word. You won't care for the outcome."

"Then give me something to try to save some lives before we go forward. The mounds out there are most probably pyramids, but the interesting pieces that don't fit are the stones with different hieroglyphics that aren't Mayan or Incan."

"One of my men told me about the snakes in the first chamber that killed the men who went down first." Alejandro waved him to a chair, and this time he accepted the drink. He was surprised when he tasted his favorite scotch. "Do you believe in magic, Doctor, or what some call witchcraft?"

"Even in the Mayan times the powerful shamans were nothing more than talented magicians. They convinced their royals of their power, but it was all based on sleight of hand and nothing more." He wanted to curse his father for getting him into this situation, especially for not telling him there was no out. "The events at the site are strange, but I haven't seen anything that can't be explained scientifically."

"You're so much like your father was in the beginning when he had the same arguments with my father. Open your eyes, Oscar, before something you can't explain plucks them from your skull."

"How does that help me?" This was a complete waste of his time.

"The places I will send you are under the protective spells of an organization called the Genesis Clan, or so we believe. That's who's mentioned in the early writings of the Order of Fuego. The key to breaking them has to be in the glyphs, but up to now no one's been able to decipher them. There's no Rosetta Stone for this."

"Then, with your blessing, I want to head back to the university and research them before anyone else dies needlessly."

"You have a week, and then back to the jungle."

Oscar nodded, then left without another word. The helicopter was ready to depart, and only when he was out of sight did one of the back doors open. Pauline came out and kissed Alejandro's cheek.

"Is he going to be a problem?" he asked.

"He's simply worried about the lives we lost. Oscar has a soft heart but a brilliant mind. If anyone can come close to breaking the code in these stones, it's him."

"My apologies if you heard me earlier when your name came up."

She bowed her head slightly and smiled. "We may not have spent much time together, but I haven't forgotten your love for me. France was a dead end, so I appreciate you letting me come home, Father. You and the order are all I have left now that my mother is dead, and I'll serve you as faithfully as she did."

"Good, so go back and do everything you need in order to keep Petchel in line."

"He'll probably never fully convert, but he'll be useful."

He stood and kissed both of Pauline's cheeks. "Good, and his reward will be to fly off my perch out back along with his father. It'll give my birds something to feast on that's not from my hand," he said, remembering Oscar's insult. "He'll learn the hard way that no hunter can be totally tamed."

CHAPTER FOUR

Piper sat outside on the balcony and held Hali as she stared unseeingly at the levee that banked the river across the road. She let her mind wander like Bruik had taught her and did her best to put order to the thoughts that came like a mudslide, in that it was a jumbled mess with a lot of images to process. She concentrated on Hali's breath against her neck and smiled despite her semi-conscious state.

"That bitch has much to pay for" was the one statement that caught her attention, so she closed her eyes and tried to pinpoint that one thing by peeling away the rest of the noise. Bruik's instruction was that all her insights were like walking through a mansion with a multitude of rooms. Each room had a separate conversation going on, so if one was of more interest than the others, she should sit there and listen while trying to drown out the rest of the din.

With time and practice, he promised she would hear only the noise of the thousand things when she wanted to. When he sat to let his mind wander he always had a particular destination in mind. She knew instinctively that the statement was about Kendal, but the woman who said it stayed in the shadows. This wasn't a sight from the future—this had already happened, and all Piper could see was the large, straight scar on the back of the woman's hand.

"Who are you?" she said as she sat in her mind's eye and tried to gather more information.

Macedonia, 142 BC, The Korab Mountain Range

Erik Wolver rode up the steep incline he was on as fast as the horse could handle the terrain. Once the ground leveled off some, he dismounted and let the horse loose to graze where he wanted. The only thought in her mind was how far the days of the pharaoh's forces were behind her. Wolver was a good alter ego for Asra as she traveled to do the Clan's bidding.

The flat sands of Egypt were only a memory now as she looked out at the valley with sporadic signs of fire from the people living and trying to make their way here. Snow mixed with ice crunched under her boots as she tried to find a way to start her mission. Up to now she had used her skills only to hunt Ora's fledglings who'd become a nuisance, but this was a different scenario she couldn't quite believe existed.

Men and women who could shape-shift into a wolf in a way defied even her imagination, but Morgaine had assured her they did in fact exist and were terrorizing the villages along this area. It wouldn't be long before someone tried to keep them away from their livestock and they'd acquire a taste for human blood.

"So where are you?" She leaned against a tree and decided to wait for the upcoming night.

It took three days, but she stood between a cave entrance and the four unnaturally large wolves trying to make it inside. At the sight of her, they lowered their heads and bared their fangs, but they stood their ground. Erik knew these were the only ones at the moment, since she'd explored their den.

"From the blood on your muzzle, I can see you've taken the life of something that doesn't belong to you," she said as she stood with her sword ready. "I don't want to hurt you, so take your family and leave. You'll find plenty of game away from here for your survival."

She spoke hoping there'd be some kind of recognition, but her experience with young vampires had taught her that the thirst trumped everything and everyone. One of the wolves started to make its way to the right, but she kept her eyes on the other three. It didn't take long for the aggressor to get behind her, but she still didn't move her head.

Patience made her wait until she heard the crunch of ice before swinging the sword down and up, catching a paw and slicing through it. The blood sprayed her face, and the other three moved a step back when their pack mate lay wounded at her feet. "All you need to do is move on," she said as the wounded were started to shift back. The tall woman held her hand against her chest and glared at her.

"Who are you?" she asked in German. "I want to know your

name, which will make sucking your eyes out of your skull all the more enjoyable."

Another one of the pack grew brave and came forward, snapping its jaws as if trying to intimidate her. "What I'm asking isn't hard, so think about it before you lose someone you care about." She spread her feet a little and tightened the grip on her sword. The one she was using was coated in silver for the occasion.

"Do you honestly think you can defeat all of us?"

"All of you are outcast from the true pack leader, Queen Beldar. I spoke to your queen before traveling here. She gave me permission to kill every one of you if I wished. She has no use for your disobedience."

"You know nothing," the wounded woman yelled as Erik moved toward the closest wolf with her sword ready for a killing blow. "Wait," the woman screamed louder. She then spoke some kind of language that sounded inhuman and guttural. After hearing her, the other three shifted and stood naked before Erik.

"Start out in the morning and never return here. Start on the path you were meant to run, and Beldar will welcome you home. Your mother misses you." She took a small jar from her bag and gave it to one of the young men. "Convel, use that, or the silver will eventually poison your blood. The salve will stop it, but it won't do anything for the scar it'll leave."

"This won't end here."

"If you want, next time I'll sink my blade through your heart and leave the job of redeeming your family name to your sister."

Oakgrove, Present Day

Piper opened her eyes when she felt the baby move, and she hoped Kendal would come back soon. Erik Wolver seemed to be a persona Kendal had used over more than one lifetime and had more than "his" share of tales to tell.

"At least your mom didn't have some sex scene in this vision," she said to Hali, who was awake and puckering her lips at her. "You are so beautiful."

Hali favored Kendal more in coloring and eye color, but Piper could see herself in this child she'd been dreaming about from the first night she'd been conceived. She'd known for months it'd be a girl, but Hali's future had stayed a dark mystery to her no matter how many times she'd wanted to catch a glimpse of it.

She thought of her own parents and how different her life would be if they'd lived. Pain, though, got you to where you needed to be to recognize true happiness. That's what Kendal had given her, she'd thought, when she'd wiped out their debt, but in reality they could be penniless and she'd still feel the same. She heard something in the distance and made out Kendal and Charlie galloping toward the house.

"Look, Hali." She held the baby up and set her on her lap. "With that sword and her comfort in the saddle, you can see that soldier in shining armor beaming through."

"What did you say, sweetheart?" Piper's grandmother, Molly, asked as she came out and took the baby into her arms.

"I was saying that it's not hard to see the pharaoh's elite soldier if you look that way." She pointed to the right.

"She does inspire you to either become a writer or just kiss her senseless," Molly joked.

"If you were five years younger, I'd worry about you," Piper said, kissing Molly and then Hali. "Will you two behave until I get back?"

"Are you sure you should be riding so soon?"

"The sunrise made it like it never happened. These healing powers make me want to fill up the bedrooms in the house, but for now I'm going with that kissing-her-senseless idea you had." She waved and headed down before Kendal dismounted.

"Charlie," she heard Kendal say before he made it out of the front drive. "Make sure those guys take their patrol seriously. I don't want my family harmed."

"I'll let you know if we find anything. Good morning, Mama," Charlie said when she stepped outside. "Congratulations, and I can't wait to meet her."

"We'll all have dinner tonight, and you can fight my grandparents for her, Uncle Charlie." She held her hand over her eyes to cut the glare and smiled up at Kendal. "You're using a saddle today? Is there room up there for me?"

Kendal dismounted and removed Ruda's saddle before lifting her up. They headed for the gate and the levee, which was now one of the areas their new staff was patrolling and making off-limits to any outsiders. Ruda made quick work of the slope, and Kendal held her as she headed for the clump of trees that went all the way to the waterline.

She fell into Kendal's arms and followed her to the most secluded spot Kendal had carved out for them. "Did you find anything?" she asked as Kendal spread Ruda's blanket out.

"We might have a wolf problem," Kendal said, sitting with her back against a big willow.

"That makes sense." She straddled Kendal's legs. "I had another waking dream about Erik Wolver and his many exploits."

"You're not pinching me, so it couldn't have been too bad," Kendal joked.

"You're hilarious, but no. You were in the mountains, and you fought a big wolf and cut her. The wound caused her to shift to human form, and you warned her to move on. Even though she's a werewolf, you scarred her. We'll get into how I've only seen that in a movie later."

"Convel Lupo is who you're talking about, and I was sent to hunt her and a few of the weres who'd left with her. They'd broken from their leader because she showed too much restraint when it came to respected territorial boundaries. If you saw her, it's probably who hunted down a deer on our property after cutting through the fence."

"Is she dangerous?"

"She doesn't like me very much, but she knows better than to challenge me again."

"She actually hates you, and I can't understand it," she said, unbuttoning her shirt. "I find you utterly adorable."

"It's good to know you aren't bored with me yet." Kendal glanced down as Piper started on her shirt next.

"I loved being pregnant, but I'm glad to have the body you're used to seeing back and to not have anything between us." She leaned closer and hummed when they met skin to skin. "I will never get enough of you."

"You are the main reason I'd love to have the ability to dream, but not sleeping means I'll enjoy every moment of my life with you." Kendal placed her hand on her ass and picked her up so she could kiss her.

"That's mighty sappy of you, baby." Her crotch pressed against Kendal's abdomen, and she held on to maintain the pressure.

"No one but you believes I'm capable of it." The way Kendal

kissed her always made her feel possessed. It was as if Kendal needed her to realize how much she wanted her, and for the first time in her life she felt wanted and incredibly sexy. No one could fake that kind of response over and over again.

"We aren't going to be surprised by one of Rolla's people, are we?" She ran her hand up Kendal's hair from her neckline and moved her head closer so she could kiss her again.

"Do you need me to touch you?" Kendal tightened her hold on her ass, and Piper sucked in her bottom lip.

"I want you to put your mouth on me and make love to me," she said, hissing when Kendal laid her back and sucked in a nipple. "Shit."

"Sorry. Too hard?" Kendal laid her down and stretched out next to her.

"No. Not too hard, so take your pants off and let me feel you."

Kendal stripped for her, then helped her take off her jeans. She loved seeing Kendal standing naked with the sun shining through the trees, appearing as if she could conquer the world as easily as she had her heart. The emotion that swamped her at times when she saw the way other people looked at Kendal had a way of disappearing when Kendal's eyes met hers. No matter the years that stretched out before them, Kendal would be hers forever.

"You're beautiful no matter what. At least I've thought so from that very first day when you sat screaming at me." Kendal touched her, never really lingering in one spot. She seemed to want to revisit every inch of her, and the calluses on her hands from thousands of years of wielding a sword raised goose bumps wherever she touched. "I love you with all my heart."

"I love you, but I can't wait anymore." She spread her legs as Kendal hovered over her with a ravenous expression.

Kendal twirled her tongue around each nipple slowly until both of them were hard and dark pink, but she resisted when she put her hand behind her neck to keep her in place. "Slow down, my love," Kendal said, coming back up to kiss her.

"That's a hard demand." She reached down and touched herself, wanting to get her fingers wet. "See what you do to me." Kendal closed her eyes when she painted Kendal's lips with her wetness before allowing her to suck her fingers in. "You make me wet...you make me crave you...and you make me want to beg to be fucked."

She reached down again and circled her nipples, this time getting the result she wanted when Kendal sucked each one hard enough to make her hips buck up. She'd had other people in her life, but not one of them had ever made her this crazy for their touch. The only answer that made sense to her was that she'd never been in love. That was very true now with Kendal, who fueled every fantasy she'd had from the first time they'd gotten naked together.

"You never have to beg me for that, *mon amour*." Kendal moved down her body and used two fingers to open her up, but then she only looked down on her.

"Is something different after the baby?" She began to close her legs in reflex when the old fears that the elixir hadn't really worked on her came back. No matter how many times the elders had told her she was as immortal as they were, the fact that her eyes were still green haunted her.

"No, but I missed seeing you like this." Kendal dragged her tongue from her opening slowly over her clit. "I missed the taste of you and how wet you get for me." Kendal repeated the move with her fingers positioned to keep her open. "That you want me this much makes me hard and crazy."

"God, when you talk—" She didn't finish her thought when Kendal flicked her tongue rapidly over her clit and slammed two fingers inside her. "Shit," she said again, but this time Kendal knew not to stop. The way Kendal filled her made her wish she had the patience to make it last, but she could already feel the tightness in her belly as the orgasm started to burn through her as fast as Kendal's tongue moved over her clit.

She put her feet on the blanket and thrust her hips into Kendal's mouth and fingers, wanting everything Kendal was offering.

"Oh God, don't stop. Don't fucking stop," she said, her voice strangled and oxygen-deprived. "Ah," she said as she reached that place only Kendal had brought her to.

The last thing she saw before she closed her eyes was a few birds startled out of the high branches as she screamed Kendal's name when she came. The sensation of the orgasm made tears run down into her hair, but Kendal seemed to understand that their appearance had nothing to do with sadness or a problem as she moved up and held her. That innate knowledge was one of the best things of being in love.

"I love you," Kendal said softly as she strengthened her hold.

"You certainly know how." She kissed Kendal's collarbone and moved so she was lying on top of her. "And you're certainly good at it."

"Thank you, love. It's always my honor to touch you." Kendal smiled, seemingly content to stay just like they were, but she wanted her content for other reasons.

"It's no wonder my grandparents love you almost as much as I do." She ran her fingers along the curve of Kendal's cheek and almost cried again at the way Kendal looked at her. "Almost, since I want to be the only one who gets to touch you like this."

"I'm yours, Piper, forever. Never think otherwise." Kendal rolled them over, and she went willingly.

She reached down when Kendal kissed her and found what she knew was waiting, smiling at the wet hardness she found. They had to break their kiss so she could reach comfortably, but this was all the proof she needed that Kendal did indeed belong to her.

"I want you," she said, moving the pad of her wet fingers over Kendal's steel-hard clit. The military training Kendal had received all those years ago helped her with that cool-and-in-control façade she displayed in every aspect of her life except here. Piper had a way of making her lose that tight hold and let go, and she knew she had done it again when Kendal brought her hips down hard. "And I want all of you."

The way she stroked her with no gentleness made Kendal flare her nostrils, but when she smiled, probably too smugly, Kendal held herself up with one hand and touched her. After the orgasm she'd had she shouldn't be this turned on, but she was ready again, and it was a good thing Kendal was so damn strong.

"I can wait, baby," she said, and Kendal smiled and pinched her clit hard enough to make her almost come.

"Can you?" Kendal tugged up and down.

She put her feet on Kendal's ass and shook her head, trying desperately not to lose complete concentration as she touched Kendal in return. "I can't, please," she said, her voice pitching lower as her need grew again. "Please, baby, keep going."

Something about making love like this and seeing Kendal's strength on full display really turned her on, and she kept her eyes open to see Kendal go over the edge. She followed right after her and wrapped her arms and legs around Kendal when she fell into her.

"You think we'll be okay?" The question came out without permission, but Kendal didn't move.

"We'll be fine, and nothing will come between us," Kendal said, kissing the side of her breast. "Your waking dreams have the ability to be changed, so no matter what comes, we'll take care of it."

"When you say it like that, I believe you."

"Good, but you don't have time to worry about anything." Kendal raised her head and slipped her tongue into her mouth. "Not for the rest of the afternoon anyway."

CHAPTER FIVE

Rolla opened his eyes and stared at Bruik for a long moment before he sighed. "How can they have gotten so close? I thought we put measures in place and had a watcher in the region?"

"This generation's family are the ones who called me," Rawney said as she brewed more tea for him to bring back his sharp intellect. "We've always known the Order of Fuego exists, but their numbers have dwindled steadily through the centuries. The last few are the true believers of the old fairy tales that most have forgotten, or believe to be simply that."

"So our watchers eventually came to think the same since they waited until someone actually started digging before they bothered to send a message?" Rolla sat back as one of his attendants wiped his chest clean with a warm towel. He wasn't used to such doting, but his new man, Louis, seemed to enjoy touching him whenever he could.

"They will be dealt with, Rolla, but one of their sons was killed at the dig site. We'll send someone to speak to the head of the family before they're stripped of their land and wealth," Bruik said. "It shouldn't come as any surprise since each new head must sign a pledge before he or she takes control of the largesse of the Clan in return for their vigilance."

"Don't wait too long," Rolla said as he buttoned his shirt. "If they didn't know the ramification of their laziness and disloyalty, the future won't change that."

"Aishe is in the area awaiting your order." Rawney tapped her fingers together. "She knows what to do to avoid any problems going forward."

"She's ready for something like this?" Rolla asked.

"She's learned the old ways from me, so she won't disappoint you."

Rawney was invaluable, and he'd given his blessing to her apprentice turned lover because she'd never given him reason to doubt her. "My apologies, but I think we all know the consequences of failure."

"The easiest route is to kill every member of the Order, but for every member we know, I'm afraid there are four unknown. They would burn the world down to avenge any attack on their ranks." Bruik sat with his legs folded under him, appearing relaxed, but Rolla knew the truth of what he'd said. His old friend very seldom made idle conversation.

"We need to talk to Asra and especially Morgaine. There has to be a way to stop all this before it becomes disastrous." He stood and walked back to his window.

"There's one more thing, sire," Bruik said.

"Something you've seen?"

Bruik nodded and took a deep breath. "It's about Piper's grandparents, and Piper's future."

"Their future will be to remain here with their businesses," he said, missing the solitude of their main complex in Egypt. Scrolls and old books were so much less complicated than all these people Asra had surrounded herself with. This had been one of her habits from the beginning, and none of them had been able to steer her away from her nurturing nature.

"I don't think you fully understand their importance, my friend," Bruik said, glancing at Rawney. "The Marmandes' history is an interesting one, and when I came here, I started to understand better how something or someone altered their history to lead us to this day."

"What do you mean by altered?" Rolla asked.

"Rolla, the Clan is ancient and its resources vast, but we don't hold the only talent in the world," Rawney said as she combed her hair back. "For each of us there is a counterpart that might or might not be working with us. That is our strength, I believe. We work always with good in mind, but more importantly, we work together."

"You can see what Rawney means when you compare her gifts with those of Vadoma. If that's true, then there's no reason there can't be someone as talented as me when it comes to sight. We're witnessing it in Piper as she starts to understand her gift." Bruik stood and walked to Rolla's side. "When Piper lets go of her hesitancy and fear as to what the future holds, she will surpass me."

"If that's true, what does it have to do with her or the Marmandes?" he asked, knowing he probably wouldn't like the answer.

"I asked Piper to show me the spots on their property she enjoyed the most as a child. Physically touching and standing in those places made some of my visions come into focus."

Rolla smiled at Bruik's habit of meandering around the truth when he thought it'd displease him. "What did you see?"

"The death of Piper's mother was, by all accounts, an accident. The man blamed for her death was found in a trance, the police report said, and her death drove her grieving father to the brink of madness. He took his own life by ramming his car into a tree."

"Asra told me Piper's story when she came to be named an elder. Piper's misfortune, I believe, ended when she met and fell in love with Asra. Together they'll be an unstoppable team that will faithfully serve the Clan." He took Bruik's hand and led him back to where Rawney was seated.

"The first thing that changed Piper's fate was the death of her mother," Rawney said softly. "Her mother sacrificed her life to give birth to a beautiful daughter."

"The sight of his child with the love he'd lost drove her father to his own death," Bruik continued. "It left a shattered family that clung to what little they had left, keeping Piper exactly where Asra would eventually find her."

"So what exactly are you two saying?"

"That what happened with Angelina DúPon dictated what Piper's future would be. Angelina proved that Asra had weak spots, and Ora tried her best to exploit them for the future. Whoever she used to look for a way to defeat Asra with her soft heart found the one woman who Asra would have no choice but to notice. Piper was a gift from her greatest enemy to date, and the ploy would've worked had Asra not been the disciplined soldier she is."

Bruik seldom had the ability to shock him with such an intriguing story, but he felt like a schoolboy waiting for the teacher to finish the book he'd been reading from. "She's planned for every contingency except Piper's life," Bruik said, having Lenore tell him this chapter of Asra's story. "Asra would've sacrificed everything to save Piper."

"She can't help who she is, Rolla, and that's what's kept her safe and our servant. The only weak spot in Asra's talent as a slayer is those she loves," Rawney said. "Ora's seer was right about that, but they didn't count on her love not only for Piper but for Charlie. She gave him what she'd dreamed of for centuries and let him kill Henri. The loss of the Marmandes will devastate Piper and, in turn, Asra's ability to go forward."

"Stop speaking in riddles and tell me what you mean."

"That Kendal will give up everything to make Piper whole, and that could take a few lifetimes. It will be too late for what you saw today," Bruik said, spreading his hands out.

"But Ora is dead," he said, though the reality made him sigh.

"She is, but she left Piper as a shining beacon for anyone who wants and has the talent to look." Bruik handed him a scroll with his visions and placed his hand on his shoulder. "Because of Asra's threat, the Marmandes lost so much, and we can either do something about it or let the threat stand."

"It's never been done, Bruik."

"No, but Piper is touched by the goddess, and Piper loves the wielder of our justice. To keep balance, we have no choice."

"They found it," Onai told Convel after she'd run home from Oakgrove. "I made it through the fence right ahead of the security forces."

"Was she out there?" Convel stretched her hand out and grimaced as if Kendal had sliced through it in that moment.

"She was, but I didn't stay to watch her. You said to stay out of sight."

"Has Sepf returned?"

"Not yet, but I put out a call," Lowe said, shaking her head. "Why put them in danger if we don't have to?"

"Onai. Head back outside and wait for Sepf." She put no anger into her tone, but when they were alone, she turned and glared at Lowe until she dropped her eyes to her lap. "I love you, but never question me in front of anyone again."

"Something has changed in you since we got here, but it's not a good thing." Lowe stood defiantly and turned her back on her. "Your anger will get one of us killed, and you don't seem to care."

"You don't understand."

"You're wrong. I understand perfectly. Your revenge is more important than me or anyone here. We joined you because you gave us a home and a family, but you don't have the right to sacrifice us one by one."

"We've hunted on her land and she doesn't suspect anything, so stop giving her so much credit. The slayer's only talent is to surprise her victims, but it won't be that easy this time."

"Have you read none of the letters from your family?" Lowe placed her hand on the side of the window frame and seemed to be holding herself up. "You met her as Erik Wolver, but the slayer has killed Ora and a slew of others. The old queen of the vampires was a formidable enemy, and she's dead."

Convel slammed her fist against the desk and growled. "So you want me to run and hide? If that's what you're after, you don't know me at all."

"I want you to wake up before it's too late." The softness of Lowe's voice almost cut through the anger, but Convel didn't get up until Lowe gasped.

"What?" she demanded.

"She found what you left, and it's led her right to you."

Convel stood and shook herself with a smile. The others could think whatever they wanted, but she intended to enjoy ripping pieces out of the slayer and watching her bleed. She stepped outside and stood in the circle the others had made after they'd shifted. Their growls and snapping jaws didn't seem to faze the large horse the slayer was riding.

"Hello, Convel." The voice and those eyes were the same, but this wasn't Erik Wolver. "You want to call off the puppies before someone gets hurt."

"You're not welcome here," she said, not about to do this woman's bidding. "I know how much you respect boundaries and rules, so leave."

In a fluid, smooth motion the slayer drew her sword and cut the bag hanging from the saddle. The bloated deer head dropped close to Onai and was immediately covered in flies. "You come to my home and do that, and you expect me to respect your boundaries? Have you learned nothing since I saw you last?"

The man with her dismounted, took something from his belt, and started to swing it over his head. She was about to laugh at the primitive weapon until it left his hand. The bolas wrapped around the circling hawk's feet and knocked it from the sky. Just as quickly, it was in the man's grasp with a knife against its neck.

"Should we start with her before I pile the rest of your family at your paws?"

"Let her go," Convel screamed.

"Yield, and I'll let you all go, but if you choose to fight, I'll kill every single one of you."

"Our queen would never allow it," Lowe said, sounding almost urgent.

"I know your queen." The slayer took something from her belt and held it out as if daring Lowe to take it. "She and I have an understanding."

Convel glanced back at Lowe and nodded. "What understanding?" Lowe asked.

"You choose to live outside the authority and reach of your queen, which gives you the freedom to do as you please. When that freedom brings you to my home, close to my family with the intent to harm, I can kill you without breaking the Clan's truce with the were queen."

Lowe took the scroll, signed by Queen Tala Bashar and addressed to Asra, and handed it to Convel. "This might be true, but does the word of Rolla mean nothing to you?"

"The word of Queen Tala is favored here. Make your choice, Convel."

"I choose to accept Rolla's invitation, so let my pack go," Convel said and had Lowe hand her the invitation. "He gave his word, which forbids harm to any of us. You do otherwise and you go against the great Rolla."

"Let's find out if he knew about your trespassing, so bring only one with you. You try to trespass again or have anyone try to watch me," Asra pointed to the hawk, "and I'll respect only your queen's wishes."

"Until I'm on your doorstep, Asra," Convel said and laughed.

"Or hanging from the end of my sword." Asra smiled. "In either case I see you've wasted your years, since you still need the pack to make your threats. I faced you alone and with honor, but you need all these pups to prop you up."

Convel tensed in anger, feeling the need to shift. "You know nothing about me."

"I know enough." Asra mounted again, along with her companion, after he released Sepf. "I've wasted enough time here, so remember what I said. Come with only one or risk everyone."

CHAPTER SIX

Kendal rode back silently, furious that Rolla hadn't bothered to tell her he'd invited Convel Lupo to her home. That wasn't his place, and it never seemed to bother him that he never cared about the enemies she made in his name. People like Convel wanted to take their pound of flesh from her, not the man who sent her to do his bidding.

Morgaine was waiting in the barn when she returned and stayed there until the grooms led the horses away. "Rolla will be here tomorrow, but he wants to see you before he meets with all of us."

"I'm in no mood for Rolla and his minions," she said, starting back to the house.

"He apologizes for reaching out to Convel first, but he wants to talk to you about Piper."

That stopped her. "What about Piper?"

"He said his words are for you only," Morgaine said.

"They may be, but I'd like to come with you," Piper said when she joined them in the yard. "He's afraid of how to tell you something without pissing me off."

"What?" She was getting angrier that the birth of their daughter was getting mired in all this crap.

"Hali's too young to know everything you've faced today, so lose the frown and take me into the city." Piper got close enough to tap on her sword hilt and shake her head. "Leave the hardware. You won't need it."

"You can read my mind now?"

"Not very often, but I get lucky every now and again." Piper waited until she handed Morgaine the sword, then hugged her. "It's how I know how much you love me, so don't forget that."

"I guess you know what he wants, then?" She kissed Piper, then walked with her to the closest available vehicle and helped her inside. "Morgaine and Charlie, watch over my family and yours until we get back."

"You have our word," Morgaine said.

"Do I get any hints before we get there?" She waved off the driver and faced Piper before she took off.

"It just popped into my head when I was feeding Hali, and I think Rolla wanted to tell you first so you could soften the blow. I should've known when Bruik took me on a few walks and asked a lot of questions. He figured it out at the tree swing next door, since it's the one place I have the most vivid memory of my father."

Piper told her what she'd seen in her vision as Ora put her plan into motion. The face from Kendal's past that would make such a difference to her future was no coincidence. "I was supposed to be your weakness, baby, not your wife. If Henri had succeeded in turning me, you would've been easier to bring down. That was the vision the seer gave Ora when she demanded it. You were getting too strong and good at your job for her not to try to destroy you."

"Her seer was wrong, then?"

"Not necessarily." Piper closed her eyes as they passed the spot where her father had died. "Her seer and I have something in common."

"The visions and their outcome can be changed," she said, placing her hand against Piper's cheek.

"It seems to be a family flaw." Piper kissed her palm. "If given the power to change that about this gift of mine, I'd keep it the same. I think, though, I won't have a choice, and this will be how it always is."

"That's something I can accept if you can." She turned onto the interstate and relaxed when Piper took her hand. "But what do you mean by family flaw?"

"I'm not the first seer in my family, and my distant grandmother is who expanded her sight for Ora. But I don't know if she got it wrong because of me, or she didn't mention the vision could have another outcome."

"What does your gut tell you?"

"That it was both. She tried to protect me by omitting enough to keep me safe and leaving out the part that it could end differently."

"So because of me, you had to grow up without your parents," she said, and some of her anger returned. "I'm so sorry, Piper."

"Don't say that. This, not any of it, is your fault," Piper said passionately. "Ora was a sick bitch that stole something precious from me and my grandparents, but I choose to not see it like that. You are my fate, but your love for me is real. It's not because of some spell or magic. All that pain that at times almost drowned me brought you to me. That seer saw it, and so did Aphrodite, so you should be angry that your life was planned out for you in a way."

"I'm under no one's spell but yours, my love. My feelings for you are mine, and they're real."

"That's true, so how can I be anything but happy about that. You gave me a child and a life I didn't think possible, so whatever comes next will be more than I deserve."

"You deserve every bit of happiness I can give you, and I'm going to do that every chance I get."

"Then don't be mad about Rolla and the rest. He might be aggravating, but he really cares about you. It's one of the reasons he's forgiven you every time you've broken a rule. His world is more complete with you in it, even if you never raised another sword."

"You might be overestimating his fondness for me."

"You'll see, so I'll keep telling you until you believe me."

They kissed when Kendal arrived at the Piquant, and Piper held her for a moment before they got out. "Will you believe something for me?" Kendal said as she looked into Piper's eyes.

"Name it."

"You are my fate, that's true, but you're also my love. You own my heart, and there will be no other for me no matter if my days are short or long." She framed Piper's face with her hands before she kissed her. "I fell in love with you because my heart couldn't survive without you."

"Did you hear what I said?" Piper finally seemed to let loose some of her insecurity. "If I hadn't looked exactly like Angelina, you wouldn't have ever noticed me."

"Give me more credit than that. You're not a replacement for Angelina. You are the woman I waited lifetimes for. For so long I've been taught that for everything there is something out there that balances it. For all the bad there is equal good, and my job has been to try to tip the scales for good." She kissed Piper again, and it broke her heart to see her tears. "If that's true, then the gods have finally taken mercy on me, and they created someone who balances me."

"I'm sure you'd survive without me," Piper said, but she sounded like a woman who wanted desperately to be convinced.

"I'll keep telling you until you believe me," she said, repeating Piper's words. "You are my wife, my love, and the one person in my life who knows all of me. I love you for that, but especially for standing beside me."

"I'm starting to believe you, so forgive me for being such a dope. I think it's the hormones the sun couldn't take care of."

❖

"Piper." Bruik took both of Piper's hands and kissed her forehead. "Do you finally see it?"

"Took me by surprise, but it's a new concept for someone to be able to plan this far ahead." Piper hugged Bruik, then held her hand out to Kendal. "Immortality has been something so many have searched for, but it finally hit me today what all of you have seen and been through. It's just as shocking that someone would've seen me or my family that far back."

"The time period we're talking about is just a blip in time, but your family's talent seems to be strong, so I hope you can forgive your distant grandmother for what she did and the reason Ora went through such trouble." Bruik kept them by the door, and Rolla seemed not to mind waiting.

Piper nodded and kissed his cheek. "To condemn her or Kendal for something they had nothing to do with would be like holding Hali accountable. I love her too much to blame her for Ora's evil nature." They followed Bruik into the main room of the large suite and accepted Rolla's embrace.

She smiled as Rolla kept his hands on Kendal's shoulders, smiling up at her. Kendal liked referring to Rolla as the old man, but he actually looked like a young, nerdy college professor. His appearance definitely gave no hint of the thousands of years he'd roamed through time. The woman with him in a way reminded her of Vadoma, which put her on high alert. The main difference was the light-blue eyes, marking her as part of the Genesis Clan, and her being here with Rolla wasn't part of a friendly visit.

"Rawney," Kendal said, kissing the woman's hand. "This is my wife, Piper." Kendal took a step back so she could come closer. "Piper, this is Rawney Lumas, the Clan's head Romani shaman."

"It's a fancy way to say witch," Rawney said, framing Piper's face with her hands. "You're as beautiful as Kendal said, and congratulations on the birth of your daughter."

"Thank you." She didn't move since the woman's touch was strangely soothing.

"Please sit," Rolla said, and she and Kendal took the small sofa. "And please accept our congratulations on Hali's birth. You certainly have bent some of our known reality since you arrived in Asra's life. This is your first lifetime, Piper, but you will always walk in the light in full sight of the gods who bless you and those you love."

"Thank you, and I'm sure I wasn't your choice to join your ranks, but I appreciate your acceptance. None of this was expected, but I'm happy, and when you see Hali you'll see why." She took Kendal's hand and smiled. "She's definitely ours, both Kendal's and mine."

"We'll head back with you, but that's not why we asked you here first," Rolla said as Rawney stood and started brewing tea. "Today you looked back and saw the lengths evil will go to in their effort to win. We may not understand their reasoning, but their drive to plunge the world into darkness is constant."

"I'm not gullible enough to turn away from Kendal and her job, if that's what you're worried about."

"That's the last thing we're worried about." Rolla leaned forward and rested his hands on his knees. "As I was saying, you looked back, but you need to consider another aspect."

"Rolla, I love you, but spit it out," Kendal said, and Piper laughed.

"Be nice, babe."

"Good luck trying to calm this one down, Piper." Rolla shook his head but appeared to relax. "We also need to look forward, which is, for me, the scariest place. You have that gift, and your sight can be altered."

"It was key in defeating Julius before he gained the power of the serpent sword," Kendal said.

"The coming months will bring danger that will make Julius's betrayal appear minor. The bond you and Piper share is essential to the same successful outcome." Rolla appeared almost uncomfortable in getting to the point.

"I already told you that I don't blame anyone but Ora for my parents," she said with conviction. "I sense that you don't believe my commitment to Kendal and to you."

"Your parents have already been stolen from you, Piper," Bruik said, patting Rolla on the back. "After staying with you and Kendal, I've started to see a new set of visions that at first made no sense. They didn't because I didn't have all the information."

"And do you now?" she asked.

"If you accept what the Clan will ask of you, Kendal, Morgaine, and Lenore, you will lose your only living relatives, Mac and Molly."

"Then forget it," Kendal said, but Piper squeezed her fingers.

"We cannot ask you to make that sacrifice," Rolla said as he moved to kneel before her. "I cannot ask that of you even if the others had disagreed with me."

"I appreciate you saying that, but I imagine you will ask us to go back into the devil's teeth if you need us, no matter what the sacrifice is."

"I can if I can promise your grandparents' safety."

"How?" She knew the question was unnecessary because the truth suddenly popped into her head.

"Tonight as you allow us to celebrate the birth of Hali and Anastasia, we will mix the elixir of life, if Mac and Molly agree. You and Kendal are committed, but we all realize from now until always, your family will be the reason you both will be successful." Rolla placed his hand on her knee before he stood back up.

"What did you see?" Kendal asked Bruik.

"I'm not trying to put either of you off, but please wait until we're all together tonight."

"It has to be something for you to break the most sacred of rules," Kendal said.

"What rules?" Piper asked, still shocked at Rolla's words.

"No matter how much we love our families, we can't mix the elixir to keep them with us. My father was killed, and Henri was the only family I had left, but had my father lived, I couldn't have saved him. We must all, no matter our position, accept the natural order of things even though we are, in a way, an affront to nature."

"I understand what you're saying, but we must always put the greater good before rules and everything else. This isn't simply about trying to make up for what Piper has lost. Mac and Molly are a part of what's coming." Rolla accepted the cup from Rawney and stood waiting for everyone to take one. "We will all respect their wishes, though, because we can't force this on anyone."

"But how are the other elders, like the ones who were more than happy to allow Travis to rise after his betrayal, going to handle this? If the Marmandes accept, I don't want to have to battle the old and unbending guards in our ranks," Kendal said, then took a sip of the tea after sniffing the contents.

"You have nothing to worry about. Once you understand the stakes, you might usurp me." Rolla sounded totally serious. "I would gladly hand over my title."

"Keep your crown, old friend. My coming days will be filled with enjoying the child and woman of my dreams."

"If any of us deserved to have the ability to have brought children into the world, it is you, Asra. I'm happy for you both." Rolla smiled, and it was the happiest Piper had ever seen him.

They left knowing Rolla and the others wouldn't be far behind. Piper got in after Kendal opened her car door and stayed quiet until Kendal was next to her. "What the hell was that?"

"If Satan exists, we're getting ready to meet him. It's the only explanation for the old man to agree to this." Kendal finally drove out, but not before she reached over her. "Rolla is a lot of things, but he doesn't have a rebellious bone in his body."

"Interesting, but let's get home. I have to feed Hali and give Pops and Gran the news of the most interesting gift they're ever going to get." She kissed Kendal's palm and laughed. "And if we really get to meet Satan, he's going to regret ever inventing hormones in recently pregnant women."

Oakgrove was lit up when Kendal and Piper returned as the staff prepared for the dinner guests they were expecting. One of the men took the car after Kendal had helped Piper out, and no one else bothered them as they headed up for the master suite and Hali.

Kendal opened the door and found Molly inside, walking around with the baby and trying to calm Hali's crying while Mac sat nearby smiling, even though his great-granddaughter seemed none too happy.

"Sorry we took so long," Kendal said as Piper relieved Molly so she could feed the baby. "Has she been crying long?"

"Only a little bit, but who could blame her? She was hungry," Mac said, ready to leave when Piper started unbuttoning her shirt after she'd sat in the rocker Kendal had bought for her.

"You don't have to go, Pops," she said, and a second later the room grew quiet as Hali got what she wanted. "We actually have something to talk to you about." She glanced at Kendal, who nodded and waved her on. "I think you should start, love."

"Is everything okay?" Molly asked as she moved next to Piper and took her hand.

"Everything's fine, but we have a few things to discuss with you, and you should both understand you're under no obligation to do anything you don't want to." Kendal shrugged when Piper laughed at her rambling. "I'm doing my best, but the rest might be a little bizarre."

"You're over three thousand years old, you got my granddaughter pregnant with the help of the goddess of love, and you've made Piper immortal. What, pray tell, can be more bizarre than that?" Mac asked as Molly joined Piper in laughing. "I'm also going to forget for now that you got Piper pregnant without any kind of ring or wedding, so let's hear it."

"All of it?" Kendal asked Piper.

"They deserve to know. The more I think about it, the better I feel about the situation." She caressed Hali's cheek and didn't try to think about her father holding her like this, if he ever did. Was the spell or curse they'd been subjected to been stronger than the love he'd felt for her? "None of us are to blame, so it made me think differently about the whole thing."

Kendal sat and started talking about what had happened to their only son and the woman he'd loved. "If you can't forgive me, I'll understand, but you have to know I would've sacrificed myself to give you all back what you lost. Ora cared nothing about the pain she inflicted, but I would've changed the outcome had I known."

"Piper's right, Kendal," Molly said, her tears falling. "I've spent every day from the second I heard my son died thinking of where I'd failed him. Mackey was so lost after Jen died in labor. He simply gave up after that, and we blamed ourselves for not seeing what he was going through…for not seeing his pain."

"You have to understand that nothing you did or said would've made a difference," Kendal said, kneeling before Molly. "Look at that beautiful baby and know the power of magic possible in the world. It's a balance that has both blessed and cursed you, and the only thing they have in common is me."

"Asra," Mac said, placing his hand on Kendal's shoulder. "That was the name your father gave you, and then he was ripped from your life by the woman that took my son from me. That's the only thing all this has in common. If I cursed you for something you had no idea of, then I curse Piper and your daughter along with you."

"Thank you," Kendal said, and her tears mixed with Molly's when she hugged her, then Mac.

Piper hadn't seen Kendal cry often, but she was glad her grandparents had come to love Kendal as part of their family. "Thank you, Gran, and Pops." She lifted the baby to her shoulder and patted her back. "You can see that Kendal showed us the way to be happy again."

"That's right, so if you were worried, don't be," Mac said. "I might've been waiting a long time, but our tides have turned."

"Rolla and the elders had something else aside from that to talk to us about," Kendal said, getting up when Piper held the baby out to her.

"Our lives are totally different now, and you'd think that since I have everything I've ever wanted, I wouldn't have anything else to worry about." She glanced over at Kendal cooing at Hali as she got ready to finish feeding her. Once she'd exposed her other breast, Kendal handed Hali back. "There was only one thing."

"What?" Molly asked.

"Losing the two of you. I have Kendal and Hali, but you're just as important to me."

"You won't find any way around that one, sweetheart. Hopefully that's a long way off, but I'm confident we'll leave you in good hands," Mac said as Molly leaned against him.

"There is a way around it, and Rolla will offer it to you tonight," Kendal said, and Piper almost laughed at the shocked expressions on her grandparents' faces. "You have to understand the elixir of life isn't mixed very often, especially by the Clan's most senior elder, so think about what you want. If you refuse, I doubt he'll offer again."

"The chance at immortality?" Mac said, sounding as if his answer would be no.

"Everyone drinks for their own reason, Mac. Mine wasn't perhaps the most noble, but I needed to live long enough to avenge my father. If I'd been offered the same chance now, I'd drink so I'd never be separated from Piper," Kendal said, and Piper blew her a kiss. "I'd never try to push you into something you might not think you're ready for, but the possibility of you two always being in Hali and Piper's lives makes me happy."

"We love you just as much, Kendal," Molly said.

"Thank you. It's nice being part of a family again. Of all the things I had in my first life, it was the thing I missed the most."

"Will you mind if we talked about it before Rolla gets here?" Mac asked.

"Of course not. Go ahead," Kendal said as she helped Molly up. "I'll come get you when they arrive."

The Marmandes walked out holding hands, and Hali finally slowed down enough to let her nipple loose. Hali blinking slowly up at her and her small mouth forming a perfect circle made her fall in love all over again. She was awed that this perfect baby was theirs.

"I thought you were beautiful from that first day when you cursed me out, but you're stunning holding her." Kendal locked their door and knelt next to her. "My two loves."

"She looks like you," she said as she ran her fingers gently over Hali's thick, black hair. "I'm so lucky."

"She looks like both of us, and she'll be as beautiful as her mother." The baby gurgled when Kendal lifted her and held her hand out to Piper. "How about a family bath?"

"You have the best ideas." Piper followed her into the bathroom, stripping off clothes as she went. "But you haven't mentioned the other new baby in the house."

"Anastasia is enjoying some time with her proud parents, though Rolla's little visit might change the dynamics of the happy day. But I'm curious to see how the babies do together." Kendal handed over a naked Hali and made quick work of her clothes as the tub filled.

"You know having kids never crossed my mind, but aside from you, it's the most wonderful thing to ever happen to me." She sat back against Kendal and laid Hali on her upturned knees. "She's ours and she's absolutely perfect."

The baby shivered for a moment, but stopped when Kendal

carefully drizzled water on her abdomen. "Whatever Rolla wants, once we're done, let's come back here and enjoy Hali until we'll have no choice but to move on."

"Like I said, you have the best ideas."

"Just wait until we get rid of all these people," Kendal said, then kissed the side of her neck. "I get my most inspired ideas when I'm alone with you."

"Let's get the show on the road, then."

CHAPTER SEVEN

The university's largest archeology lab was quiet and empty, even though the semester was under way and the specimens that needed cleaning and cataloging were starting to pile up. Oscar had informed the administration that he needed the month off to finish a grant application important for their future funding, so the rest of his staff would take over his workload until then. The only person allowed inside was Pauline, and they had rarely left after his meeting with Alejandro.

"None of these glyphs have a reference in history," he said as the computer finished another extensive search. "After we find a few symbols, we'll be able to fill in the blanks."

Pauline nodded as she flipped through the old texts she'd brought from the university's library, her place, and Oscar's. "It might not be in any recorded history, but it's someone's history. We just need to come close to a hint to what direction we need to take, and we'll be in business."

"It's a good mystery, but you've certainly bought in to Alejandro's story. You do know the Order of Fuego and the old rumors are, like most ancient stories, fantasy, right?" He rolled his chair back and rubbed his eyes. "When you first got here, I didn't take you as a fanatic."

After he really looked at her, she closed her eyes and shook her head. "What do you know of the old rumors? Your father certainly qualifies as a fanatic, so I'm sure he's tried to turn you."

"What, to there being a great treasure buried at that site?" He laughed at all these educated people who blindly believed in what was most probably a hoax. He moved to the coffeepot and started preparing a new batch. "I'm sure some hidden and unfound treasures might still exist, but we'll be lucky if that site has a few pieces of broken pottery. The other things left there are a few traps guarding nothing."

Pauline stood and sat on his lap, facing him and putting her hands against his neck. "Then why work on it at all?"

He tried to suppress his sudden surprise and excitement when she brought herself down hard on his crotch. "Whatever the pits were intended for is gone, but the history of it is locked in here." He pointed to the large blowup pictures they'd made of the glyphs. "I'll keep looking because to me the real treasure is in the knowing."

"That's it? What if all the old legends are true?" Pauline moved up so that she was firmly pressing into him.

"Then the museum people will be thrilled, and people like my father will be put out of their misery. I say that since I doubt anything we find will change the fate of man." He fought to keep his eyes open when Pauline bore down hard, making him stiff. "We might open up a new avenue of study into an unknown civilization."

"Clear your mind for now." Pauline stood and unzipped his pants so she could pull his penis free. "Just think about this and nothing else." She kicked her pants off and, when she sat back down, guided him inside. "Think only about how good you feel and believe in something. Fuck me until you believe in the possibilities."

Her words almost slammed into his head, and he stood up with Pauline wrapped around him. He set her on his desk and thrust almost savagely into her, but that seemed to be what she wanted. "Fuck," he screamed when she tightened her sex around him. All he could think about was Pauline and how good it was to be inside her.

It ended too soon, but he came with a roar and squeezed her ass to stay inside her. He was sweaty and tired, but she'd cleared his mind. As he opened his eyes, something seemed to click into place, and he pulled out and shuffled back to the computer with his pants around his ankles.

"I think I know the answer," he said and started furiously typing. "There. That's it."

"We welcome these children into our family of light," Rawney said as both Morgaine and Kendal held their babies while everyone in the room raised their wineglasses. "May they always search for the truth, as their parents have for generations. They are our future, and we rejoice in the kindness of the goddess."

"To our future," Rolla said and raised his glass higher.

Aphrodite suddenly appeared as they all drank and walked to Morgaine first and held her arms out for the baby. "Anastasia, you have my promise to always watch over you and take harm from your path if at all possible." She kissed Anastasia's head, placed a finger in Morgaine's cup, and placed a drop of wine in the baby's mouth.

Kendal watched the goddess in her own baptism ritual, and when Anastasia's lips closed around the slender finger, the baby seemed to glow for a split second. She glanced at Piper, and her love's eyebrows hiked up. Whatever Aphrodite had done, Hali was next, since Morgaine took her daughter back.

"Don't look so worried, my warrior," Aphrodite said as she kissed Kendal briefly on the lips before doing the same to Piper. "The four of you have restored my faith in mankind, and you've returned to the world two souls who truly deserve a long and joyful life."

"She's beautiful," Kendal said as she peered down at Hali. "Thank you for this gift, Goddess." She dropped to her knees and held up her child. For a very long time she'd believed only in herself, but she was willing to bend a knee if it would keep Hali safe.

"Like no other, you've served me faithfully, Asra. Despite the pain you've endured and the evil you've fought—you never lost hope." Aphrodite placed her hand on Kendal's cheek. "You have proved yourself worthy over and over again, and you love Piper the way she deserves. You were right in that in your life there'll be no other."

"If you had anything to do with bringing her to me, you have my undying gratitude and devotion," Piper said, taking Aphrodite's hands when she held them out to her.

"You've been through as much pain as Asra, but she is your true mate. She came to you not to erase your hurts, but to help you carry the burden of them. With time and belief in each other, that load will become lighter and inconsequential, no matter what comes your way."

Piper closed her eyes and knelt next to Kendal. No one said a word as the goddess placed her hands on their heads and spoke a language Kendal didn't understand but knew Piper did. Whatever it was seemed to be a good thing, since her head became warm and the sensation flooded through her all the way to her feet.

"Remember to trust in each other, to listen to one another, and most importantly, to love one another. Do you both swear to this?"

Aphrodite asked, and she and Piper said yes together. "Then you are bound for all time."

Aphrodite released them as a flash of light appeared behind her, and after it cleared a man was standing there. He was heavily muscled and wore a leather apron, so Kendal had an idea who he was. Hephaestus wasn't the most attractive of the gods, but he had married one of the most beautiful of women.

"Your grandfather was right, Piper. Every woman needs a ring," Aphrodite said as she held out her hand and the man dropped something into it. "Hephaestus made these especially for you." She gave Kendal and Piper each a ring hammered out of gold. "May they always be a reminder of the love you share."

They exchanged rings and kissed before Aphrodite dipped her finger in Kendal's wine and repeated what she'd done with Anastasia. Hali opened her eyes and raised her hand as if reaching for the goddess, and Aphrodite seemed enchanted. After a few more minutes she handed Hali back to Piper.

Kendal glanced at Mac and Molly and almost laughed at their shocked expressions. The only thing that stopped her was Piper's swift and hard pinch to her side. All this had to be otherworldly for the Marmandes, since it was still a bit strange for her, and she'd seen things that defied imagination. Aphrodite walked to them last and helped Molly and Mac to their feet. They bowed slightly, as if unsure of their actions.

"Would everyone but Asra and Piper please leave," Aphrodite said, not letting go of the Marmandes. "I know you don't need to be convinced to drink the elixir, but I'm compelled to tell you the importance of your decision. I promise to watch over your granddaughter, but she needs more than me to watch her back."

"That's the reason we decided to accept if it's offered to us," Molly said. "No offense, but all this is so very strange. We've lived next door for years and had no idea. I loved mythology as a child and would have never guessed I'd actually meet one of the gods, much less two."

"The Genesis Clan needs someone like you, Molly." Aphrodite made the name sound exotic. "Your love of history will serve your children well in the coming months."

"Thank you," Molly said, and took the hand Aphrodite offered.

"My love," Aphrodite said to Hephaestus. The Marmandes and

the two gods formed a circle by holding hands, and Aphrodite spoke the strange language again. Whatever she said made her hands and her husband's glow and spark before it shot into the Marmandes. "After tonight you'll never age, but I see no harm in turning back the clock a bit before you embark on eternity."

Molly and Mac both took off their glasses and laughed at whatever had happened. "Thank you," Mac said, his hair streaked with the same blond as Piper's.

"You're very welcome," Aphrodite said and smiled. "Just one thing left."

"You don't have to do anything else. You've already been so generous," Piper said.

"This is more a gift of necessity, like before." Aphrodite smiled at her husband. "The coming months will be filled with love, but it will be balanced, as in all things, with difficulty. You saved my realm by claiming the serpent sword, but I call on you one more time, my warrior."

"I'll do my best," Kendal said, and Piper handed her the baby when Aphrodite came closer and hugged Piper.

"The world was once our playground, and we created beings and creatures to entertain ourselves. Those days are long past, but it's not impossible to wake what sleeps. If that day comes you'll need my help again." Aphrodite motioned Hephaestus forward, and he clapped his hands together loudly.

"For you, warrior," he said to Kendal as a sword materialized in his hand. "I forged it with everything you'll need in your battles." He clapped his hands again, and two more swords appeared. "For the others."

"Your gift is a great honor. Thank you," she said as she held the sheathed sword with two hands and bowed deeply at the waist to him. "So many warriors pledged their allegiance to Ares, but mine has always been to you. The forge and what it's made possible has kept me and mine alive and well."

"You honor me, warrior," Hephaestus said and bowed back. "Not many remember the making, only what the weapons are made for."

"We must go for now, but I'm never too far away," Aphrodite said and touched their faces once more before disappearing in a gold mist.

"I'll say this for you, baby," Piper said shaking her head once just her family remained. "You certainly make life interesting."

❖

In the predawn, everyone at Oakgrove walked with the Marmandes outside. "It has been a long time since we've had so many elders welcome our new clan members," Rolla said. He watched Rawney place two cups in front of her in the field where Kendal had sent so many to their eternal rest.

"You've been bathed and cleansed to begin your new life," Kendal said as Rawney started mixing the ingredients of the elixir of life. "You already know happiness, so my wish for you is that it lasts as long as there are sunrises. You both deserve that for giving me the gift of Piper."

Piper kissed Kendal for the sweet words and waited for Rawney to finish the incantations that would bond the ingredients into cups of immortality. "Gran." She handed Molly a cup. "Pops." She handed Mac the other one. "Drink and live forever."

Like Piper had, her grandparents took a tentative sip before draining their cups. "So how will we know?" Mac asked.

Piper glanced back at Kendal, figuring she was better prepared to answer. "Come," Kendal said and knelt facing east. The sky was already a blaze of pinks and oranges, announcing a new day.

When her grandparents took her hand and joined Kendal, they seemed to move with more ease and comfort than they had in years. Their eyes were already like Kendal's and the baby's, but sometimes things were easier to accept when you were shown instead of told.

She sat in Kendal's lap once she leaned back and closed her eyes, waiting for the first sign of the sun. The morning was hot but the breeze made it bearable, and she enjoyed the feel of being held and surrounded by her family. That her grandparents would always be with her freed her mind as if it had been shackled and tethered, allowing her thoughts to wander only so far.

As the heat intensified, a jumble of images played rapidly in her head, and she opened her eyes to find Bruik staring at her as if he knew exactly what she'd seen.

"Let them enjoy their moment, my love," Kendal said, then kissed the side of her neck. "There's more than enough time to deal with whatever it is later."

"Are you sure?" She turned her head and looked at Kendal, seeing only adoration and devotion in the depths of those blue eyes.

"The way I choose to go about my life, especially now, is that everything horrible is so much easier when you aren't alone." Kendal kissed her with the kind of passion they usually shared when they were intimate. "No matter the horror, this circle proves we're not alone."

They turned when Molly and Mac gasped as the sun rose over the trees. All their ailments were now a memory, and health wouldn't be a problem as long as the sun rose every morning.

"Good God," Mac said as he flexed his hands. "This is fantastic."

"Not a bad deal," Kendal said, laughing as she stood with Piper still in her arms. "I'm so glad you both accepted."

"Yes," Rolla said, brushing his hair back as the wind picked up. "You can choose to live out this lifetime as you have, but eventually I hope you'll come to work for the clan. Mac, you'd be a great asset managing some of our many investments, and Molly, you might want to work with Morgaine in the archives."

"I'd love to get a look at the history you've all kept that seems to be a truer picture than what I taught," Molly said.

"You deserve a longer celebration, but I need to call a council to discuss some new developments." Rolla smiled, but Piper could almost sense his distress.

"Finally," she said, and Kendal pressed up against her back.

"Piper," Bruik said as the others started back to the house. "Forgive me, but I didn't want to taint your sight. In the coming days we have to work together, but we have to wait until the visions are clear before we compare what we see."

"Are...is...I mean is this even possible?" Vampires were bad enough, but what she'd seen had to be a mind trick.

"I wish I could say yes, but very few of our members remember that time, so we'll have to depend on their memories and their written accounts." He waved them toward the house and walked by her side. "I'll stay with you if you allow it."

"Kendal and I meant what we said, my friend. You're welcome in our home for as long as you like," she said, holding Kendal's hand and getting a squeeze when she issued the invitation. "Eventually you can help us homeschool the kids."

"I think little Hali will be more interested in swordplay than in the written word. She'll have the heart of a slayer, and she's lucky to have the greatest teacher."

"You've seen that?" Kendal asked, her emotions completely unreadable.

"Every vision I've had when Piper was pregnant assured me of only two things. Your daughter will be happy, and she'll come to love another as deeply and as strongly as you love Piper." He smiled in a way that seemed to make Kendal less tense.

"Will that great love be Anastasia?" Kendal asked.

"That's what I've seen, but before you accuse Aphrodite of deceiving you, Hali will make the choice. She won't simply follow a map someone else has written for her. She'll be as beautiful as her mother and as stubborn as you, Asra." He laughed at Kendal's slight frown as they reached the porch and cocked his head to the side. "You'll soon realize how patient your father was all those years ago."

"Don't pout, baby," Piper said, kissing her. "Stubbornness is a trait she gets from both sides."

"Well, if he's right and she's anything like me as a child, let's hope you're quick on your feet."

CHAPTER EIGHT

Convel came instantly awake when she sensed someone else in her room that wasn't Lowe. It was still dark outside, and Lowe lay pressed against her, naked and warm. She kept her eyes closed and tried to figure out what had woken her out of a sound sleep.

"If you let any enemy get this close to you and your little bitch, it's a wonder you're still alive, little sister."

It had been so long since she'd heard her older sister's voice, and she sat upright to see where she was. "Don't you have better things to do than to bother someone so beneath you, your highness?" Lovell had followed and obeyed their mother's wishes and married into the Bashar dynasty, and she was now consort to their queen.

"Have you no pride left?" Lovell finally stepped by the window, and she could just make out her features from the light outside. "You left us with forty, and you're living in this hovel with only six. None of those are the friends we knew back then. You add insult to that decline by poaching on the slayer's land."

Lovell walked out, but she knew it was to give her the chance to get dressed. "Lowe, wake up."

"Who was that?" Lowe asked, finally opening her eyes.

"My sister, Queen Tala's consort and royal pain in the ass." She threw on a T-shirt and the jeans she'd dropped on the floor but decided to go barefoot. It had never been her desire to impress the hierarchy.

"Why's she here?"

"Let's find out," she said, moving quietly to the main room. She faced off against Lovell and curled her fingers, ready to fight. "The next time you enter my home or insult my mate, I'm going to forget we're family."

"Your problem, cub," Lovell said, using the hated nickname she had used when they were children, "is you never have learned your place." Lovell was on her with her teeth at her throat before she could get more than four feet from her. "Tell them to back down or they'll be dead before they can growl," Lovell said of Convel's pack. All of them had shifted, but Lovell had surely not come alone, so the threat was real.

"Go outside, all of you, and be careful," she said, extending her neck back in a sign of submission. "What do you want?" she asked once everyone but Lowe had left.

"Tala sent me to deliver her final warning so you understand the seriousness of her order."

Lovell released her, and she glared at the ease with which her sister moved and attacked. Their queen had been blinded by the great Lovell Lupo from the first time she noticed her as they trained to take their place protecting the pack. She'd actually met Tala first, but her sister was hard to compete with in any arena, and she'd become invisible to Tala from that day forward.

"She disowned me, hell, all of us, so what else can she do to us?" She dropped into the old, torn sofa, wanting this over with.

"Tala has been more than patient, Convel, so stop acting like a pup that needs weaning. You left, so try not to rewrite history, and you never have made any move to reconcile with the pack. Our mother still cries for you, and we all miss you, but none of that matters to you."

"I didn't fit in there."

"You never tried, so save your weak excuses." Lovell dropped the scroll she'd brought at her feet. "You abandoned your family, and you've tried your best to break our treaties with the Genesis Clan. That alone should've resulted in your death at the hands of the pack, but you're my sister." Lovell's voice grew softer and almost tired.

"What's different now than when I left?"

"Asra let you live this time because Tala and I asked it of her."

"That bitch cut me." She held up her hand as she yelled. "I don't care what Queen Tala or you want. I'm going to kill her."

"The slayer kept her word to Tala, but you'll be released from our protection. Asra will not hunt you all down, but another infraction against the laws of the pack and she has permission to finish what she could've all those years ago." Lovell looked at Lowe, but her face showed no emotion. "You and the others outside are invited to join us if you swear loyalty to our queen and the pack."

"I've never lived with the pack," Lowe said quietly. "If not for Convel I'd be dead. That's true for all of us."

"There's freedom from our rules, Ms. Carey, and there's the love and support of our family and community. I'm not here to force you into anything, but realize the consequences of refusing."

"How's Mama?" Convel asked as a way to change the subject. Losing any of her chosen family or Lowe would destroy her, but her mother still weighed heavily on her conscience. Unlike the Genesis Clan, they did not live forever. Their lives were much longer than those of humans, they could be killed, but they did eventually grow old and pass like every species of wolf.

"She still loves you, but why do you care? It's never mattered to you enough to check on her, Mother, or Felan, even though they still miss you."

She laughed at Lovell's omission. "And you don't miss me?"

"Tala and I have two pups, so actually I think of you every time I'm with them," Lovell said, staring at her like she could see into her soul. "The thought they'd leave me without a backward glance tears at my heart. I didn't understand Mama and Mother's pain until Tala gave birth to our daughters."

"Is Felan mated?" The guilt of never reaching out to her family swamped her.

"She'll marry Chann in the fall. Tala's sister is her second in command and loves our sister the way I love Tala."

"The Lupos are climbing closer and closer to the throne," she said, bitter that she was stuck here while even timid little Felan had a place in the world.

"I wish I knew what had happened to you, so I could save you from yourself."

"As if you don't know. Come on. Finish what you came for, Lovell, because it's not to brag about your idyllic life."

"I know why you lost your way, but take Rolla's invitation and accept his offer. You do that, and Tala will welcome you back. Before you think of running or defying the treaty, you will do it alone. Your little brave pack out there will be sent north to join the others." Lovell snapped her fingers, and Convel heard the yelping outside. "They'll either conform or die."

"They're innocent," she said, standing up.

"They followed you through that fence and wherever else you deemed yourself the right to go. A pack of thieves cannot be called innocent."

"What does Rolla want?" she asked, trying to at least save Lowe from being taken away from her.

"I'm sure it's not the need for a lapdog, so whatever it is, your answer will be yes."

"How do you know the slayer?"

Lovell smiled, but the expression didn't seem to have to do with her. "She's an old friend and honorary protector of my daughters."

"You chose the slayer for that honor?" The naming of a protector was sacrosanct in the pack.

"Your life and that you still have it proves how honorable she is, so she was Tala's and my first choice. Your *choices* have led you to different places, but I try my best to always look after my family." Lovell placed her fist on her heart. "Asra of the house of Raad is no different, and in my soul I know she'll stand by my girls and keep them from harm if I but ask."

"You're a fool."

"Make your decision tonight, or wake up alone tomorrow."

"I won't leave her," Lowe said.

"Not everything is of our choosing, Ms. Carey. Sometimes you leave the decisions to others when you're too stupid to make them yourself," Lovell said, then departed, leaving an empty, quiet house behind.

"What are we going to do?" Lowe asked.

"You heard her. We go and listen, and if it's not reasonable, we run and never look back."

"I can see why you left," Lowe said as she started toward her.

"No, I don't think you do. Lovell is strong, but Tala is stronger in her own way, and I loved her."

"Loved her as in you and she were lovers, and your sister took her from you?" Lowe seemed to change her mind and moved away.

"Not exactly." She rubbed her hands over her face as if the motion would take away her shame. This confession, though, would be better coming from her and not some of her so-called old friends who'd rejoice in the telling. "Our mother worked closely with Tala's mother, so we became good friends. I thought it was more than it was until I kissed her. That's when I found out her feelings for Lovell. There'd never been room for me with her or anyone else there, so I left."

"You can't blame yourself for a misunderstanding when you were much younger. This is your chance to go back to your family. It sounds like they miss you a lot." Lowe smiled at her and sighed. "Tala and Lovell seem happy, so maybe it's time to move on to something else."

"I have," she said, walking to Lowe and pulling her up so she could hold her. "I found you and I love you. That's all I've needed."

"You know where I came from, Convel. They'll never accept me." Lowe rested her head on her shoulder, and she saw the shimmer of tears in her eyes.

"What happened to you isn't your fault, and I won't leave you."

"From what she said, that's not true. Lovell and the rest of them know I'm nothing but a whore. That's not something I can deny."

"You did what you had to in order to survive. Being bitten by a rogue were doesn't make you any lesser than me or anyone else born into the pack. Believe whatever you like, but the most important thing is that we belong together. I love you, and you're mine just as much as I'm yours." She wiped Lowe's tears and held her.

"What about the slayer?"

"Let's see when we go there, and I'll answer you then."

"And you won't leave?" Lowe asked, sounding like the lost young girl she'd found in Arizona a few years before. When they'd first met, her love had rolled to her back and exposed her belly in an instant act of submission, as if begging her not to kill her. A prostitute who'd been bitten by a rogue were and survived didn't understand what had happened to her until Convel had taken her in and fallen in love with her.

"You're my mate, so only death will take me from you."

"Rawney, would you begin, please," Rolla said, and Piper leaned against Kendal as they all gathered in the large front room.

Ever since Rolla had arrived with his entourage, as Kendal loved to say, Piper had been curious about the beautiful woman who loved to brew things and always seemed to be studying everyone around her. Kendal had told her Rawney's position but not her story. Every one of the Clan members had interesting beginnings when they were as old as Kendal, but Piper understood that Rawney was much older than her partner.

"We've watched and tried our best to tip the balance toward the light. People like Ora can be killed, but the followers she left behind are too numerous to completely get rid of. Right now we face other problems, ones we thought we'd dealt with years ago, but it seems they were only sleeping and waiting," Rawney said, her voice almost mesmerizing.

"Was that supposed to mean something, or are you being overly cryptic because Molly and I are new?" Mac asked, and Kendal snorted. Piper was used to his up-front, no-nonsense style, having learned the business from him, but the elders appeared shocked.

Rawney seemed miffed, but Rolla and Bruik laughed. "Sometimes we're used to stating everything in the flowery way we use for the archives, Mac," Rolla said. "You've seen vampires, but there's a lot more out there that makes you wonder who had imagination enough to create them."

"Years before Ora and her kind came along, the few members of the Genesis Clan dealt with something we had very little resource to combat, but with Rawney and her family's help, we did away with them," Bruik said.

"Tell us the what before Mac beats you with a wet noodle," Kendal said, and Rolla clapped.

"Dragons," Rawney said, as if that would explain everything.

"Dragons?" Kendal asked as if that was the most ridiculous thing she'd ever heard. "The big fire-breathing lizards from the storybooks?"

"Kendal, you're old enough to know that all the fairy tales are based in reality," Rolla said. "They existed, and the problem they posed caused Rawney to join our ranks. The big lizards, as you describe them, were her first test."

"If she killed them all, I don't see a problem," Kendal said, and Piper bit down gently on her shoulder to keep her quiet.

"It wasn't that simple." Rawney folded her hands and rested them on her lap. "They're not dead—they're sleeping."

"If you had them in a position to kill them, why didn't you?" Kendal asked, ignoring Piper's subtle request to let the elders finish.

"I've heard you say not everything deserves killing, love, so pay attention," she said, and Rawney bowed her head slightly in her direction.

"They are magnificent creatures that were a sight when they dominated the skies. All those stories about them as unthinking killing machines that people sacrificed their virgins to weren't all that true. From what I saw and subsequently read, they were protective of their families, and they loved their children," Rawney said as one of her assistants brought in a few thick books.

"Some figured out how to kill them, but it was important to us to preserve as many as we could," Rolla said.

"Why?" Kendal and Morgaine asked together.

"Because the woman who gave them life did it by sharing a piece of her heart. Kill them all, and you kill their mother, or weaken her to the point of crippling her," Piper said, and Bruik nodded. "We either have to stop them before they wake or find a way to do what Rawney's family did back then."

"Who in the world would've created dragons?" Mac asked, and Piper agreed when she saw them in flight in her mind, but they'd have no choice except to accept Rolla's request.

"Aphrodite," she said, and Kendal sucked in a breath. "She did say that the gods created different creatures to entertain themselves, but she really did see them as noble creatures who could teach the importance of love of family."

"She couldn't have tried something cuter, like unicorns?" Kendal asked, and Piper pinched her again.

"Why can't we just do what you did before?" Morgaine asked Rawney.

"Because I didn't work the spell that trapped them so the goddess would live."

"I thought you—" Kendal said, but Rawney raised her hand.

"I was given the elixir in that time, but my mother cast the spell that locked them in perpetual sleep," Rawney said as Lenore started to flip through the books. "I was learning back then, so she took up the challenge."

"Why were they put to sleep?" Molly asked. "If Aphrodite

created them for those reasons, wouldn't they eventually have been worshipped?"

"They were by some, but many more thought their blood and various parts held the key to eternal life," Rolla said. "Rawney's mother worked a spell that would rid the world of them after they'd grown vengeful once others started to hunt them. The group that worked against her and eventually killed her consisted of the men of the Order of Fuego."

"The Order of Fire," Kendal said and shook her head. "Never heard of it."

"That's not surprising." Rawney's auburn hair fell onto her face when she leaned forward. "They've kept to themselves all this time and have been working very secretly for centuries. The elders and slayers at the time thought they'd gotten them all, but that obviously isn't the case."

"So how do we know they're working now, except for my vision of them doing just that?" Piper asked, and her grandparents still appeared shell-shocked since she'd become a seer overnight.

"This was something unique, so after the spell was cast, we left watchers in all the areas the dragons were placed. Our watcher in Costa Rica sent word after his son was killed at the dig site," Rolla said.

"Like after they actually started digging?" Morgaine sounded disgusted.

"They know the consequences of their actions, but yes," Rawney said.

"No matter the century, these things always play out the same. They've been watching something on the Clan's payroll, but they stopped believing in why they're doing it a long time ago." Kendal's assessment made everyone nod. "I guess the power behind the Order of Fuego offered enough money for them to think they were fools for adding to their wealth over what they thought was a whole lot of nonsense. It's not the first time that's happened."

"That's true, but with one big difference. These idiots have actually done the unthinkable and broken the first set of locks," Rawney said.

"How many layers are we talking about?" Lenore glanced up from the book she'd opened.

"It's hard to say," Rawney said, and Kendal grunted. "My family always taught us slowly so we understood and respected the power the books contain, so my mother's writings are as foreign to me as they will be to whoever finds them. Every one of my ancestors believes that only with age comes the wisdom to wield the book of spells, and I was too young then."

"What about her sister?" Piper asked.

"She perished with my mother, but her daughters survived. Unfortunately they weren't much help in breaking the code some of the book is written in. Now we need to turn to whatever help we can find, and that includes enemies from the past." Sitting for so long seemed to bother Rawney, so she stood and paced. "Do you think Vadoma would answer your call again?"

"We're not exactly pen pals, but I can contact her and see," Kendal said as Piper stiffened in her arms. "Is this why you invited the fleabag to our home?" Kendal asked Rolla.

"Convel Lupo is no one's first choice, Asra, but unfortunately we'll need her in the hunt for a few things that have been lost in time. Queen Tala asked us for help in bringing Convel back into the fold and thought this would be a good first step, but she'll send a few more if we need them." Rolla sounded almost weary as he sighed. "To include Convel in something like this makes me nervous, but it's hard to refuse Tala."

"What does Lovell have to say about it?" Kendal asked, and Piper raised her head to glance up at her. "Lovell Lupo is bonded to Queen Tala and Convel's older sister."

"She knew you'd ask, so the royal family is here, and they'd like to meet with you if you're so inclined. I was forced to invite Convel, but I'll leave Tala and Lovell up to you." Rolla stood, and Piper knew the meeting was over.

They really didn't have much more information than when they'd started, but that dragons were real was enough. "Thank you, and I'd like to have Queen Tala and her consort here when we meet with Convel. She's been on her own for years, but let's hope she still has some respect for her queen and family."

"From what I've seen, don't count on it," Piper said. "You might end up needing to put a choke collar and a leash on her."

CHAPTER NINE

"What is that?" Pauline asked as she stared at Oscar's computer screen.

"It's the answer to understanding the glyphs we found, and it's amazing," Oscar said as he started printing. "The area and the time period when the site was built should've been exclusively Mesoamerican, but if this is true, then what we found is incredibly out of place. It's a totally new, never-before-seen revelation."

"Tell me what you mean." Pauline pulled her pants back on and picked up the papers from the printer.

"I think the extensive glyphs are a form of Romani language, but that's impossible. They would've had no way to get from Europe to that jungle that long ago. The only known inhabitants of Mesoamerica were the ones we know already." He set another search with new parameters. "There's no way for them to have traveled, or communicated, but here it is. It's hard to argue since it's literally carved in stone."

"So you can translate it?" Pauline glanced up from the pages and stared at him with an almost predatory expression that came close to frightening him.

"Not yet, but maybe."

"Why the hell not?" she snapped.

"Because the Romani language is fluid even today. It's unique to each particular tribe, so while they had a common way of communicating with each other, each symbol on these stone markers and its exact meaning might be known to only a tribe member. That's true even if it's the same symbol from one marker to another, if more than one tribe was involved."

"How do we find where to at least start looking to decipher

it?" She folded the sheets in her hand and pointed them at him like a weapon. "And don't think you can hide anything from me."

"What are you accusing me of? You know everything I do."

"You're right. I'm sorry." She changed her approach instantly and placed her hands on his shoulders. "Do you think you can find the key? If you're right, we've at least narrowed the field."

"Maybe, but you have to realize these people were a very closed society. If there's a record, we'll find it only within their ranks, and it'll be hard to uncover." He moved away from her and poured himself some coffee. "Let the computer work, and let's take a break."

"You go ahead, and I'll see you later." Pauline smiled almost too sweetly and left before he did.

She'd saved him the trouble of having to come up with an excuse to get away from her for his own answers. He changed his search again so it'd find what he had already, not trusting Pauline's motives any longer. The aggravation of getting mixed up in this had blinded him to the beautiful assistant who'd miraculously shown up to help him and had quickly fallen for Alejandro's bullshit.

He made sure the security system was running before he shut off the lights and locked up. It was probably over-the-top paranoia, but something about all this wasn't what it seemed. The only person who'd be honest with him was his father, and he wasn't sure about even that relationship. Sometimes devotion to something superseded every obligation, including family.

"Are you home?" he asked his father once he was outside.

"Yes," Sebastian said, but he sounded distant.

"Wait for me in the park, and, before you say no, it's important."

"Don't worry. I'll be there."

Oscar glanced around him, sensing eyes on him, watching to see what his next move would be. He went into the parking garage and waited in the stairwell to check if his imagination had run wild after being locked in the lab so long. After a few minutes two men entered and walked close to his car, then started toward the other exit. They were talking to someone as they hurried to the other side, where the taxis usually queued up.

"What the hell is going on?" he muttered as he waited to see if anyone else would come. It didn't totally surprise him when Pauline appeared with two more men. The only person he figured who'd want to keep this close a tab on him was Alejandro. With any luck, his father had left without all these people trailing him as well.

He went to the third floor, where the garage attached to the administration building, then took a cab to the cemetery five miles out of town. He and his father called it the park because of all the flowers and silence, and they often visited his mother's grave together. Missing his mother was one of the only things they had in common.

Sebastian was already sitting on the bench directly in front of his mother's grave. It was one of the only ones in the place that didn't have flowers, but it was clean and well maintained by the man Oscar paid to tend it. He'd often wanted to bring a bouquet but remembered his mother always saying to give flowers to her in life so she could appreciate them, not in death.

"What the hell is Alejandro looking for? And what have you gotten me mixed up in?" He didn't give his father the chance to skirt the issue like he always did. "People are following me, and Pauline seems to be in on whatever this is." His father appeared to shrink away at his tone, so he took a deep breath and combed his hair back. "Look, I know you care about this cult more than you ever did about me or Mama, but tell me what's going on."

"Your mother did everything to keep you safe and turn you from what was supposed to be your true calling, and I've tried to keep my word to her the best way I knew how." Sebastian's expression appeared to be that of a man either drugged or dazed by something equally potent. "You just need to finish, but that's the last thing I want you to do."

"Either tell me, or I'm leaving, and you and that freak will never find me," he said, standing up and moving away from this stranger masquerading as his father.

"No," Sebastian said in a harsh whisper. "He'll find you no matter where you hide. This is too important for him not to give up the hunt for you or the answers you're meant to find."

"Tell me or I'm gone."

"Thousands of years ago, history tells us that man was a simple creature without much thought process, but that's not true. Man evolved much sooner than the currently accepted timelines, and in those early days the world was much different, in that dragons existed." Sebastian spoke so softly he had to sit next to him to hear.

"I thought you were going to be serious," he said as disgustedly as he felt. "Dragons?"

"It's the Order of Fuego. What did you think they're looking for? Matches?" Sebastian asked, pulling him back down. "Sit and listen while there's still time."

"Go on," he said, seeing that his father's expression held no teasing despite his words.

"The dragons were revered, but someone finally found that if he ate their heart, including the fire glands, if he survived, he would become immortal. Only a few survived the ordeal, but they didn't share the secret of how they'd done it. That's all that was mentioned in the old books." Sebastian glanced around them before he went on. "The old writings went on to say that it only took a small amount of time for the dragons to disappear from the skies and from the world, but that's not exactly right. They were gone, but not totally."

"What do you mean?" He thought about the large, sunken rooms he'd found at the site. Depending on their size, it was a perfect pen. If they held dragons, it would also explain the blank walls.

"I thought you didn't believe, mi hijo." Sebastian smiled as he called him his son, like he had when he was little.

"It shouldn't make sense, but what we found didn't make any sense either."

"The old priests wrote about the dragons' disappearance, but not their deaths, so they had to be located. When they could be woken from their sleep, they would bring their saviors a new kind of power." Sebastian moved to speak right into his ear. "When I was younger I found something that Alejandro and his family had searched centuries for. It led you to that site, even though I knew you wouldn't find anything."

"What is it?" He moved closer to his father and took his hand. "And why are you involved with these people?"

"I know you always thought I was more devoted to the Order than to you and your mother, but you should know the truth." Sebastian's eyes filled with tears, and he ignored them as they fell down his face. "I did everything for Alejandro to keep you and your mother alive. He doesn't motivate with reward, but by punishment."

"Why didn't you tell me, Papa?" He put his arms around Sebastian and cried with him. "I think I found something too, and Pauline was with me."

"You must not give them any more, Oscar, and be careful with Pauline. I can't prove it, but she's connected to Alejandro somehow." The way his father covered his face with his hands made Oscar feel his guilt. "You have to believe that I did everything to keep you alive and safe. I was planning to run to get away from this madness, and they killed your mother. After that I thought we were stuck."

"We can still go," he said, but Sebastian shook his head.

"It's too late for me," Sebastian whispered in his ear, the grip on his arm tight and painful. "One of the things I found was something called the Genesis Clan. Try to leave the city and contact them. I pray they'll keep you alive and away from Alejandro's madness."

He wanted to curse himself for not having this conversation sooner, but overwhelming fear did strange things to people. "It's not too late, Papa. We'll go together."

"We have no time," Sebastian whispered harshly. "That bastard seldom lets me out of his sight."

"I've got contacts in the US, and we can be on a plane tonight."

"No, Oscar, you don't understand," Sebastian said, much more calmly. "The only way you can get away from this is for me to let you go. Find the leaders of the Genesis Clan and tell them what you know—everything you found. If I stay here, I can keep them away from you long enough."

"I'm not leaving you. Mama's gone, and you're all I have left." The fear of being alone seized him, and he felt like he was ten watching his mother die some pain-wracked, horrible death.

"It's the only way. Alejandro is a powerful man who knows it's his destiny to find what no one in his family has been able to. He'll kill anyone to accomplish that, and I refuse to let him. Losing your mother was bad enough." Sebastian pressed his hand to his cheek and studied him as if this would be the last time he saw and touched him. "Remember always that I love you, and how proud I am of you."

"Papa, I'm sorry I wasted so much time because I didn't understand." He couldn't stop his tears and smiled when Sebastian wiped them away.

"I gave you no choice, so you're not to blame. Everything I

taught you was to prove to Alejandro that I was initiating you into the teachings of the order, but also making you suspicious," Sebastian said and chuckled. "You were safe until you proved yourself brilliant, so now he sees you as the key that unlocks the door that's been bolted shut to him and his ancestors."

"The glyphs at the site are extremely out of place, but I believe they're Romani in origin."

"See, brilliant. It took me years to figure that out. Now go." Sebastian kissed his forehead and hugged him tightly. "When you find these people, tell them the truth lies with the dead."

"What do you mean?" He didn't want to part with only questions between them, but he felt ignorant since he had no idea what his father meant.

They heard a few car doors slam in the distance, and Sebastian's breathing picked up as if he were panicked. "Run, mi hijo, and don't look back. I love you. Forgive me for not being the father you deserved."

"Please, Papa, come with me."

"Go down four rows that way and look for the tomb with the name Conception. The door locks from the inside. Don't come out no matter what until past midnight. Go, and honor me by staying alive."

He left reluctantly, and Sebastian stayed on the bench, his attention on his mother's tombstone, and only briefly glanced his way. Deep somewhere in his heart and in his mind he knew that expression of longing and pain etched on his father's face would haunt him for the rest of his days because it'd be the last time he saw him alive.

The tomb his father mentioned was like all the others on that row, and the door opened silently, as if someone oiled it regularly. A bag sat in the center of the floor, and he found everything he'd need for the days of running ahead, including a fake passport, credit cards, and a book with contacts in it. "You thought of everything."

At the bottom were two letters, and he touched the neat, beautiful script his father had perfected and used instead of the computer in his office. He opened the one that seemed lighter and had to clear his tears when he heard three gunshots outside.

Mi Hijo,

When you read this, my life will have ended, but don't waste time grieving for me. I hope I had the opportunity to tell you how much I love you. In all my career, the greatest treasure I ever found was the overwhelming joy the first time I held you.

Inside are all the things you need to find the people who'll help you in the war to come. Leave once you know it's safe, and I'll watch over you as always, even from beyond the grave. Once you find the person you trust with the information you have, remember to tell them that the truth lies with the dead. I hate to be so cryptic, but I can't afford for Alejandro to find what he needs to succeed.

Know one truth above all others as you begin this quest. You were loved and so very wanted, despite what you may have believed. My heart goes peacefully and quietly because I know what kind of man you are, and I'm proud to think I had some small part in that.

The other truth is, if we've reached this drastic juncture, then you've taken the first steps toward finding what must stay buried. Do what you can to keep that away from Alejandro, and don't stop going until you are safe.

I love you,
Papa

The muffled voices outside made him stop breathing as he went and locked the door. He didn't care about anything now but finding a way to kill Pauline, Alejandro, and everyone else who'd taken everything from him.

"Well?" Alejandro asked as soon as he answered the phone.

Pauline knew he was already pissed when she'd reported they'd lost Oscar, and Sebastian had slipped his watchers for far too long not to have contacted his son. "Sebastian has been dealt with, and we're still looking for Oscar. Do you want me to take care of him once we locate him?"

"No, you idiot. I need him alive to finish what that old fool wouldn't or couldn't do. Find him and bring him here. With some proper motivation, he'll get the work done."

She glanced at the blood that had trickled from Sebastian's wound and knew that might not be possible. Her father at times had a way of letting his temper set them back. "We've killed his last bit of motivation, so he might not cooperate."

"There's death, Pauline, and then there's pain. The kind of pain that will make you do anything to make it stop, even beg for death. But there'll be only one way out, and a bullet isn't it." He paused, almost as if he was reminding her that she wasn't immune to the same treatment. "Get this done. We've wasted enough time."

"Yes, sir."

CHAPTER TEN

Kendal walked to the bassinet and peered inside as Hali made her presence known with some loud crying, as if all were not right with her world. She and Piper had been sitting outside watching the boat traffic on the river and talking. They were waiting for her old friends to arrive, and Piper told her every bit of her vision.

She lifted the baby and held her at arm's length, and the movement made Hali open her eyes and stop crying. "What's wrong, princess?" She finally cuddled her and moved her to the changing table, studying everything Piper had put within easy reach.

"If all the creepy crawlies that shake at the mention of your name could see you now," Piper said as she started to change Hali's diaper.

"Very funny," she said, reversing the diaper when Piper indicated she had it backward. "I can help with this part since the follow-up is all you."

"You look incredibly sexy as a parent, baby."

"Thank you, and I'm still trying to convince myself that it's all real and she's here."

"You've given me so much, but I know what you mean. It's like my life before you is a distant place I never want to go back to." She walked into Kendal's arms when she finished and turned around. This was where she belonged. Kendal treated her like every woman dreamed of, and it'd been that way from the day they'd met. "I was such an ass in the beginning, so thank you for sticking with me."

"You weren't an ass." Kendal kissed her temple and lowered her hand to her backside and squeezed. "More like a pesky little thing—"

"Buzzing around your ear," she finished for Kendal with a smile. "I remember, and you're too nice."

"Not too nice, my love," Kendal said in a tone that made her raise her head and peer into the eyes that dominated her thoughts. "It's such a cliché that I almost hate to say it, but you're unlike every woman I've ever known. You captured me without trying, and believe me, I spent some days wondering how to rip you from my head and, more specifically, from my heart."

"You had to know."

"I do now, but not then. That you loved me enough to drink has made my whole life complete. Hali only adds to that, so like always, I look forward to my tomorrows."

"Me too, and I have to admit, warrior mine, you make beautiful babies."

"You two can make even me nauseous with all this sweet talk," Aphrodite said as she materialized before them. "Though you empower me more than anything in the world, so don't ever forget what you mean to each other."

"Does it empower you enough to give us another one of these in a few years?" Piper asked as she laid her hand on Hali's back.

"I doubt the big stud needs much help," Aphrodite said, and Kendal cleared her throat. "But we've got plenty of time to negotiate that gift later. I wanted to check to see how you felt about our conversation earlier."

"We still don't have a lot of information to go on, but I do have a question," she said and glanced at Piper when she pinched her hard again.

"Don't worry, Piper. I'm long used to her. Warrior minds are focused and hard to bend, but that's why we love them so much." The goddess came closer and placed a hand on Kendal's cheek. "I couldn't have picked a better champion, though, and your mate also belongs to me. You two make me the envy of the other gods, especially my brother, Ares." Aphrodite let go of her, and where her hand had been left a trace of heat. "So go ahead and ask whatever you like. I have a feeling I know what it is, but ask."

"Why dragons of all things?" she asked, and tensed for Piper's deadly pinch, but it never came.

"There were so few humans back then, and we did things to gain followers after we realized the temples and the worship made us gain strength." Aphrodite stopped and held her hands out for the baby. Kendal smiled as she handed Hali over, not worried in the least.

"You're a beauty, baby girl," Aphrodite said, cradling the baby and cooing to her. "I had a feeling that mixing a half from each of your moms would result in a gorgeous kid."

"So really, if we ask again for a repeat performance, would you do it?" Piper asked, and the goddess laughed.

"Do you think she'll get better at changing diapers?" Aphrodite winked at her.

"She'll do fine, and Hali and Anastasia need someone aside from us and each other to love them." The way Piper said it, Kendal knew it had to do with what had happened to her and that she was an only child.

"When you're ready, you ask, and I'll be happy to if it's within my power," Aphrodite said and caressed Piper's cheek.

"Can I ask what the sword is for?" Kendal wanted that question answered before the goddess disappeared again. "I don't want to do anything to weaken or somehow destroy you."

"The sword is a precaution of what might come of all this, but it will kill a dragon if you're able to make a fatal blow."

"I've taken plenty of killing blows that the sun has taken care of, but I doubt if I can come back from a pile of ashes, so I'm going to try my best to stay away from dragons, much less try to destroy one."

"They won't hurt you, Asra. They're a part of me, and they'll know that, but I don't believe that's what these people are after. And before you accuse me of being evasive, I really don't have the answer. I created them, but as with everything, some men can find a way to pervert it no matter how noble."

"Do you have a guess?" she asked.

"It's not for the dragons alone, since only Ares and I can control them."

"Ares?" Piper said softly.

"They can't be used for war, so don't worry. Everyone in the family knows Ares's ambition, so while they could destroy the world, they're not violent unless someone—anyone messes with their families." Aphrodite handed Hali back after she kissed her forehead.

"Thank you, and our devotion to you will never end," she said as Piper pressed to her side. "I won't forget it in the heat of battle."

"I know. You never have, so the devotion isn't one-sided." Aphrodite started to fade. "And don't forget to listen to Piper." With that, she was gone.

❖

Hillary Hickman stopped at the front gate to Oakgrove and found it locked for the first time since she'd been coming after she accepted a job from Kendal. The house was lit up, so she pressed the buzzer and waited. Something about Kendal and the other people who worked for her left her with a lot of questions, but Piper wouldn't have hooked up with some flake, even if a vampire had been involved. That night was still vivid in her mind, and she was having problems trying to come to some comfort that what she'd seen was real.

That Piper had chosen a woman who wasn't her stung, but her old friend was clearly in love and surprisingly pregnant. She almost didn't recognize Piper, even though they'd known each other for years.

"It's time to move on, Hill," she said softly as she waited for someone to answer and let her in.

"Good evening, Ms. Hickman," someone definitely female said as the gates started to open. "Won't you come in?"

She understood the appeal of Kendal Richoux, but it amazed her at how many beautiful women Kendal surrounded herself with. That was something else that made her uneasy for Piper's future. It was evident by how some of them stared at Kendal that they either had a past sexual relationship or wanted one. How long would it be before Kendal strayed?

Now wasn't the time to think about that since Kendal was waiting on the large porch, Piper seated right behind her. "Hey, sorry to come so late, but…" The air in her lungs seemed to seep out slowly on the last word as she saw Piper nursing the child at her breast, and to her embarrassment, she started to cry.

Kendal rubbed Piper's shoulder and went inside, as if all Hill's jealousy and misery was plain to see, and she was giving them the chance to bury old feelings. "God, I'm sorry."

"Don't apologize, Hill," Piper said, tickling the baby's cheek. "Come sit and meet Hali."

The baby was beautiful in profile, but she didn't look too long, since Piper's breast was exposed. "She's beautiful—congratulations."

"Please sit. I really did want to talk to you." Piper smiled when Hali let go and gave a full-body stretch. "I wanted to because I think it's me who should apologize to you. Believe me, Hill, none of this was planned, and I never meant to hurt you."

"You didn't," she said quickly and wiped her tears. Fuck, even she wouldn't have believed her.

"Come on. We've known each other for years, so you can be honest." Piper held the baby against her shoulder and gently patted her back. "I've always known you might've been interested in something more, and I'm sorry I couldn't give it to you."

"Why her, then?" The question ripped from her soul even if it was petty and immature. "What's she got that I don't, aside from a lot of money and stuff?"

"She's mine, and she owns my heart. I couldn't have been happy with only half the equation. It sounds so trite, but finding the right one really has completed the person I'm supposed to be."

"What about all that weird stuff that happened in England? Why raise a baby if that could happen again?"

"Hill, you're my friend, so I'm going to forget you said that, but don't make that mistake again." Piper's voice rose and startled the baby. A moment later the door opened, and Kendal appeared, not looking too pleased.

"Problems?" Kendal asked and took the baby when Piper held her up so she could get her clothes in order.

"Not really," Piper said. "We were just getting some stuff straight."

"I'm sorry I upset you, Piper," she said, her eyes not leaving Kendal and the child she held. "Good God. She looks just like you."

Kendal and Piper shared a glance, and Kendal nodded at the unasked question. "She does because she's hers," Piper said, staring at her with an expression that dared her to say otherwise. "Hers and mine."

"I know you're better at business than biology," she said, smiling to soften the insult, "but that's impossible."

"Sort of like vampires don't exist?" Kendal asked with no emotion on her face. "Either wrap your head around the unthinkable or leave. At this point you really don't have any other choices, Hill."

"What are you?" It was the one question she'd been dying to ask since that night in England. Kendal and Piper had left her and Piper's grandparents in California after that bizarre night, and she'd walked around that beautiful house at the center of Kendal's vineyard studying all the pictures. The few of Kendal didn't make any logical sense because she hadn't aged. The property's caretakers, Sparrow and her boys, had aged, but Kendal looked exactly the same.

"I'm an old soul who's in love with Piper. Believe me or not, that's not my decision to make for you, but Piper is mine. The baby's ours, and I belong to her with everything I am and have in this life and all others that will follow."

"Do you mind if I talk to Piper alone for a few more minutes?"

Kendal smiled at Piper and took the baby with her back inside.

"She's not the jealous type?"

"She's more the drive-a-sword-through-your-forehead type if you get stupid, but she does get jealous on occasion. Listen, I appreciate everything you've done for me, but she's right. If you can't accept this," Piper said, glancing at the front door, "then you have to go. I'm not going to change my mind no matter how much you want me to."

"This is about me, so I'd like to stay if you don't mind it, and if she lets me. If she makes you happy I'm not going to be an asshole about it."

"You're not staying to keep an eye on her, are you? I wasn't kidding about the sword thing."

"I'm staying to keep an eye on you. One look at that baby, and I believe she belongs to both of you, but there's a million other things I want to know before we get to that." She smiled and did her best to bury her feelings for Piper.

"What you need is to find a nice girl and start a family. I can totally recommend it."

"You're a riot," she said, glad she wasn't losing Piper as a friend. "But now I've got to go see the boss about a report. Hopefully when I'm done she'll still be my boss."

They went inside, and Piper led her to the large study at the front corner of the house that once had been Jacques St. Louis's office. The furniture was still the same, with the addition of the line of electronic equipment, since this had become Kendal's new headquarters for all her business dealings. Eventually they'd have to decide what to do with Marmande Shipyard, but the staff was doing a good job of dealing with the day-to-day operations with both her and Mac gone.

"Honey," Piper said as they entered together and caught Kendal making faces at the baby. "Hill's got a report for you."

"Is Hill's head screwed on right?" Kendal said, holding her finger where the baby could clamp down on it.

"It never really was, but I think you should let her do her job anyway," Piper said, kissing Kendal and pinching her cheeks.

"Leonardo came back," Hill said, and Kendal nodded. "He asked if he could meet with you to discuss business. He never mentioned what that might be, but he was pretty insistent he get to meet with you."

"Did he leave a way to contact him?" Kendal moved her hand to the beautiful sword sitting on the large desk.

"It's all in here, but I don't think you should go alone." She shook her head when Kendal started to say something. "I know you can take care of yourself, but you're paying me to do it." She stepped closer and studied the blade. "It's beautiful. Where'd you get it?"

"Walmart," Kendal said, and Piper snorted. "I'll call when I set something up."

CHAPTER ELEVEN

Rawney stood outside with a smoldering bunch of sage and seemed to be mouthing a spell of some kind in a language Piper didn't understand. Kendal stood next to Piper, holding her hand, and smiled as if signaling that everything was all right. The car that had driven slowly up the drive came to a stop as Rawney finished, and she bowed as the back door was opened. The two women who emerged bowed back, and they seemed regal and powerful to Piper.

Kendal tugged her gently so they could descend the stairs together, and their guests' expressions changed to true happiness. The two blondes came forward, and when the taller and stronger-looking one held her arm out, Kendal grasped it, wrapping her fingers around the woman's forearm. As imposing as the woman was, Kendal was taller and more solidly built, even if her body was hidden by the heavy linen shirt she wore.

"Lovell, welcome to our home," Kendal said, and went willingly when the woman tugged her into a bear hug. "I've missed you, old friend."

"Save some of that for me, Asra," the smaller woman said as she opened her arms.

"Queen Tala, it's great to see you again. How are the children?"

"I'll bore you with pictures later, but introduce us," Tala said.

"This is Piper Marmande, my mate," Kendal said, having told her that in Tala and Lovell's world, that's what Piper was to her. She'd explained so she wouldn't be insulted by the title even if it'd been used by others before now, but hearing Kendal say it made her love her more. It fit perfectly as to what Kendal was to her.

"Over three thousand years," Tala said, taking Piper's hands, "and she finally found you. Congratulations, Piper, and I hope we can become friends. It'll be good to have someone to talk to about the big bears we married."

"Yes, your highness, it will. Please come inside," she said after shaking hands with Lovell.

The table in the formal dining room was set, but she invited them into the large living room for a drink. Tala and Lovell seemed like every other couple, but Kendal had told her they could shift at will into wolves that were larger than any known species. They could also mate despite their sex and produce offspring like the twins Tala and Lovell had brought into the world.

She accepted the baby from the young woman they'd chosen as their nanny and turned to Tala and Lovell. "This is the newest addition to our family, Hali."

Tala held her arms out and Piper handed her over, not sensing any danger. "She's beautiful," Tala said, glancing up at Kendal when she held the baby closer. "She's yours," she said, not in question form. "How?"

"It's a long story we can tell you at dinner, but it's her dinnertime first. Would you like to come up with me?" Piper asked, taking Hali back.

Tala followed her upstairs after placing her hand on Lovell's chest. "Thank you for putting the smile back on her face, Piper. Asra deserves the kind of peace only a true mate can bring into any life."

She opened her shirt and cradled Hali against her breast. "How long have you known Asra?"

"I met her a few years before she came here and built this place. My mother was queen then, and Lovell had first started showing interest in something other than the hunt and patrol." Tala laughed as if recalling something really humorous. "She'd probably still be loving her unencumbered life running through the wild if it hadn't been for Asra."

"She has a talent for matchmaking too?"

"Lovell challenged her when Asra came to a meeting with my mother in the name of the clan. If my mate expected a fight, Asra disappointed her by not drawing her sword and instead told her to look at what she had to gain by staying alive and whole. We were bonded less than a year later."

"You waited all this time to have children?" she asked, finding Tala easy to talk to.

"My mother died in a freak accident not long after that, and I faced rebellion once I'd claimed the throne. Now seemed a better time because I wanted to raise them in peace."

"I understand that," she said as Hali slowed. "Thank you for being her friend."

"She is that, and I owe her my throne as well as for giving Lovell a kick in the rear, so I've loved her for a long time. You have to understand that Convel met her before that, and it was Asra who spared her that first time at the request of Convel and Lovell's mother, Melle. Every time after that it was because Lovell and I asked it of her."

"She's come here," Piper said, not knowing exactly how to finish.

"We must all eventually choose what's right, Piper, and Lovell's made that clear to her sister. It will kill a part of her that won't be able to be restored, but she sides with our children's protector. So do I."

"I'm sorry if it's hard."

"Our mates and our children are why we live full lives, my friend. Asra is no different. Let's hope Convel comes to the same conclusion before it's too late, but you have nothing to fear from me or my pack. Asra has come and fought for my mother and me whenever we've asked it of her, so she'll face no betrayal from me or Lovell."

They went down and joined Lovell and Kendal in the dining room, where Piper told them the story of the goddess and their reward for helping her with the Sea Serpent Sword. Both Lovell and Tala listened like children being told an adventure story, and they exchanged an interesting but unreadable glance when she finished.

"Is something wrong?" she asked, but Tala waited until the dishes were cleared before she spoke.

"The Genesis Clan has Bruik and the other seers as well as the archivists who record their visions of the future, but so do we. Anatol Bashar, Lovell's other mother, brought an old prophecy to my attention recently." Tala took a deep breath but smiled as if to put her at ease. "This is from some of our first ancestors and was told for centuries until, like all far-fetched stories, it faded from history."

"How far back?" Kendal asked.

"Before you and most of the elders existed," Lovell said. "Back to a time when people still believed in fairies and in us. Before we were hunted and had to live in the shadows."

"In the time of the gods and dragons," Tala said, staring at them as if expecting them to laugh.

"That time may come again," Kendal said.

"Aphrodite told us someone is trying to find her dragons and awaken them. For what, though, she doesn't know, but it's not for the dragons themselves," Piper said.

"Our prophecy says something similar and that one from our kind will join the hunt because waking them will bring us out of hiding and into our rightful place," Tala said.

"Which is?" she asked.

"Rulers of mankind." Tala said it almost as if she didn't agree, but the pieces were starting to fit.

"So why would Rolla invite Convel here?" Kendal said, her frustration evident.

"Because we needed someone who'd fulfill the vision but would be dispensable once they'd found what can't be found," Lovell said, and Piper could almost feel the pain in her voice. "You know Convel and her total disregard for her pack or her family."

"My promise to you still stands, Lovell. I won't kill your sister, even with the blessing of you and Tala. You can unbind me from my promise, but we can't go back after that. I warned her to stay away from my family, but I'll cause her no harm." Kendal spoke to Lovell, and her words made Lovell's green eyes water with tears that wouldn't fall. "I know that pain, so I won't do that to you, Melle, Anatol, or your children."

"You might not have a choice, Asra, so promise me you won't expose my children to Convel's stupid delusions of grandeur. Promise me," Lovell said, bowing her head.

"I promise, and I'll watch over your children like I would if they were Hali."

"Good, so if you'll allow us, we'll return tomorrow and meet with your elders and share our writings with you," Tala said. "But before we go, we'd like to offer you what you did for our children."

"It would be a great honor," Kendal said, lowering her head in Tala's direction in what seemed to be a posture of respect.

"Piper, if you'll allow it, we need to bare our true selves to your daughter so our animal spirit will know her. No matter how much time or distance, we'll come if she needs us."

"Thank you. You'll be something like godparents then," Piper said, but thinking the Catholics didn't have this in mind.

"In a way, yes," Lovell said as she stood and offered her hand to Tala.

"Turn around, love," Kendal said, walking to her and holding her against her chest with her hands on Piper's abdomen. "They have to get naked for this next part."

Behind them she heard the sudden sound of what seemed to be breaking bones and grunts before the room grew quiet again. Kendal kissed the back of her neck before whispering, "Don't freak out, okay."

It was a hard thing not to do when she turned around and saw two wolves sitting where her new friends had been. The only thing that hadn't changed was Tala's pale-blue eyes and Lovell's green ones.

Kendal bowed again and held her hand out, motioning for her to do the same. Both wolves sniffed and barked softly, so Kendal moved and opened the door so they could lead them up to Hali's room. Each wolf stared at the baby before sniffing her as well. They seemed to be committing her to memory, and when they were satisfied, they went back down. By the time Kendal and she made it to the living room, Lovell and Tala were dressed.

"Thank you," Piper said as Tala hugged her.

"We're family, so no need to thank us. Until tomorrow."

"That was truly bizarre, but cool," she said once they were alone in their bedroom.

"You mean you didn't entertain werewolves before you met me?" Kendal said, unzipping her when she presented her back.

"Kenny Delaney doesn't count, honey," she said of the man who'd truly tried to steal their business. "And I never heard from him after you shoved his head in the toilet."

"I'm horrible for your dating prospects, so hopefully old Kenny has put the word out."

Piper laughed as her dress fell from her shoulders and pooled at her feet after Kendal pushed it down. "I'm glad you're possessive since that's how I feel about you. You're mine and I don't share."

"Not ever, my love." Kendal picked her up and carried her to the bed. "Not ever."

❖

Aishe sat on the wall that surrounded the Rodriguez estate in Costa Rica and idly ate an apple. From the size of the main house and pool, the family had lived well off the Genesis Clan's money. They'd been paid millions over the decades to watch a parcel of land the archives called Ventanas de Fuego.

Windows of Fire was catchy, she guessed, but right now all it contained was vegetation and the kind of unnatural wildlife that would make anyone have nightmares, but someone was indeed digging and uncovering things these people should've been reporting. So far their silence had cost them their son, but the rest of their toll was coming.

"Anything yet?" Rawney asked her lover in lieu of a greeting.

"They posted a few guards around the place today, but I'm not sure why. The only people who've come in or out are the staff and the cemetery representatives, though I'm not sure why they're bothering. From what one guy willing to talk to me said, everyone who died at that dig is dust on the jungle floor." She finished her apple and leaned more into the shadow of the branches that hung over the fence. "Let me call you back."

"What is it?"

"Someone new with a car that screams how important he is just drove up." She dropped down into the yard and waited to make sure there was no movement around her. "Let me see who this is. It might be what we've been waiting for."

"Be careful and don't linger."

"You know you're the only one I linger on. Don't worry, but I have to get closer." She cleared the number off her phone and turned it off before moving nearer the side of the house and climbing onto the roof that was draped in shadows. Franco Rodriguez came out and kissed the man's hands as he bowed over them, like whoever this man was, he deserved the overexaggerated greeting.

"Señor Garza, thank you for visiting my home," Franco said as he still held the man's hands.

Aishe mouthed the name and thought, but nothing came to mind. No one, from what she'd learned so far, had that name. She was in luck, since whoever Garza was, he sat on the large porch out front instead of going inside.

"It's the least I could do, Franco, since your son died in service to our cause. I wanted you to know that I'll erect the memorial to him myself so your wife will have somewhere to go and express her grief. His spirit lies, though, in the one place that holds the secrets we most want to know. Hopefully you understand why we had to do what was necessary to keep the site a secret."

"I understand that, but I don't understand how this could have happened. My boy was not new to digging, so that he'd have been killed by a trap doesn't make sense to me," Franco said, holding his head. "He was my only son, and my heir. Without him I'll have no one to carry this on for me."

"These people who set the traps are to blame, my friend, so it's time to tell me the story you've been reluctant to up to now. Either you believe or you don't." Garza leaned forward and placed his hand on Franco's knee. "And stop all this whining. You still have your daughter, and with time she'll be proud to carry on your name and traditions."

"You have to understand that, while I believe, my family has been charged with keeping those secrets, and have been for generations."

Garza leaned back and sighed. "Then your loyalties lie elsewhere. That's a pity, since I've trusted you with what set you free of the chains these people have put you in. The Genesis Clan hasn't been around here, from what I can tell, in years, but I'm here and with you in your grief. Where are they?"

"Alejandro, please understand that my vow is sacred to my family, and breaking it means we lose everything if they find out. Even if my daughter wants to stay here and take over, if I say anything, everything we have will be lost."

Alejandro Garza, Aishe mouthed as she moved a little closer, not wanting to miss any part of this conversation. Whoever this guy was had to be in the middle of what they needed to find to locate everyone involved in trying to wake sleeping giants. It was surreal they didn't understand the dragons would in no way fit into the time period in which they would awaken.

"I understand that you value that more than the work of the Order. Keep your word, but if you share what you know about me, you and the rest of your family will never live to regret it."

Aishe wondered what Order he was talking about and moved a little closer since she was near another tree that would hide her even though she was almost on top of them. She barely noticed the small capuchin monkey that she startled awake, though, and after one small popping noise everything went black.

CHAPTER TWELVE

Kendal lay on the floor on her stomach, watching Hali sleep on the blanket Molly and Mac had brought over from Piper's baby things. Piper's mother Jen had made the colorful quilt with animal characters in each square when she'd found out she was pregnant with her first child. Piper's eyes had welled with tears when she'd seen it, and she'd run her fingers over the folded material as Molly had handed it over before spreading it out on the floor of their room.

"Are you watching her so closely because she's learned some tricks?" Piper asked when she stepped out of the closet in a robe, holding the outfit she'd chosen.

"She's like her mother in that she's too beautiful not to stare at, so leave me alone," she said and winked. "And why the hell are you over there and not over here kissing me if you're naked under there?"

"Because I'm not getting you all excited with the baby this close to us, so behave and get dressed. We've got a bunch of werewolves visiting today, and I'd like to be prepared before they arrive." Piper dropped her robe, and Kendal groaned at the black panties and bra.

"There's no way I want to waste time talking about Convel when you're dressed like that."

"Suck it up, baby, and get going," Piper said and stepped into her jeans.

"Suck it up is exactly what I had in mind," she said, hopping up and pressing Piper to her.

"Not what I meant and you know it. Get dressed, and let's sit outside and have coffee so I can ask you a bunch of annoying questions." Piper laughed when she picked her up and kissed her neck. "I promise I'll make it up to you later."

"What do you want to know?" she asked, stripping off her robe and smiling when Piper put her hands on her ass. "If you're worried about Convel, don't. She knows better than to try anything, especially since Lovell's on a very short leash where's she's involved. If she gets out of line, her big sister will save me the trouble of killing her."

"I'm not worried about that," Piper said, pressing up to her back after she'd followed her into the closet. "I don't understand why I can't really see forward. All the images I've been able to make out are of the past. Ancient history won't do us any good right now."

"Stop trying to see the future and concentrate on what you can see. Sometimes the best way forward is through the past. History helps us all not repeat our mistakes, if we're smart enough to learn anything from it."

"I know only darkness can take you away from me, but I'm afraid of sending you somewhere without knowing what you're getting into. Your loss before Hali would've devastated me, but now with her, I don't know if I could go on." Piper squeezed her harder. "After I fell in love with you, I understand my father so much better now. All those days I spent cursing him for leaving me seem like such a waste." Piper couldn't seem to lift her head as she said the words, and as always when she spoke of her parents, something in Kendal hurt like someone had driven a sword through her gut.

"Believe me, my love, if I could go back in time and change what happened to them, I would. What you lost is so unfair, and that you've carried the hurt all this time is what I find the most painful, but it's not something I can do anything about." She raised Piper's head with a couple of fingers under her chin and smiled at her. "That above all else is what hurts the most."

"You do the most important thing by loving me. I'd go through all that again a thousand times if I get this life at the end of it. When I became your partner in every sense of the word by drinking from that cup, I thought all the adventures we'd have together would fill up another one of Lenore's books, but now, I'm terrified something may happen to you."

"Nothing is going to—" Someone started knocking loudly on the door. "Doesn't everyone in the house get that we have a baby now?"

"Finish putting your pants on, and I'll go see who it is. Whoever's out there had better pray that the sun will cure them after I stick something sharp in their eye if they wake Hali." Piper rubbed Kendal's side as she left her in the closet.

"Piper, I'm so sorry," Rawney said as Piper tied off her robe. "Is Asra here?"

"What's wrong?" Kendal said, her shirt not tucked in as if she'd hurried dressing.

"Aishe called last night to report that everything was quiet at the watcher's home, but then she said she'd get back to me when someone new arrived to visit the family. She hasn't called, and she made me promise I wouldn't contact you if I didn't hear from her so as to not lead anyone back to us."

"She didn't recognize who it was?" Kendal asked.

"She said something about a big car and the kind of man who drove around in one."

"The kind of guy who might be in charge of the dig these idiots are supposed to be guarding against anyone going near?" Kendal asked, and Piper thought the game or whatever the hell this was had started in earnest.

"What do you think happened to Aishe?" Rawney asked, and Piper could hear the worry in her voice. It didn't matter that no amount of physical harm could come to their loved ones because of the elixir, but the concern was still there.

"Let me make a few calls and see what I can find out. I still have some contacts in that area through Richoux International. If not, it's not a long flight from here, and I have to check out the area anyway."

"Not without me," Piper said, and Rawney seemed almost uncomfortable with having to come to them, but Piper couldn't blame her for asking. If Kendal had been missing, she would've demanded every single elder hunt her down and not stop until she was found.

"We'll eventually have to go, but I'll try to find her without leaving. I don't want to go until we know exactly what the hell is waiting for us either. Did she mention anything else? Who are these people that the Clan has watching the site?" Kendal kissed Rawney's cheek before sitting to put on her socks.

"Franco Rodriguez used some of the stipend the Clan pays him to open a resort close to where the site is. It's one of those places for nature lovers who enjoy being in the rain forest, and it did well until a few years ago, when a group of tourists died falling from one of the hanging bridges on the property. That's what everyone thought at first, but when they fished them out of the ravine they noticed that all six of them had been shot." Rawney sat, glanced down at the sleeping baby, and smiled.

"That's unusual for Costa Rica," Kendal said, sitting back. "Did they ever find whoever was responsible?"

"No. From what Aishe found, the investigation is still open, but Franco's business never recovered."

Piper put her hand on Rawney's shoulder and squeezed. "I take it the falloff in business is what pushed him to something else like going into business with the guy in the big car?"

"That's what Rolla and the others think. Please, you have to help me find her. I sent her there, and maybe she wasn't ready," Rawney said, and Piper had to agree with her feelings of something being wrong. It wasn't anything she could really say for sure, but whoever these people were, they were dangerous. "Please help me find her."

"We'll do whatever it takes," she said as she took Rawney's hand. "While Asra makes some calls, I'll sit with Bruik and concentrate on finding something we can use."

"Thank you, Piper, and if I haven't said it before, I'm glad you and Asra found each other."

Rawney left, and she seemed to be trying to hold her emotions in check. "They can't really do anything to Aishe, can they?" Piper asked once the door closed again.

"I'm not sure that the watchers realize exactly what we are. Any interaction between the elders and a family like this doesn't require a lot of contact. Whoever Rolla put in charge will meet with the family so infrequently, they'll never know they're dealing with the same person throughout the duration of their job." Kendal held her as if understanding that her worry was starting to grow.

"These people and the guy leading them aren't going to give up easily, and they won't be easily beaten," she said, kissing Kendal's hand. "You know that, right?"

"Will you do me a favor?"

"For you, anything. What do you need?" she asked, and Kendal kissed her forehead.

"While I'm making calls and Hali is sleeping, try to see something, but when you do it, let your mind wander wherever it might want to go. Don't try to guide the path. I trust your sight, and I'm curious as to where it'll lead you."

"Do you think that'll help?"

"I think you need to start trusting yourself. You belong with me, and more importantly, you belong in our ranks as much as anyone."

❖

"Who is she?" Pauline asked when Alejandro's men carried the dead woman to the back of the house where the platform over the cliff was. The bullet hole in the center of the woman's head was a sure sign of finality, so they'd have no way of finding out anything more.

"Who the hell knows? The idiot Franco hired shot the bitch before we could talk to her. I bet she's with the Genesis Clan, and we've missed our chance to find out who these people are and what they're about."

The men came back with the body of the guard who'd shot the woman, and the man also had a bullet hole in the center of his forehead, put there by one of his people for his stupidity. His men tossed the guy over first, and the fall was too high to hear the body drop below, but the area was so remote the animals roaming the mountainside would take care that no trace of him would ever be found.

"Make sure you check all her pockets before you get rid of her," Pauline said and took the phone the closest man handed over. "It's not locked, but it's completely empty too," she said as she scanned through the device. "She erased all the calls and messages in here."

"Then her only mistake was not seeing the monkey close to her," he said, and grunted in disgust. "At least they have smart people working against us." He glanced at his daughter, and she made the right move by lowering her head. "Try to learn from this and keep the mistakes to a minimum. Find Oscar and bring him to me. That's the most important thing."

"Yes, sir," she said before kicking the dead woman over the side and taking a deep breath.

"Don't worry," he said and smiled widely. "If you suffer the same fate, I promise you'll get the same kindness of a bullet to the head before I push you off for the birds and wild pigs to finish you off."

CHAPTER THIRTEEN

Thanks, Rueben," Kendal said as she leaned back in her chair in the office. "Pull that badge out of mothballs, and go over there and scare the hell out of them. These idiots aren't going to know any one police officer from San José, and Aishe was there last night. Push until they give you something."

"You got it, Jefe," Rueben Margoles said, and after hearing the intakes of breath, Kendal knew he'd lit one of his favorite cigars. "I'll call you if I find anything."

"Try and get out there today if you can manage it. I know it's a trek from the capital, but it's important."

"I might get there late, but I'm leaving now."

Kendal stood when she was done and held her hand out to Piper, who'd been listening in one of the chairs opposite the desk. "Who was that?" Piper asked, glancing back at the bassinet in the room where Hali still slept.

"Rueben is an old friend who did some legwork for me when I bought some abandoned factories outside the capital." She squeezed Piper's fingers and smiled. "Don't worry. There were no pretty girls mad at me for trying to steal their businesses."

"Lucky for me then, since you've got a soft spot for that type. I would've lost out."

"I refitted the places and put them back to work without ever going in person. I thought after Kendal Richoux had run her course, I could set up my next identity there."

"We'll still keep this place once we have to move on, won't we?" Piper came closer to her and slowly ran her hands up her chest. "I love the fact we've started out our life together here."

"Of course, and you know that every house, no matter where it is, will be our home. And if you decide on somewhere I don't already have one, we'll have fun picking one out together for us and our family."

"Will you sit with me for a little while?" Piper asked as she moved her hands farther up and locked them around her neck.

"Our guests aren't due for a while, so I'd love to, but let me tell Rawney that I've got Rueben going out and checking."

Piper gave Hali's nanny some instructions while Kendal chatted with Rawney and smiled at the young woman as she took Kendal's hand and walked to the back of the house and out to the yard. Kendal had surprised her one day with a nice, secluded retreat in the spot where she and Hill had hidden to spy on her all those months ago when they didn't know each other well. They walked there holding hands and not really needing to fill the air with a lot of small talk.

The area had a large chaise lounge covered by a big umbrella that was there more to keep the leaves off the chair than for shade, since they were in the center of a bunch of old maple trees that bordered the lake out back. "I love you," she said to Kendal when she picked her up and laid her gently on the seat.

"That's what will make any place home, love." Kendal sat at the foot of the chaise and took Piper's shoes off. "And it's time to show you how lucky I think I am."

"That's not why I brought you out here," she said but didn't stop Kendal when she stood, leaned over her, and reached for the button on her jeans.

"You're turning me down?" Kendal said as she moved to the next button of Piper's pants.

"I didn't say that, but I don't want you to think I want you only for your body," she said and winked as Kendal almost pulled her off the chair getting her pants off.

"I still remember that day out here when you slammed into Hill after I caught you peeking at me," Kendal said, starting on her shirt buttons next. "You were scared first, and then, just as fast, you were pissed. No matter what I think, you are one passionate woman, Piper Marmande, and I'm happy you're mine."

"I couldn't take my eyes off you that day," she said as Kendal straightened up and started to pull her own shirt off, but Piper knelt and moved toward her, slapping her hands away. "The way you move and that cocky attitude of yours hooked me into coming back again and again."

Piper slowly undid her belt and unfastened the buttons on the jeans Kendal was wearing, glad she'd forgone the suits for now and dressed more casually around the house. She got the fly open, and Kendal stood still as she pulled the pants and underwear down to her knees. No matter what else was going on in their lives, Kendal was always ready for her. At times like this she was glad that Kendal couldn't hide how she felt.

"You want me, baby?" she said as she slid her fingers in between Kendal's legs. She was wet, and her clit was as hard as the steel on all those swords she loved so much.

"I've wanted you from the moment I saw you," Kendal said, lowering her head and kissing her in a way that made her feel like Kendal couldn't get enough.

Piper pushed her down and finished the job of taking her pants off so she could kneel between Kendal's legs. "I'm all yours, but first I want you to come in my mouth. I want you to remember that you belong to me, and that I don't want to be left behind when we have to start whatever this is."

"You don't have to do that for me to remember that, love. I know you're mine, and where I go, you'll come with me. No matter what, I won't leave you unless you want to be left." Kendal closed her eyes and mouth when she lowered her head and licked from the opening of her sex up and over her clit.

She did it a few more times until she took Kendal into her mouth and sucked her in until her clit was against the roof of her mouth, and then she sucked harder, using her tongue to create more pressure. Kendal stayed quiet, like she usually did when they made love, but her fingers had threaded through her hair, and she used the leverage to keep her in place. No matter how many times they'd been together, she loved having Kendal like this.

The slayer that had terrified so many who lived in the shadows with the stories of her deeds was the first person in Piper's life who made her feel this cherished and loved. Kendal, no matter what else was going on, was always tender and loving because she wanted to be, not because it was expected of her. When she had Kendal in this position, she liked to take her time, so when Kendal pressed down on her head, she pulled back a little and teased her with just the tip of her tongue.

"Now you're being cruel," Kendal said as she looked down at her.

"Slow down, baby, there's no rush," she said softly, then circled Kendal's clit with her tongue. "With everything we know is coming, it might be a while before we can take our time."

Kendal placed her hands at Piper's sides and picked her up again so she could sit her on her lap. "I don't give a damn what's coming. I'm not going to stop making time for you." Kendal kissed her and gently glided her fingers from her collarbone down to the tips of her nipples. "You can't think that all of a sudden I'd want to stop doing this." She went back willingly when Kendal held her at an angle and sucked one nipple, then the other, into her mouth.

"You're making me crazy, and I said I want you to come in my mouth first," she said as Kendal bit one nipple hard enough to get her attention but not to hurt her. The sensation made the wetness between her legs double, and she almost begged Kendal to touch her. "Lie back, and let me have you."

"Just as long as I get to finish what I started," Kendal said as she let her nipple go with a pop.

She didn't always waste a lot of time thinking of the few lovers she'd had in her life before Kendal, but when she was this desperate, she was glad she'd found someone who made her totally crazy for her touch like no one before her ever had. Kendal made her crazy enough to almost become selfish, so she liked to take control every so often so Kendal would get the same satisfaction she always did.

"Do you want me to suck this until you come?" she asked as she pinched Kendal's clit. The reaction she got almost made her smile, but she didn't want to get too cocky too fast, or Kendal would turn the tables on her. "You're so hard for me, so let me have you."

Kendal lay back again, and she took it as a sign of surrender. She moved back to kneel between Kendal's legs and didn't make her wait for what she really wanted and took Kendal into her mouth and sucked hard enough to make Kendal's legs open wider. It surprised her a little when Kendal groaned louder than she ever had before and her toes curled under.

"Don't stop," Kendal said, her voice sounding strained and hoarse. "Fuck," she said, and her hips bucked up. "*Je jouis*," Kendal said as she stopped moving and became rigid. It was the first time she'd been so vocal about coming.

"I'm so glad I paid so much attention in French class," she said as she kissed the inside of Kendal's thigh. "Were you feeling especially frisky today to announce you were coming?"

"I've never been noisy, but sometimes it's hard to keep everything I feel for you locked inside. I need to let it out and tell you how completely nuts you make me." Kendal smiled when she slid along her body until she was lying on top of her with her head pillowed on her shoulder. "You have a way of breaking new ground when it comes to me."

"That's because up to now you've been waiting for me," she said and fanned her fingers out over Kendal's breast. "I love you so much."

"I have been waiting for you, and I'm sorry it took me so long," Kendal said as she moved her hands down her back to her ass. Once she got her hands there she squeezed possessively and pushed Piper up a little. "But I've found you and you're mine. I'll always love you, and I'll never disrespect you, but you're mine."

"I know, baby, and I'm glad. It's good to come in from the lonely cold," she said as she pressed her sex down on Kendal's abdomen. If anyone had told her she'd be this crazy about someone until just recently, she'd have laughed them out of her office. Until Kendal, the only things she'd ever cared about were her grandparents and her job. "I am yours, and I'm happy I can make the same claim."

"Anyone who can turn me into a pile of jelly deserves every bit of me," Kendal said with a smile and pulled her up a little so she could reach between her legs without lifting her up. "So let's see if I can reciprocate."

"You know you don't have to try very hard to do that," she said as Kendal's fingers went down until they landed on the base of her clit. She raised her hips, wanting Kendal's fingers to slide over the one place she needed her the most, and Kendal didn't disappoint by waiting until she'd reached the spot that made her hiss before flicking her finger a couple of times over her clit.

"I love how wet you get for me." Kendal kept her on top, moving her hand constantly, and raised her head to kiss Piper.

"You should be used to it by now, since you've kept me in some state of horniness since we've met." She moved her hips up and down, enjoying riding Kendal's fingers at the pace she wanted. Lately they hadn't had the opportunity to make it last, so she tried not to move too hard or too fast. "You make me want to rip your clothes off at least a couple of times a day," she said as she lifted her ass higher and pushed more into Kendal's touch before backing off again.

"Tell me what you want," Kendal said as her movements got faster but lighter.

"I need you to go inside...I need you to fill me up," she said, not wanting Kendal to stop but needing Kendal to put her fingers in and bring her to the brink.

Piper sat up and looked at her as she pressed down on Kendal, needing the contact. She took Kendal's hand when she held it up and sucked in two of the long fingers to the knuckle. Kendal closed her eyes as she ran her tongue along the tips.

"Fuck me, baby," she said, getting Kendal to look at her again. Kendal moved her hand down and placed her fingers so she could come down on them. The comment wasn't one she used often, but she needed to come before she hurt something inside if she didn't.

Kendal placed her thumb so that on every down stroke she slammed into it, and even though she wanted to speed up, she kept it slow and steady. She wanted to hold off until the last moment, but the tightness in her belly meant the orgasm she was hurtling toward wasn't something she could hold back, and she gripped Kendal's wrist to keep her hand in place.

"I'm coming, baby," she said and bucked her hips as fast and hard as she could manage. "Ah," she said as she came down and stopped groaning while Kendal's thumb massaged her clit, making the walls of her sex clamp down as she enjoyed the last of the wave of pleasure. "Stop before it falls off," she said, joking, as she fell like a rag doll to Kendal's chest. She was done but wasn't ready to give up the fingers still inside her.

Kendal kissed her and rubbed her back soothingly. "Close your eyes, sweetheart, and relax."

She heard Kendal's voice, but it sounded so far away. When she did as Kendal asked, she saw the canopy of dense trees and a ceremony going on in a large stone city.

"Come," a woman with dark skin and beautiful blue eyes said as she took Piper's hand. When Piper looked down at herself she was dressed in a leather skirt and a very brief top decorated with what looked like jade and turquoise.

"Where are we going?" she asked, glancing behind her and looking for Kendal, but she'd disappeared.

"To see what you need to know so you can help my daughter," the woman said, and she followed, knowing this experience might open her mind to the answers she was seeking.

❖

Costa Rican Rain Forest, 6132 BC

The beautiful dark-skinned woman with wavy auburn hair with red highlights led Piper along a long avenue of pyramids, stopping once to glance toward the heavens, but then kept going until they were near the fire burning on a stone platform in front of one of the pyramid structures with another large platform on top. Mayan people were dancing around the fire, their bodies oiled and streaked with sweat from the heat of the tall flames. An older man with a cape of what appeared to be straw and colorful stones threw something in with a flick of his wrist, and the smoke turned yellow.

"It's something I taught them," her guide said, taking her hand and looking into her eyes. "It's the fire ceremony."

"Where are we?" Piper asked, glancing around and listening to the chanting. The words were foreign, but she understood them. These people were calling their gods to show themselves, and from the fervor of their singing it sounded as if they fully expected them to appear.

"The jungle very rarely has a name for any one place for these people. They were living in small tribes before I got here, but with the help of my sister we've taught them to band together." The woman placed her foot on the narrow steps of the pyramid and held her hand out to her. "The ones who came before us taught them to build this place for what's to come."

"Who are you and how did you get here? You don't look like anyone here." As they started up the steps, the dancing stopped, and the people clustered around the structure fell to their knees, then pressed their faces to the ground.

"I am Lumas, mother of Rawney. You will soon come here with

the slayer, but this is what this area was used for. This night will help you understand." Lumas took something from her belt and showed it to her. It looked like a tuning fork with a small hammer attached to the end.

"When in time is this?" Even this far up, Piper could feel the heat of the fire, and the stones decorating her top seemed to grow warm enough to make her breasts hot.

"If you read the history books we're over four thousand years too early for the Mayan existence, but there they are. It will take them more time to start their quest to build more cities like this, hoping to call their gods back, but there'll be no waking them from their sleep."

They reached the top, and Lumas held her hand up with the tuning fork, and the crowd stopped their chanting. The sun was starting to set, but the dense vegetation that encircled them was as quiet as the observers down below. Whoever the man in the straw cape was, he bowed to Lumas and threw more powder into the fire so the smoke that billowed up was now red.

"You have done well and finished the home the gods will use for their eternal rest." Lumas's voice carried over the main square, and a few shouts went up after she spoke in the language the people understood. "You will celebrate this day with the fire ceremony, even if your children will not fully understand what it means when the time of the living gods is over. All of you will remember them, and you will teach your children, but you must leave this place and let the jungle have back what rightfully belongs to it."

"They're still here? The dragons, I mean."

"This is the first step of your journey, Piper. My daughter must follow the crumbs I've left and understand how they fit into the book of spells that belongs to our family."

Lumas hit the side of the tuning fork, and for something so small the sound was loud enough to hurt her ears. When the vibrations stopped she hit it again, then one more time before a shadow overhead blocked out the remaining light for a brief moment, and Piper looked up in awe. At least twenty of them had appeared, and they were huge.

"Are those—" Piper didn't want to sound stupid, but it wasn't every day that she saw a mass of dragons flying in a cluster with a kind of graceful ease she didn't think they were capable of.

"The children of the goddess," Lumas said and tapped the fork one more time. The largest of the dragons circled and landed on the platform where they stood and let out a cry to the others, who perched on the other structures around the square. There was a pyramid for each of them.

The large beast shook its head and folded its wings against its body before lowering its head to Lumas. It closed its eyes when Lumas placed her hand on its snout and rubbed the spot between the large slits that were its nostrils. Piper smiled that this thing acted like a pet dog that enjoyed a good scratch.

"Drakon, open your eyes and see your mistress," Lumas said, and the dragon opened his yellow eyes and moved his head to Piper.

She lifted her hand slowly, and the dragon moved his head until it was pressed against the spot where Lumas had touched him. He opened his mouth, and she could see the fire that was right at the surface, hotter than the one below, but she wasn't afraid. When she showed no fear, Drakon moved his head as if to look at her closer, seeming to memorize every part of her face. That she couldn't know for sure, but it was something she felt in her gut.

Drakon rose to his full height and roared loudly, shaking his head when the others answered his call, then moved to the side, leaving them at one end of the platform as another dragon landed next to him and nuzzled the side of his neck.

"This is his mate Peto. They're the pack leaders and life mates. Their love for each other and for the children they have had together is a beautiful thing, but only two of their children remain. When they sleep, they will do so together for all of time." Lumas waved her hand, and another attractive woman with a large book started up the steps. "This is my younger sister, Rowen, and she's learned the secrets of the book at my side. The truth of this will die with us."

"You don't have to," Piper said as both women put a hand on her shoulders.

"In our time we didn't know that was our fate, but our ashes still carry the history of our betrayal and of who we were. The Order of Fuego was born here, and the ember of those who follow them has been kept burning until your time." Lumas kissed her cheek. Rowen did the same, and then they turned and opened the book Rowen had brought up with her. "This is a copy of my family's treasure that my daughter now has. Tell my Rawney how much I love her, how proud I am of her, and that I have every confidence she'll find the key."

Rowen opened the book, and Lumas started to read from the very last page. This time Piper had no idea what the language was, since it sounded foreign and strange to her. "The only thing you need to remember, Piper, is that even though Drakon is here, the words I speak will carry to every corner and forest in the world. Tonight all the goddess's children will find the peace of sleep."

Lumas finished her spell, and the dragons seemed to start fading from sight. When they were translucent in the waning light, Drakon aimed his head down and shot out a stream of fire that heated the stone they were standing on, but it wasn't an unpleasant feeling. Piper spread her arms out to keep her balance when the platform started to rumble as if in an earthquake, but the same thing was happening on every one of the platforms around them. When it stopped the dragons were gone, and at the base of each one stood a stone carving of a dragon head with its mouth open.

"How did you even get here, never mind how you did that?" Piper asked when the impossible was over.

"They brought us," Rowen said, waving to the newly decorated pyramids. "We left our families to come to this place, and here we'll stay until we welcome the darkness. It was our fate, but the goddess promised good fortune going forward for our families and for our rest."

"Don't forget anything that you've seen here, Piper, except the words of the spell. They will not travel forward with you, so don't feel disappointed. Those words are for Rawney to find, but you must tell her all the rest." Lumas glanced back, and the men carrying sharp sticks and bows were almost at the top after scaling the other side of the structure. Their chests were painted red, along with what looked like a flame on their forehead. "Remember, you must promise me," Lumas said as a spear came through her chest.

"I promise," Piper said as Rowen suffered the same fate. One of the attackers took the book, but he didn't seem to know what it was so he threw it into the fire burning below.

The scene was chaotic and violent, and the people scattered into the trees, not fighting back, and she didn't understand. When the killers had finally left, the worshippers had come back and lowered the two bodies off the top and placed them on the funeral pyres that had been erected. The old man with the straw cape gathered their ashes and the charred book and glanced at Piper as if in silent request for her to follow him. He took everything into the jungle and put the stone jars along with the book in a small stone vault buried in the ground.

He led the others away into the darkness after they covered it, and Piper instantly knew they'd roamed for centuries until generations later decided to start building on the stories of those long-ago times that had sprouted from this place. In all those years of the construction and expansion of the Mayan empire, this place was forgotten. The last time it was inhabited for anything was the fire ceremony that Lumas and Rowen had begun but had died before the fire went out.

CHAPTER FOURTEEN

Oakgrove, Present Day

Piper opened her eyes, and she lay still pressed on top of Kendal with Kendal's fingers still buried inside her. Life sometimes surprised you in ways you couldn't imagine, like showing you very detailed memories of things you had never experienced yourself, but lying in the arms of the person you loved was more of a dream that never failed to bring joy into your existence. She lifted herself up and combed Kendal's hair back and kissed her.

"Are you okay?" Kendal asked softly in that deep burr that seemed to seep into her chest and heat her blood.

"Considering your fingers are in the right place, I'm perfect." She kissed Kendal again and started to rock her hips. "Being with you like this opens my mind to all the things I need to keep you safe...to keep us safe." She exhaled deeply when Kendal squeezed her ass hard enough to get her attention. "I love the way you love me, but right now I need you over me and holding me."

Kendal flipped them over and held her weight off her by resting on her elbow, but her other hand stayed in place. Having Kendal between her legs made her nipples come to hard points of need, and she ran her leg up the back of Kendal's thigh. "I want you to make me yours all over again." She knew they had to go back soon, but not before she had her fill of Kendal's fingers inside her and the way they slid in and out, making her crave the orgasm that wasn't too far off.

"That's it, baby," she said, putting her fingers in Kendal's hair and tugging her head down, biting her lower lip. "Don't stop."

She placed her feet on the backs of Kendal's legs, making it easier to thrust up into the hand between her legs as she kissed Kendal hard and long. This time it wasn't about slowness or control but belonging to someone so completely that it robbed you of any inhibition you thought to have.

"Oh my God," she said as the rush of pleasure made her clamp the walls of her sex around Kendal's fingers, and the orgasm swept through her so fast she stopped moving. Kendal seemed to realize it, and she stilled her hand as the last of her spasms pulsed in her sex. "Good Lord, the things you can do to me," she said when Kendal finally pulled her fingers free.

"I do feel like beating my chest every so often," Kendal said and laughed. "But then you do the same things to me, and I think it's time for that right now before we go back to the house."

Piper pushed on Kendal's shoulder and got her to roll over so she could move, and when Kendal was on her back she straddled her thighs low enough that she'd have access to the wetness she knew was waiting on her. "Do you remember the day I came up to your room at the Piquant?"

"That's a hard day to forget." Kendal's eyes drooped until they were only halfway open, but she figured it was because she was stroking her clit. "It was the first time I got to see you in your underwear, and it took everything I had not to drop to my knees and beg you to let me touch you." Kendal took in a sharp breath when she pinched her rigid clit and tugged hard a few times.

"I think that was the first time I realized that I needed you to touch me, and I'd pray you never wanted to stop. It was a little scary since I didn't know what the hell I was doing, but you reached inside me and claimed some part I'll never get back." She returned to her soft stroking and saw that Kendal's breathing was starting to deepen. "It was okay, though, since that part was waiting on you, and I almost cried at the joy of being found."

Kendal raised her hand and moved it up her body to one of her breasts and smiled. "You are so beautiful."

"No need to flatter, baby. In this position I'd think it's clear that you're getting lucky."

"It's not flattery if it's the truth. You're many things to me, love, but that doesn't blind me to the fact that you're incredibly beautiful."

"Declarations like that deserve to be rewarded," she said and lowered herself until she could put her mouth on Kendal again and bury her fingers inside her. She moved at the pace Kendal had set and came close to patting herself on the back when Kendal let out a groan so loud she felt it in her chest. Just as quickly as she came, though, Kendal was sitting up, seeming to put her body between her and the path that led to the house.

"Wait right here," Kendal said, getting up and handing her the shirt that had fallen to the ground.

"Where are you going?" she asked, but she spotted Hill through the trees standing like a statue but not averting her eyes. "This is ridiculous," she muttered as she put her shirt on and searched for her underwear, having to hold Kendal back when she finally got them on. "No matter how satisfying you might find it, warrior mine, you can't kill her."

"Says who?" Kendal said, her hands on her hips and obviously not finding Hill a threat.

"Let me get some things straight with her, and if she doesn't get it, then be my guest." She kissed the middle of Kendal's chest above her breasts and sighed. "Now will you get dressed before I have to kill her myself? I don't like to share."

"I wasn't spying on you," Hill said to Kendal's retreating back when she walked past her without a word after she'd dressed. Piper hadn't seen her mad very often, but having someone, no matter if it was an old friend, see something so intimate was probably what set Kendal off, and she couldn't blame her. This part of their lives wasn't for anyone else but them.

"Hill, what the hell are you doing out here?" she said as she turned around after buttoning up her pants. The briefs Kendal had worn still lay on the chaise, so she folded them into a small bundle and wrapped her fist around it. "I thought I made myself clear before. There's nothing between us, there never has been, and no matter what, there's never going to be anything between us."

"I told you I wasn't spying. That's not my style unless someone hires me to do it for a cheating spouse, and even then it's not my favorite thing to do." Hill shoved her hands low into her pockets and couldn't seem to look her in the eyes. "You made your choice, so what can I do but accept it? I may have wanted something different, but I'm not an asshole that's going to try to mess things up for you."

"Do you remember watching her that day we were out here?" she said, not believing she was asking the very same question but for different reasons.

"Yes. She cut my camera in half."

"You should remember that if anything like this ever happens again. Kendal Richoux is a little different than your average businesswoman, so try not to get on her bad side. You won't get another chance to make it up to her." She started walking, not caring if Hill followed her or not. "And this better be the last time you come somewhere you're not invited. Do you understand me?"

"Perfectly, and I'm sorry. Trust me, that's the last thing I needed to see, but maybe it's a good thing I did."

She stopped and glared at Hill like she'd completely lost her mind. "What the hell does that mean?"

"You really love her, and maybe I didn't believe it until right this minute. I'm sorry, and I hope you'll still be my friend."

"I never stopped being your friend, even after I knew you wanted more, so it wasn't for me to make that decision for you. All I can do is be perfectly clear that I love her, and more importantly, I belong to her. I'm never leaving her unless she sends me away."

"I doubt that'll ever happen."

"You're right, and don't forget it."

They walked back into the house, and Piper stared at the skinny, bald man sitting in their living room with his eyes closed. She wasn't worried about who he was yet, so she climbed the stairs, leaving Hill to deal with him since she'd obviously brought him.

Kendal was already in the shower when she entered their bedroom, and she stripped, dropping clothes on the way to the bathroom. She was immediately picked up so she could wrap her legs around Kendal's waist, so she kissed her, feeling the residual tension in her body. All she could do was kiss her until Kendal relaxed.

"Does she finally get it?" Kendal asked when she let her down and put her head under the spray.

"It doesn't really matter, since the only one who needs to get how much I love you is you." She squirted some bath gel onto the sponge and washed Kendal's back before turning her around. "But she does get it, and I think she was only there to tell us she brought that guy Leonardo. Or I'm guessing that's who the guy downstairs was."

"Just as long as she knows I don't like sharing, much less letting anyone see you naked. That really pissed me off."

She kissed Kendal's bicep and smiled. "I know, baby, but it could've been worse."

"How do you figure?"

"I could've been right in the middle of what I was doing," she said and winked.

"If that had happened she'd be sporting a dagger out of her forehead," Kendal said, and Piper didn't think she was kidding.

Convel stayed on her porch with Lowe as the four large cars stopped in front of their place. She figured they'd be forced into one and their next stop would be the slayer's home, where she'd have to tamp down her desire to kill, if only to keep Lowe from suffering from the one thing she wanted to do more than anything. When the door to the second car opened, she was surprised to see Tala emerge in a pair of jeans and a white linen shirt.

"My queen," she said, lowering her head and glad to see Lowe do the same.

"It's been a long time, Convel, but I hope not so long that you've forgotten how to greet an old friend," Tala said with her arms open.

"How can you be so forgiving?" she said as her feet betrayed her and she moved closer. She'd loved this woman for so long, and it had killed a huge part of her heart when she couldn't have her. It felt good when Tala's arms came around her in a friendly embrace, and she let go only when Lovell emerged from the car.

"Because I'm your queen and protector no matter how far away you are from me, and more importantly, you're my family. The children Lovell and I have will bind us together just as much as it did Lovell and me." Tala took her hand and squeezed it. "It's time to come home and know them. You've kept everyone waiting long enough."

"Sometimes there's no going back, no matter how much we want it," she said, and Lowe rubbed the small of her back.

"That's only true if you're not wanted, cub, but that's not the case, and you know it," Lovell said.

"And who's this?" Tala asked, as if to change the subject.

"This is my mate, Lowe Carey," she said, and Lowe lowered her head to Tala and Lovell.

"It's good to know you," Tala said as Lovell took her hand. "Before we go, I'd like to talk to you inside."

The people in the first and last car came out and surrounded the house to keep the two royals safe, but so many people didn't make sense considering no one here knew who Tala and Lovell were. When they entered the run-down small house, Convel felt shame for the first time for how far she'd drifted away from her family and friends only to end up somewhere like this.

"You left the pack because you didn't want to live by the rules that govern all of us, and I can understand that," Tala said to begin after she'd chosen the small dining table to sit at. "You are under no obligation to follow my order, but I'd like you to listen to me before you refuse."

"If you need something, just ask. I had plenty of reasons for leaving, but lack of loyalty to you wasn't one of them," she said as Lowe took her hand.

"Wasn't it?" Tala said, but with no trace of malice. "Sometimes, no matter who we are, we want things we can't have, but I think it's fate's way of telling us that perhaps we shouldn't get everything we desire. In the long run it's not what we need. From the look of things, we've both ended up with who we need to make us complete as far as mates, but it still pains me that you haven't come back."

"I don't think I can now. Too much time has gone by," she said, and Lovell sighed. "I know you don't have any patience for me, sister, but I never could measure up to you, and I'm too old to start trying, even if I wanted to."

"You know that each of us has different talents," Tala said, as if she had all the patience and time in the world. "On the battlefield, perhaps Lovell is the strongest, but that's not what we're asking you to do."

"Then what?" She spoke sharply, and Lowe squeezed her hand hard enough that she felt her nails dig into her skin.

"You need to travel with Asra and help her with the threat that's coming to all of us."

She laughed, thinking Tala was joking, but from the firm set of her mouth, that wasn't the case. "I know she's your friend, so send Lovell if you want, or ask me anything but that."

"Lovell will do her part in this, but I need you to go with Asra and her mate when the time comes." Tala's voice was now devoid of any kind of emotion, and Convel guessed she was trying her best not to end that statement with "it's an order."

"If I go, am I coming back?"

"Nothing in life is a guarantee, but I'm sure you're smart enough to make it back," Lovell said.

"Where would I be going?"

"That we're not sure of yet, but once our elders and theirs get together, I'm certain they'll tell us the first destination. If you agree, you have to promise you'll keep your feelings for Asra under wraps. You've already broken a treaty that's punishable by death, so don't add to that by trying to provoke her into a fight you can't and won't win."

"You have so little confidence in me?" she asked with a smirk.

"Asra probably doesn't need any help, but there's more than one slayer in Asra's house, so I doubt you'll get even a tooth on her," Tala said with a shrug.

"And if you do, I'll rip your throat out myself," Lovell said.

"With such an enticing invitation, how can I refuse?" she said and bowed her head.

CHAPTER FIFTEEN

I appreciate you coming here to see us, but if I could ask you to wait in Charlie's place outside," Kendal said to the man who jumped to his feet when she and Piper entered the room. "Hill can show you where it is."

"I really need to talk to you as soon as possible," the man said. "My name is Leonardo, and my employer made me promise I'd find you. It's a matter of saving someone's life."

"Please give me an hour. Then I'll come back with my wife, and we'll do what we can to help you." She took Piper's hand and studied Leonardo. He appeared a little different from the first picture she'd seen of him sitting in Hill's office. Why he needed to talk to her or had gone to the trouble of finding her was a mystery, but right now she didn't have time to satisfy her curiosity. A meeting with her persona of Kendal Richoux shouldn't have made the difference in keeping someone alive.

"Please, if you can give me ten minutes as soon as you can." Leonardo pressed his hands together and seemed genuinely concerned about something.

"I can't put off the meeting I have coming up, so either wait out back or we'll reschedule, but if you'll excuse us," she said when the front-gate bell rang. She pointed Hill toward the back and left to meet Tala and the others who'd come with her, fully expecting Hill to take him out.

"I'll wait, however long it takes."

Rolla was already outside, and he nodded to her and Piper. "Who was that?" He pointed to the living room.

"Someone who's been asking questions about me and Piper from the time we started trying to uncover the secret of the Sea Serpent

Sword and somehow found Hill. He wants to talk to me about someone who's in trouble, I guess, but I have no idea who."

The cars stopped, and she suddenly had an urge to strap a sword on. From the way Piper held her hand, she figured she'd read her mind. "It'll be okay, so relax," Piper said softly before standing on her toes and kissing her cheek.

"Asra, thank you for inviting us," Tala said when she stepped out after Lovell. Kendal bowed and straightened when Convel appeared with the young woman she'd seen when she'd followed their trail back to the house close by. "We all come in peace. You have my word."

"Our friendship means you have no need to give such promises, your highness. Welcome to our home, all of you," she said, waving them inside.

Tala had brought a few people aside from her security people, and they all followed one of the staff to the dining room, where lunch was waiting. She sat at one end of the table and Piper at the other, since Piper had requested that seating arrangement to better observe everyone who'd come. It didn't happen often, but sometimes Piper experienced an instant flash of something when she was sitting around someone, and this was the perfect relaxed setting to allow it to happen.

Convel ate only a little, and she gripped her fork like she was getting ready to try to bury it in Kendal's forehead. Kendal watched as she ate slowly. The anger that seemed to come off Convel like a bad odor almost made her laugh. What had happened between them had been so minor that she was amazed Convel had never let it go. After Convel finally dropped her fork, she stood and asked Convel to join her in the other room and put her hands up to keep everyone else in their seats.

"I was sent to do my job all those years ago," she said when Convel slammed the door of the study closed. "Not only the clan but your queen sent me, and at that time I had no choice but to obey because I'd given my word to carry out my duty. The were queen was tired of you skirting the line, but despite that, she wanted to respect your need for freedom while keeping you out of trouble that would eventually come back on the pack."

"You weakened me to the point that, afterward, I lost most of my friends to hunters. They depended on me to take care of them, and you ruined that ability for me."

"Your friends died because they continued to take what wasn't theirs. The direction I pointed you in was full of game and everything you needed to survive, but you all thought the livestock was rightfully yours to take." She spoke as she drew closer to Convel, and she could see how she was starting to shake her head as if she couldn't control herself. A little more pushing and she'd shift. "You and everyone who followed you thought you were better than those people, and you took and took until they had no choice but to fight back. I bet the most surprising thing was that you weren't invincible."

"So I killed my friends?"

"I have no idea. Only you can answer that by remembering the type of leader you were then and are now, but maybe it's time to let the anger go. You're no pup any more, so grow up. I haven't thought about you since the day we met, but it seems like you've carried this load all that time. Hate me if you want, but if you can't dial back some of the hostility, then tell Tala you want no part of this. I don't have time to fight you and whatever else is waiting for me out there."

Convel lunged at her with her fists curled tight and tried to connect with her jaw, but she sidestepped it and hit the side of her face near her temple. She pulled back at the last second, not wanting to break the skin, but Convel would have a hell of a headache for the rest of the afternoon. "Or don't grow up and add some more scars to your collection. I have too many precious things in my life to let you anywhere near me. Next time, I'm not going to stop until you beg me to. And if you're too full of pride for that, you'll die at the end of my fists. I don't need a sword to finish you off."

She left Convel in the study and met everyone in the living room, where the staff was serving coffee and Rolla was talking to Tala and Lovell. Morgaine lifted her eyebrows in her direction, and she shook her head when Convel followed her in, rubbing the side of her head, the bruise already darkening. Lenore sat with the archivists from the were pack, and Bruik was whispering something into Piper's ear. The scene seemed like some average dinner party, but it was time to get to why they were there.

"Queen Tala, will you share with us what your seers have predicted?" Piper asked, and Kendal moved to Piper's side.

"Trudy," Tala said, and a young woman came forward whom Tala introduced as their seer. "Trudy was the one who found the old scroll about this situation and has worked ever since to try to find more answers to what sounded like an incomplete riddle."

"All I've seen so far is the actual dragons in flight. What happened to them or any other clue as to where we need to start looking hasn't come to me yet." Trudy opened a leather briefcase and handed a folder to everyone present. Inside was a copy of the old scroll Tala had mentioned, which was a record of the dragons throughout Europe a little before the site in Costa Rica had come into play. The were had worshipped the creatures, and the dragons in turn had come to befriend them in their animal states.

"I think we have something to add to that," Bruik said, and he nodded to Piper.

"This morning I had a vision of the night the dragons were put to sleep and of your mother, Rawney. She and her sister were there, she said, because the dragons had brought them, and she knew that once she was done, death would come right after. Even if it hadn't, she would've been lost to you with no way to come back from that distance with the ocean separating you."

"Did you see the actual ceremony of how she did it?" Rawney asked.

"It's the one thing she wiped from my mind—not the actual moment, but the words she'd said to do what she needed to do. All I know is that in every family there's always a strong leader like Tala, but that night she put Drakon and his mate Peto into an everlasting sleep, and the dragons seemed to understand and accept that move." Rawney joined them on the sofa after Bruik had moved, and Piper slightly shook her head as if signaling not to ask her any more about what she'd seen.

"If you look at page six of the file," Trudy said, opening it to that page, and they noticed the highlighted section. "Eventually the children of fire will try to undo what's been done, and only a force of unlikely comrades can stop that from happening."

"Would that have something to do with me?" Convel said, finally opening her mouth and making Lovell look at her like she wanted to add a bruise to the other side of her face.

"To find the children of the fire, and I mean all of them, will take more than what Asra and her slayers can do alone," Trudy said, pointing to the page. "We need the powers of the children of the night to mesmerize information out of potential members, and we need you or another willing were to track what's been lost. I wish I could tell you what that might be, but that's all the scroll says."

"So I'm going as a sniffer dog? Can't they just get a bloodhound and be done with it?" Convel said, sounding totally disgusted.

"I don't think that's what it means." Tala shook her head. "When I read it, I took it to mean that Asra or Vadoma's people would be spotted and immediately put them on the defensive. But a wolf, while foreign to the area, wouldn't raise the same alarm."

"So where are we going if this doesn't even give a clue?" Convel asked.

"Costa Rica," Kendal said. "We'll land in San José and take a smaller plane north."

"Do you have any idea where this is?" Tala asked.

"I do have a centralized location, but the watchers who were supposed to be guarding the area will lead us there, or they're going to lose more than just the comforts of the house we've paid for," Kendal said, and everyone nodded. "I'll need to know who'll be going from your end, Tala, and if we get all our paperwork in order, we can leave in about two days."

"That sounds good. Lovell and I will stay until then, so we'll head back to town until we're ready to go."

"Actually, highness," Molly said. "If you and Lovell would like, you can stay next door. It's empty, and we have enough rooms for all your staff. I'm sure the hotel is comfortable, but our home will give you more privacy."

"Thank you, Mrs. Marmande. If you really don't mind, I wouldn't mind stretching my legs, with Asra's permission," Tala said with a smile.

"If you head west from the back of the house, you'll find plenty of interesting things you might like in the woods. Just try not to spook the horses," she said teasingly.

"We'll try our best, but it depends on how frisky Lovell's feeling."

Piper checked on the baby after her grandparents left to get Tala's people settled. Lenore promised to meet her upstairs once she'd gotten Anastasia for her afternoon feeding so they could sit and talk. She was sure her grandparents didn't really know what Tala meant by stretching their legs, and Tala asking for Kendal's permission meant they'd be doing their own brand of hunting.

Hali was awake but not fussy, so she took time to bathe her and change her outfit before she sat in her rocker and got ready to feed her. No matter what, she wasn't leaving their daughter behind, so hopefully Kendal was on the same page when it came to that. "Wherever we're going, sweet girl, you're coming with us."

"You know there's probably not going to be anything sweet about them in five years or so when they're both following our beloved spouses around begging for little swords," Lenore said when she came in holding Anastasia. "Let's trade before we start, to see if yours looks as much like Kendal as this kid looks like Morgaine," Lenore said, laughing.

"Down to the cute butt, so you're probably right." She laid Anastasia down on her empty lap until Lenore took Hali. "She's beautiful," she said as she ran her finger along the wisps of blond hair the same color as Morgaine's.

"Same goes here," Lenore said, holding Hali in her lap so she could really examine her. "How lucky are we?" She touched Hali's cheek and laughed when the baby raised her arms. "She does look a lot like Asra, and she'll have a ready-made friend in Ana. Hopefully they'll be as good friends as Morgaine and Asra have been."

"Let's hope they wait on that really-good-friends part until they're older," she said, and smiled teasingly at Lenore. "I was jealous of your partner for the longest time, but she seems more settled and happy with you."

"I didn't think she could be, but she's a completely different person, especially now that the baby is here. I finally believe her when she says that she loves me and, more importantly, only me."

"So, do you think Aphrodite lied a little bit when she said these guys won't be a complete reincarnation of the two souls trapped in the Sea Serpent Sword?" Anastasia started to fuss, so she traded with Lenore and led her outside to the comfortable chairs on the balcony.

"We have to take her at her word, but that wouldn't be so bad, if it came to that. Would it?" Lenore sucked in a breath when Anastasia started nursing, and then she glanced at her with a serious expression.

"No. I want them to be friends and anything they want to be to each other, because you and Morgaine mean so much to us. But I hope it's their choice, and Kendal wants that as well."

"They're Morgaine's and Kendal's children, and you think they're not going to have their own minds?" Lenore said and laughed. "Those two are as hardheaded and opinionated as they come."

"That's what they probably say about us when we're not listening." She laughed until someone cleared their throat from the doorway. Rawney stood there with an almost haunted look, and she felt for her. It sounded like her mother had simply left one day, and Rawney and her cousins had never gotten an explanation of what had happened to them.

"Is this a bad time to talk?" Rawney asked.

"Please sit, Rawney, and I'll tell you what I saw. It'll save me from having to repeat it for Lenore." She patted Hali's bottom as she started her story, and Rawney had tears rolling down her face when she finished. "I think Aphrodite and her fellow gods existed even then but didn't make themselves known to very many people. Your mother and your aunt must've been some of the people blessed with her presence, but carrying out her wishes cost you something precious."

"She died right after the spell?" Rawney said, wiping her face.

"The men of the Order of Fuego killed them both once it was done, but I think she knew it was coming and did it anyway because Aphrodite made promises about you and your cousins." She glanced down and smiled when Hali sucked like she couldn't get enough before slowing down and glancing up at her. "She told me the one thing you have to remember is how proud of you she was and how much she loved you. She also said she has every confidence in you to find the key."

"The key to what?" Rawney said, sounding lost.

"She didn't explain, but now that I know where she is, maybe I'll get to go back there, only earlier, and ask her some more questions. Believe me, my sight isn't perfect, and while I mostly just witness something, every so often I'm able to interact with the people in the past. Your mom was a special woman, and the other interesting thing she said was that their ashes still carry the history of their betrayal and of who they were. I'm not sure what she meant by that either, but it sounded like it was important for you to know."

"Please don't let Asra leave without me," Rawney said, tentatively stretching her hand out until it was on her forearm. "I have to find the answers or the crumbs she said she left for me. Like your Kendal and how long she lived for the one true purpose she had before you, I've lived all this time to carry out the job my mother and the clan set aside for me."

"We're going to be a big traveling group, but no one is staying behind," she said, gripping Rawney's fingers. When they touched she saw a young woman waking with a gasp as she touched her forehead. Her head of thick black hair was matted with blood, and the clear blue eyes of the clan darted around as if she was confused as to where she was.

"Piper, are you okay?" Piper heard Lenore ask from what sounded like downstairs.

"What does Aishe look like?" she said, peering at Rawney, and she gave a description of who she'd seen. "I'm not sure where she is, but she's okay. She just woke up from whatever happened to her, and she's desperate to talk to you, so you won't worry anymore."

"Thank you, Piper, and I'm so glad you accepted Asra's proposal. If I could cast a love spell that would result in what you have for her, I'd be a rich woman," Rawney said and smiled. "The love she has for you, though, can't be cast. It has to be born in the heart and expressed through the soul."

"I'm a lucky woman," she said and closed her eyes when Rawney kissed her cheek. Her skin was warm, and she smelled like jasmine after a summer rain.

"I'm sure she'd disagree with that assessment, and that's why it's so real you can almost touch it. The same goes for you and Morgaine, Lenore." Rawney stood and touched both babies on the head. "I don't think the goddess would've given you these beauties if that wasn't true."

"I wonder what that thing about the ashes means?" Lenore asked when Rawney left.

"She said it so casually when I was standing on that platform with her that I didn't think about it until just now. Now, though, it seems like one of the most important things she shared with me."

"Do you think there's anything left to be found there?" Lenore asked as she burped Anastasia.

"The pyramids hold the dragon pack leader and his mate, as well as some of their offspring. I'm not sure if the people who dug there realized that, but they're actually hidden in plain sight."

"Let's hope they don't figure it out until we get there, and let's hope we figure out why we have to tote that ass Convel along with us."

"With the side of her head bruised and swollen like that, I'm sure she'll be a pleasure to be around."

"I'm sure, but let's pray the answers come faster and much more clearly than they did the last time we did this," Lenore said, and Anastasia spit up on her. "Or it could be as messy as this."

She laughed as Lenore grimaced at how well covered she was in baby vomit. "We'll have to wait and see, but you know how patient we all are, so our job will be to keep Kendal, Morgaine, and Charlie from slicing everyone they see with those spiffy new swords."

"Thanks, Gran," Piper said as she handed Hali over while the nanny Lydia cleaned the changing table. "We have to go meet this guy Hill brought over, so call if you need anything. I won't be far."

Kendal was waiting for her in the kitchen with a cup of coffee in her hand, reading the file Trudy had given them one more time. The white linen shirt she had on let some of the tattoo on her chest show through, and Piper put her hand on it when she got closer. "Pick out anything new?" she asked.

"It must've been a rule back then to make things as foggy and cryptic as you could manage when putting these scrolls together," Kendal said, placing her cup down but keeping the file.

"I guess they didn't think some of this stuff would come true, so they didn't put a lot of effort into it, or maybe they had to go to the trouble of finding the answers, so they didn't want to make it easy on us."

"Probably, which makes some of our ancestors assholes," Kendal said, making her laugh. "Let's go see this Leonardo guy and hear his sad tale."

"Mind if we come with you?" Morgaine asked as Lenore walked at her side. "Since we'll be in this together, we might as well start to get on the same page as far as information-gathering."

"I doubt this guy knows anything about this," Kendal said. "He's been after Hill to introduce him to Kendal Richoux and Piper Marmande longer than all this stuff came along."

"He got half the equation right anyway," Piper said. "Should we bring him back in here or go to Charlie's place?"

"Let's go out there," Lenore said. "There's too many strangers in the house to take chances."

The staff had cleared the land around Charlie's home, and the big farm garden for the kitchens was starting to take shape. Charlie had gladly given up the care and maintenance of the gardens to the new staff, but he still kept the home he'd shared with his family. He was the overseer now but concentrated more on his defense lessons than anything else.

Kendal waved to him when they saw him sitting outside the cabin, and he followed them inside, where Hill was keeping an eye on their guest. "Leonardo, I'm Kendal Richoux, and this is my wife Piper." Kendal sat across from the man.

"I need to talk to you alone," Leonardo said.

"Since you're the one in need, it's all of us or nothing. You choose," Piper said, sitting on the arm of Kendal's chair.

"Fair enough, ma'am. My employer—"

Kendal put up her hand to shut him up. "I need names from here on out. You know me and my wife, so 'your employer' isn't going to cut it."

"The man who hired me is Dr. Sebastian Petchel. He's the retired department chair of the archeology department at the university in Costa Rica, and he was a member of the Order of Fuego."

"Shit," Kendal said, and Piper squeezed her shoulder when she thought the same thing. How the hell had this guy found them?

"I'm sorry," Leonardo said.

"Never mind that. Please go on," Piper replied.

"From my understanding, Sebastian was killed just recently, and the reason he hired me is running as best and as fast as he can to find you," Leonardo said, wiping his head with his handkerchief. "He told me he'd stayed in the order to keep his son safe, but the fact that he couldn't keep Oscar safe became apparent in the last few weeks. With my help, we put together a bag that would help Oscar get out of Costa

Rica and come here. I haven't heard from him since Sebastian's death, so I need your help finding him."

"Is Oscar also a member of this order?" Morgaine asked.

"Oscar is more a professor than a believer of anything, but he did what his father had asked. I think he only did it, though, to dig up the past, not anything to do with any cult, as he liked to say."

"Was he involved in a dig in northern Costa Rica recently?" Kendal asked.

"I don't know how you found that out, but yes. From what Sebastian said, some of his men died in the pits they found there, and Oscar left to do more research before going back. The last time we talked, Sebastian told me that whatever the leaders of the order were looking for was about to be uncovered."

"We'll help you any way we can, but how did you find me?" Kendal asked. "Why come to me and Piper?"

"Sebastian also found old documents about something called the Genesis Clan and somehow tracked you down, but we know there are others, though we haven't found them yet."

"The bag you put together for his son, what was in it?" Kendal asked.

"A passport, money, and a ticket to New Orleans." Leonardo pressed his hands together. "I gave Sebastian my word I'd keep his son alive."

"Charlie, get the information from him and check. I'll be right back after talking to Rolla," Kendal said and kissed her before leaving.

Piper wasn't going anywhere, knowing Kendal would fill her in on what she needed from Rolla later. Leonardo gave Charlie the name on the passport and of the airline that had issued the open ticket for when Oscar needed it. Morgaine kept Leonardo occupied while Charlie printed the information and gave it to Piper. The ticket had been used, and the man who was traveling was actually arriving in a few hours.

"Keep looking, Charlie, and let us know if you find anything," she said, slipping the paper into her pocket. "Lenore will keep you company, but Morgaine, you need to come with me."

Rolla appeared aggravated when they went up to his room, where Kendal was already pacing like a caged animal, but he had no idea how

Sebastian had found anything about the clan, much less Kendal herself. "Who exactly is this guy?" Rolla said, smashing his fist into his palm.

"Right now all we have is what he's told us and who hired him, and whoever Sebastian's son is, he's getting here soon so we can ask him." Piper handed over the information Charlie had found. "I'm sure if Leonardo is a private eye like he said, he didn't need us to look for that. He should've known it, so I have to question his motives."

"I'm sure it's a setup," Morgaine said. "If they lure us out to pick Petchel up, then whoever's behind this has a way to get to us and whatever information we have, not that it's much. So how do you want to handle it?" Morgaine glanced at Kendal.

"We could threaten to remove his kidneys in the most painful way possible, but I don't think they know exactly what the Genesis Clan is. If they think it's something like the Order of Fuego, then Leonardo knows the answers won't be easy to come by, so let's go pick up Oscar. If you're right, it'll be a hell of a surprise when we don't go all that willingly."

"So you don't believe any of his story?" Piper asked.

"I believe that Sebastian probably is trying to save his son and that Oscar is running from something, but Leonardo's part doesn't ring true. No one hired for something this important is that incompetent, or maybe he is. We're not going to know for sure until we see what happens next," Kendal said.

They all went back to Charlie's place, and Kendal nodded slightly to Charlie, so he printed the same thing again. "Found it, and it looks like he made it out."

"He's coming?" Leonardo asked, pressing his hands to his face. "When? I need to be there when he gets here."

"Morgaine and I will go get him. You stay here, and you can talk to him when he arrives. If his father thought it was important for us to meet, then that's what we'll do."

Piper saw the swift panic that flashed across the man's face, but he hid it well and nodded. "You're right. I'll wait here and trust you to find him."

Kendal was right that Leonardo wasn't all he seemed, and hopefully they'd know what his game was as soon as Oscar was found. "Relax out here, then, and I'll have something brought out to you. I'm sure a nice meal and some wine will help you pass the time," Piper said, and everyone stood. "Charlie, you don't mind, do you? We'll give him some privacy."

"Sure. I'll even leave the computer up, if you need to use it for anything," Charlie said, and was the first one through the door.

They left Charlie to watch the monitors strategically placed in every room of his home after Kendal had suggested using it as a guest cabin every so often until some more places could be built since Charlie didn't mind staying in the house when asked. For something like this it was easier to keep an eye on someone than if you gave them full run of the house and property, and Leonardo didn't disappoint when he immediately got on his phone.

"He made it out, so I'll have him back by the morning, along with whatever information Sebastian thought these people had. They didn't exactly seem surprised when I mentioned the dig and Oscar's part in it. Bring enough men so we don't have any problems."

"Bastard," Kendal said, shaking her head. "And you offered him dinner too."

"I guess it takes more than Southern hospitality, baby," Piper said and pinched her cheek. "Charlie, can you figure out who he was talking to?"

"That'll take more time, so it might be easier to go in there and beat him to death with his phone," Charlie said. "I'll have Hill help me with that."

"Okay, but I doubt we'll find out who he was talking to if we go that route, and I think that's who needs to be beat to death," Kendal said, watching Leonardo walk around opening each drawer and reading what he found. "Go ahead and take him the meal Piper promised him before he gets to your journals. If he doesn't know what he's looking for now, those books will give him all the answers. I'm not willing to give that up to him or anyone involved with him."

"You got it," Charlie said, standing next to the young woman putting a tray together. "Should I babysit until you get back?"

"If you don't mind. I'll make it up to you later," Kendal said and patted him on the back when he followed the man carrying the tray. When they were out, she held her hand out to Piper, and Morgaine did the same to Lenore. "The kids okay for now?"

"Fed and napping, so we're up for whatever you have in mind," Piper said.

"How about a trip next door to set up our torture chamber?"

"Torture chamber?" Piper asked, more curious than upset.

"Would you talk if I threatened to beat you up?" Kendal said and laughed. "Or would you talk if you thought a pack of really big scary wolves was about to rip you to shreds before they enjoyed a little bald appetizer on my command?"

"I see your point," Piper said, shaking her head. The members of the Order of Fuego were playing with matches when it came to butting heads with her partner, so they were going to learn the meaning of getting burned.

The four of them took a car together, since Kendal told her the horses knew what Tala and the others were and got skittish around them. Tala was downstairs with Trudy, and they seemed to be looking through the volumes of new and old books, but she was glad to see them.

"You can't have missed me that much already," Tala said, taking her and Kendal's hands.

"I might have an answer to one of our unknowns sitting at our place, but he's setting me up for something along the lines of death, if I had to guess," Kendal said as they moved to sit.

"I take it he doesn't know that death isn't your thing," Tala said and laughed.

"No, and I doubt he could imagine that he's next door to *the* ultimate pack leader," Kendal said, and from the way she said it, Tala seemed to understand what she was talking about. "I have to go get someone this guy Leonardo dropped in our lap, and when I come back I need to have a talk with Leonardo with some furry backup."

"Furry backup?" Tala said, shaking her head. "You do have a way of putting things, so you should be glad I like you so much."

"Try to forgive her, your highness," Piper said, pinching Kendal's side and mouthing *Behave*. "Oscar Petchel is arriving soon, and if you're willing to help, I'll call you as soon as I hear from Kendal."

"Please, Piper, it's Tala to you, and we'll be there. I think I have enough people to make an impression."

"Leonardo might've brought some men with him, and he's in my house close to our baby," she said, and Tala took her hand again.

"Don't forget what Lovell and I promised yesterday. Hali will be fine, as will Anastasia," Tala said, glancing at Morgaine and Lenore.

"Go home and tell any staff that isn't aware of us not to worry. Lovell and I will take care of the rest."

"Thank you, highness," Kendal said, bowing over Tala's hand before kissing it.

"She does have a way of making things up to you, doesn't she?" Tala laughed before hugging Piper, then Kendal.

"She does, but you do have to give her a good pinch to keep her in line," she said, holding her fingers up in Kendal's direction.

CHAPTER SIXTEEN

M r. Pinchon," the customs agent in New Orleans said, taking Oscar's arm and leading him away from the line he was in. The airport's customs area wasn't very big, but it was crowded. Oscar had thought he was clear of danger when he went through security in Costa Rica, but something must've tipped these guys off even before he showed them the passport his father had given him.

"Is there a problem?" he asked, not trying to give any sign of a fight.

"Just come with me," the man said, and he opened the door to what looked like an interrogation room.

If they were going to arrest him, it would be in the United States, away from Alejandro and his killers. "Did I do something wrong?" He tried again, not wanting to be on a plane back to where he wouldn't live out the day.

"Not yet, but that's why we're here," the tall woman said as she handed the man an envelope and he left them alone. "Oscar Petchel?"

"Who are you?" He gripped the handle of the bag his father had given him and wondered when he'd lost total control of his life. The scary part was that he'd never get that back.

"I think I'm someone you're looking for." The woman held out her hand, and he simply stared at it but then decided to take it. "I'm Kendal Richoux, and I'm an elder of the Genesis Clan."

"My father wanted to find you, but I'm not a big believer in secret groups."

Kendal laughed and nodded. "I know what you mean, but if you walk out that door without me, a guy named Leonardo and his men are waiting to kill you. You don't know me, but I'm not some crazy who wants to do that. I'd like to know exactly why you're here."

"And if you don't like my reason, then you kill me?"

"Then I let you go to run the gauntlet on your own, and believe me, there is a gauntlet. This first step, I'm sorry, isn't voluntary. Once we talk, you have my word that if you want to go, you can."

"Why do you think my father wanted to find you?" The honesty in the way Kendal spoke made him want to know everything about her.

"I'm not sure, but he hired and trusted someone he shouldn't have. He led a man to my home who's waiting to kill us both, along with my family. Anyone who's that dedicated to getting at you and me is after something one of us has. At least he must think so."

"If what my father told me right before he died is true, I know exactly what he wants. He got killed after serving these people all his life." He was tired of crying, but that last glimpse of his father waiting to die so that he could get away was still like a knife through the heart.

"Your father died for something he believed in. At least I hope so, but I've found that whatever starts as a noble thing can become twisted and dark. If the people he followed were with this Order of Fuego, and you believe the same things, then we'll still talk, but after that I'm going to kill them one by one. Run back and tell them, but that won't change what I'm planning."

"He died trying to keep me from those idiots, so if that's where you're going, I want you to take me with you."

"Let's have that talk first," Kendal said and stood up. She pointed to the door at the opposite side he'd entered and led him out. "Do you know who Leonardo is?" she asked as they walked down a long corridor that led to a bank of elevators. Kendal punched the *up* button and studied him as if trying to see if he'd answer truthfully.

"I don't know anyone by that name, but until right before his death, I really didn't know my father at all. If he hired him to watch out for me, this man lied to him."

"Unfortunately your father made it easy for whoever is after you because they'd know exactly when you ran and what name you'd use." When they stepped out they were overlooking the ticketing area of the airport, and Kendal stopped and stared down, but not for long. "Let's go."

It was a short walk to the parking lot, and at the door a large SUV with darkened windows sat waiting for them, and Kendal made a call. The only thing she said was to tell someone to leave in fifteen minutes.

It obviously gave them a head start, but he wished he knew where they were going and who Kendal and her friends were.

"Do you want to talk now?" he asked as they headed away from the city.

"You won't have to wait long, but I'm not the only one who needs to hear what you have to say." She smiled at him, and her eyes intrigued him. "Don't worry. Your father was right to look for us."

"I meant what I said. I hardly knew anything about him, and I wasted a lot of time with him because I had the wrong impression of what his true beliefs were."

"You can make it right and ease your guilt by doing the right thing. And you're going to do that if it takes me prodding you along with something sharp pointed at your backside."

Leonardo sat and ate with Charlie and glanced at his phone every so often. When the damn thing finally buzzed, he smiled at his host and excused himself to go outside. "Did you find him?" he asked in Spanish, recognizing the number of one of his men. Leonardo had been in this place too long and was ready to go home to his young wife.

"Those two women went in, but they never came out. We've been waiting, and the line out of customs has slowed, and there's no sign of Petchel. Are you sure you didn't tell them anything?"

"I know my job, and remember that you work for me, not Alejandro. Richoux must have planned on the welcoming committee, so come back and tell the others to try to surround the house without giving these people a chance to fight back. I want this done and Petchel back in our control by tonight." He glanced up at the window of Charlie's place, expecting to see him there, but the blinds were unmoved. Whoever these people were, they didn't know crap about how to defend themselves.

"Are you sure you want us to leave?"

"They're not there, and we can't take the chance Petchel will say anything until I have some backup, so get going."

"Problems?" Charlie asked when he entered again.

"No, but would you mind if we went back up to the house? I'd like to talk to Ms. Richoux's partner before they get back." He needed to be close to the little blonde and the other woman to take control of the situation. Kendal Richoux would do whatever he asked her to when she saw a gun trained on her bitch.

"Sure, but Piper's going to want to wait for Kendal. We can wait for her inside, though, if that'll make you more comfortable."

"I'm just worried about Oscar. His father had faith that I'd keep him safe, so until I see him, I'm not going to relax." He tried his best to convey worry and emotion, and Charlie nodded, so he relaxed and placed his hands on his waist. The feel of his gun secure in the holster at his back made him smile.

Piper was sitting at Kendal's desk when they got into the house, and she waved them in without really looking up from what she was doing. "If you give me a minute, I need to approve some contracts for the shipyard," she said as she typed sporadically. When he started to touch the sword on the desk she flattened her hand over it and shook her head. "Sorry. You can look but don't touch. It's a new one, and Kendal's a little protective."

"She's a collector?" The weapon was beautiful, and the etchings on the blade were like none he'd ever seen. Whoever had made it was a master craftsman.

"A collector and a master swordswoman," Piper said, her hand not moving. "If you ask her when she comes back, I'm sure she'd be happy to show you."

It would take his men at least another twenty minutes to make it from the airport, and if Kendal had left before then it was time to explain the situation to these dumb bastards. He reached for his gun and aimed it at her head as he waved Charlie next to Piper. "I'll pass," he said, reaching for the sword. "Maybe next time, but for now all I'm interested in is Oscar Petchel and any information you have on why he's here. If you think about playing stupid and say you don't know what I'm talking about, I'm going to—"

"Kill my friend or me first?" Piper asked, way too calm. "Which is it?"

"If you think I'm kidding, how about I shoot your friend and we can watch him bleed to death while we're waiting for Kendal to get back." He pointed his gun at Charlie's head, but Piper never backed down. "Get on your knees before you get any heroic ideas."

Charlie simply looked at him with the same defiant expression that Piper had and didn't move. "I don't think so. No one has the right to make me kneel, so come up with something else."

"You don't get it," he said, his finger tensing on the trigger. "I'm not bullshitting, as you Americans like to say."

"Charlie was freed years ago, so he's right," Kendal said, tightening her hand around his and the gun. She squeezed harder than he thought any woman could manage, and his skin was starting to pinch around the metal so he lowered his hand. "Pointing a gun at my spouse isn't a wise career move on your part, Leonardo."

"You're right, I'm sorry, but you have to understand that Oscar Petchel isn't who he says he is. The man is dangerous, so I was trying to spare your family."

"I'm getting ready to use that old American saying of *bullshit*," Piper said, and Kendal laughed. "Thanks for getting here in time, baby. I really like this rug and didn't want to get any bloodstains on it."

"You aren't going to kill me," he said, laughing. "So let me go and we'll forget all about this."

"As the cobra said to the really slow-witted mongoose," Kendal smiled widely, "welcome to my lair." His world went dark right after that.

"Charlie, would you mind going out and helping the guys round up the cavalry Leo here brought with him. Tala and her people are patrolling the border between here and next door, so make sure someone takes a drive and finds the reverse of the canary in the mine."

"Reverse of the canary in the mine?" Piper asked.

"The one guy who stays behind to see if everyone dies before flying off and telling the boss we don't play well with others," Kendal said, picking Leonardo up and draping his limp body over her shoulder. "Once you think you've gotten them all, meet me on the other side of the lake."

"You got it," Charlie said as he headed out, but not before kissing Piper's cheek. "Thanks for not taunting him until he shot me. I know a quick spurt of sunbathing would've done the trick, but I wasn't looking forward to the headache."

"You're welcome, so be careful it doesn't happen in the next half hour either."

They followed Kendal outside and to the stables, where she threw Leonardo over the back of a horse and lifted Piper onto Ruda's back.

The ride was quiet, but before they could get to the spot Kendal had designated, Leonardo came to and jumped off and ran, laughing as he went.

"Is that going to be a problem?" Piper said, barely turning her head, not wanting Kendal to stop kissing her neck as they clopped along.

"Depends on how fast he runs," Kendal said, holding her tighter. "He might beat us there, but he's not going anywhere."

She had to laugh when Leonardo's chuckles turned to screams, and she heard the branches snapping as he ran close to where they were. To the right they saw him frantically moving as a very large wolf followed closely with bared teeth and snarls. "They won't rip anything off until you've talked to him, right?"

"Don't worry. They're housebroken, and if I'm right, that's Lovell. She'll be happy to give him a vasectomy later, but he'll be fine until we're done." They heard a few gunshots in the distance, and then they stopped after they heard a few howls.

"Think they're okay?" Piper asked as they stopped in an opening where Leonardo was pressed to a tree with his eyes closed, as if that would make the scary wolf go away.

"Unless these guys spent the extra money for silver bullets, everyone should be fine. They'll be pissed if they got shot, but they'll be okay after a few weeks." They slid off, and after Kendal tied Ruda to another tree, Piper raised an eyebrow in question. "I want to make sure everyone knows the pretty horse isn't lunch."

A few more men ran in their direction and fell at their feet when the wolves stopped their pursuit. "How many men did you bring?" Piper asked, stepping closer to Leonardo.

"The lady asked you a question, asshole. Answer, or my buddy there is going to rip your lips off and whistle through them," Kendal said, putting a hand on the big wolf's shoulder.

"We had ten, but two stayed behind," he said, seeming to press closer to the tree. "They're up the road."

"There's only four here, so whoever fired those shots has been culled from your herd." A smaller but still impressively large animal trotted into the clearing, and from the blood on its chest they knew what happened to the other men. "Who sent you?"

"The man who hired me never wanted to meet, so I have no idea who he is," Leonardo said quickly. "He paid the bill and had a lot of work for me, so I didn't care if we ever met."

"That's too bad," Piper said.

"Why?" He turned his head but didn't move from his position as two more wolves joined them and moved closer to what was left of Leonardo's forces. "I can't tell you what I don't know, so call these things off and let us go."

"That's too bad, because if you have nothing to say, we're done, and these guys are hungry. If you shot one of them, then your last meal will be memorable when they make it last what'll seem a lifetime," Kendal said, taking Piper's hand and moving back to Ruda.

"Wait, you can't kill us," he said pleadingly.

"That's what you said *after* you lost your gun," Piper said. "Before that, though, you were ready to pull the trigger. You were going to kill me and Charlie, but you've lost the advantage you never had, so now you'll see we do it a little differently here."

"She's right," Kendal said and lifted Piper up. "We aren't going to kill you…they are."

"Alejandro Garza sent me. He wants Petchel for some research he's doing," Leonardo screamed when Lovell moved toward him and snapped her jaws close to his head.

"It seems that lying now isn't the way to go," Piper said, shaking her head and not liking this guy at all. "So tell us, what kind of research?"

"He didn't share that with me. I swear I don't know."

Kendal cocked her head to the side as if pondering the answer and nodded. "I'm not saying I believe you about that, but I would like to know how you found me and Piper."

"You came to Hill months ago asking questions, so I want to know the answer to that too." Piper moved to get off Ruda, but Kendal patted the side of her leg to keep her put. "You came here to harm us, so start talking, or I swear I'll give the command for them to attack myself."

"Mr. Garza got some information from a woman who contacted him after some of his research led him to France. He gave me the basics of what she'd said and charged me with finding you and something called the Genesis Clan. From what she told him, there were many members, but your name and then Piper's name were all I had to go by." He started crying and bouncing a little in place, as if his fear was making him twitch.

"What woman, and don't even think of telling me you don't know," Kendal said.

"All he told me about her was she was leaving Paris and coming to New Orleans to strengthen her numbers. I guess he meant her business."

"How would Ora have met this guy?" she asked Kendal.

"Depends on what he's looking for, and if it's what we think," Kendal said, shrugging, "it still doesn't make sense."

"It's time to ask Oscar. He might have a little more to contribute than this dead end," she said, and glanced at Leonardo, then Kendal. "Whatever they wanted, it was important enough to kill me, Charlie, and you when you got back."

"Don't worry about that. Can you make it back okay?"

"He's been pretty nice to me so far, but if he gets nervous without you, I'm telling on him," she said, patting the side of Ruda's neck. "Don't be long."

Kendal rubbed Piper's leg and kissed her hand. "Depends on what happened before we got here," she said, pointing to Lovell and Tala. She slapped Ruda on the butt, and he walked off slow enough for Piper's comfort.

Lovell waited until Piper was out of sight before she shifted back. "One of his men shot two of our people," Lovell said, pointing at a now-pale Leonardo.

"What are you?" Leonardo asked, sliding down the tree until he thumped on his ass.

"Are they okay?" She glanced at Lovell and smiled when Tala moved to stand in front of her.

"In a couple of days they'll be fine, but Tala wants to deal with it. It's your land, but if you'll allow it, we'll take justice here," Lovell said, and the others with her moved closer.

"I had you bring them here because of the lake. If you can have your people not leave a trace, I'd appreciate it."

"Wait," Leonardo yelled, getting back to his feet. "You can't leave me here with these things."

She took his gun from her belt and threw it a few feet from him. "Reach deep and find that big man who pointed that at my wife earlier. If you can't find that guy, then pray they go for the throat first. The alternative will make you pray to reach that gun, but only to use it on yourself."

"You can't leave us here to die," Leonardo repeated, and the men close to him nodded as one of the wolves dropped one of their weapons out of his jaws at her feet.

"No one ever comes to visit with this kind of firepower with friendly intent. You should understand the penalty of playing a game you don't always win," she said. She gazed at Lovell, and her friend gave a full body shiver before undergoing the transformation again. Whatever justice the were royalty wanted to mete out, she'd leave them to it.

CHAPTER SEVENTEEN

You're going to have to head back to the dig site on your own and find the missing piece in all this," Alejandro said as he tapped his phone on his knee.

Pauline watched him. It wouldn't be much longer before his mood grew dark enough that she'd be willing to go anywhere he wanted as long as it was away from him. The only smile that had appeared on his face was when Leonardo had called and said he'd found Oscar. That he'd managed to get out of the country without tripping any alarms surprised her, since he was more a bookworm than any kind of clandestine spymaster.

His patience for waiting was at an end, and he dialed and placed the phone to his ear. She could hear his breathing from across the room and wondered if he'd ever succumb to the violence that seemed to constantly simmer right below the surface. The day he raised a hand to her was the day she'd leave and never see him again, even if she had to abandon the hunt. Her mother had hinted at her father's dark side, and she vaguely remembered her mother's battered face but had thought it was some confused childhood mix-up in her head.

"Leonardo?" Alejandro said, his face getting splotchy red when no one seemed to answer. "Are you there?" Again he seemed to get no answer because he took a moment to focus, she guessed, by closing his eyes and pursing his lips together tightly. When he opened them she motioned for him to put the phone on speaker, and surprisingly he did.

"Who is this?" a deep but female voice asked.

"Who is this?" Alejandro asked and only got laughter from the other side before the woman hung up. "Who is this bitch?"

"Do you think something happened to Leonardo?"

"Unless he's lost his mind, I doubt he handed his phone over to some random woman," Alejandro said through what seemed to be a haze of hate as he dialed again. "Who is this?"

"Not to get into a circular conversation with you, but I asked you first. Give me a name, and I'll think about answering you," the woman said, then laughed.

"Where's Leonardo?"

"He's having lunch with some friends," the woman said and then hung up again.

He dialed two more times, but the phone went right to voice mail. Whoever had answered it had obviously powered it off. "Get going, and don't come back until you have some answers."

"I need help. I can't go back there by myself," she said, and flinched back hard enough that it moved her chair when he punched the top of his desk.

"I'm beginning to think your mother lied about you being mine. Get back there, and don't worry about having someone hold your hand. There'll be plenty enough people from the order to help you, but I have a feeling time is running out. If it does, I'm going to kill every single person who let this slip through my fingers."

"Maybe you should come with me," she said, finally realizing that he'd never once set foot in any site they'd explored. "If whoever that was got to Leonardo, you might be vulnerable."

"Worry about what I tell you to worry about, and leave the rest to me," he said, turning his attention to something else as if they were done and whatever else she had to say was of no importance. "Go."

She left, and any illusions that he cared anything about her fell from her heart. "If I find anything at all, it's going to be mine," she said softly as she walked to the waiting helicopter. Whatever power was to be found would be hers in memory of her mother, who'd given Alejandro everything and died with only her at her side. "And if I can, I'm going to crush you with it."

❖

"Are you sure you don't want to stay here with your grandparents? I'm just going for a few days, and I'm not exactly going alone," Kendal said as she took stuff out of the drawers on her side of the bed.

"I'm not having this conversation with you again, as in never again," Piper said as she lay on the bed with the baby beside her sleeping. "You haven't been married that long, considering how long you've been alive, but there are certain lessons you should go ahead and wrap your head around now so we don't have to keep wasting time on them."

"Okay, but try to talk your grandparents into going so we don't have to worry about the baby." She got another bag out of the closet and placed it next to hers. "If Oscar got that far and shared the information with Pauline, we have to get going."

"I can't believe he agreed to go back there." She put pillows around Hali as a precaution and started packing. "Those guys today were planning a massacre, followed by dragging him home to finish what he started. From Rawney's expression, he's not wrong about the translations."

"He's not wrong, but he needs to focus if he's going to be of any use to us. Right now all he can think about is killing everyone involved with the order."

She walked around the room and put her arms around Kendal from behind. "You can't blame him, honey. It's been eons, but you must've felt the same way."

"I know, but I didn't have you and Hali to worry about back then. We don't need a hothead putting people in danger for the sake of revenge." Kendal sat on the bed, and she sat on her lap.

"I'm sure that between you, Morgaine, Charlie, and my grandmother, Oscar isn't going to be a problem. We can leave him here with Rolla and the others, but even Rawney was amazed at how much he'd figured out without any help from anyone." She combed Kendal's hair back and kissed her neck.

"What does your grandmother have to do with anything?" Kendal asked, leaning back a little so she could see her face.

"You guys can skewer whoever gets in your way, but Gran can put the fear of death into you with that mom glare. Believe me, you'll stop whatever the hell you're doing if you're on the receiving end of one of those." She pinched Kendal's cheek and smiled. "It's going to be okay, baby. We haven't come to this place in time and built what we have to allow anyone to take it away from us."

"So I'm being a little crazy?"

"I happen to like you a little crazy, but only when it comes to me, so let's go. The sooner we wrap this up, the faster we'll get back here or on a honeymoon. I'm not sure, but that ring exchange with Aphrodite means we're as married as anyone out there. And if I'm married, I want the party and the honeymoon that goes with it."

"You got it, and a Mayan ruin in a rain forest isn't going to be it."

"It's good to know that Piper got so lucky," Molly said, coming in without knocking. "I agree with her about the honeymoon, but right now finish packing, and I'm going to take my great-granddaughter downstairs and introduce her to the classics."

"She should be reading by ten months," Kendal said, standing up with her in her arms. "So let's get going before Hali is smarter than all of us and doesn't need help solving anything."

They finished packing and headed to the smaller Lakefront Airport, where Rolla had chartered a plane to take them to another small airport closer to where they were headed. Oscar seemed to be studying the group boarding, and Piper figured he was trying to put together the good-looking but different people who all had the same eye color.

Once they were in the air and Hali was comfortable, she went and sat with Oscar. The man was in pain, but he also seemed so passionate about what he did. Whatever he was looking for, it wasn't for some personal gain. "Hi," she said, sitting, and waited for him to stop typing. "Do you mind if we talk about what your father told you?"

"I still can't believe he was serious, but why would he have spent the last moments of his life spinning such a fanciful story? He must have been trying to protect me from whatever Alejandro wanted." He drummed his fingers on the laptop and glanced out the window. "He said Alejandro killed my mother."

"What do you know about Alejandro aside from working with him?" She shook her head when Kendal looked at her as if she was going to join them. "From what you said, he's affluent and dedicated to his cause, but what drives him?"

"I think he's after some kind of power he believes is buried in that spot he sent me to. If there really are dragons, which I doubt, he thinks he can control them, I guess."

"How did your father find us?" Alejandro might've found them through Ora, which she didn't really believe just yet, but Sebastian had taken another route. "Was he able to tell you?"

Oscar reached down to his bag and handed over a small journal. "He put it all in here."

She took it and flipped to the page he indicated. The most striking thing was the sketch of Kendal sitting on a horse with a cloak and what appeared to be facial hair. It was a copy of one of the pages from Lenore's book. "Where did he get this?"

He flipped the page, and she read the short history included about the first men who were loyal to the Order of Fuego. It listed their purpose, which at that time was mostly to keep the dragons with the people, and it hinted at the members of their group who wanted more power by learning to control the beasts.

In the end it was that latter group that won out, and the others were driven away or killed, but not before they'd left some hint as to their existence. It was as if they wanted someone, no matter how far in the future, to know their intentions were pure in the beginning. To them the dragons were gods, and they worshipped and took care of them. In turn the dragons had begun to trust them by coming to them in greater numbers. The old history of Kendal was a shortened version of what Morgaine had in her archives, but it listed her as an enemy to the order and their mission. There was a question as to if there were more like her, but they seemed to have uncovered the information only recently.

"This is the group I believe my father belonged to, and why our family has worked for so long in whatever this search is for. Right now, if it's to bring them back to life, I can't imagine why they'd want that, but that might be what Alejandro wants." Oscar took his book back. "Will you share with me how you know anything about this?"

They hadn't really had time to do anything else but listen to Oscar share his story, but it wasn't her place to tell him anything. "I'm sure that'll happen eventually, but you have to earn trust. You showed up at the same time as Leonardo, so we're not going to be too open too soon. That's the truth as I see it, so I hope you can accept that."

"I do," he said, and gripped the leather of the book. "If only I'd done the same thing, my father might still be alive."

"That wasn't exactly a mistake," Kendal said, having come close enough to hear that last part. "I know what it's like to get caught up in the hunt for something and believe everyone around you is after the same goal but working against you. Whoever this Alejandro Garza is, he hasn't given you even a hint of what he's after. His search will benefit only him, and everyone he's got looking will bring him the piece of the puzzle he's entrusted them to find. Eventually he'll have the whole picture."

"So how did your father find the clan?" Kendal asked, and Piper was curious to hear Oscar's answer since he really hadn't given her one.

"The beginnings of the dragons in the Mayan territory came with two different groups: the first Mayans who worshipped them and the women who came after. One group splintered into the order, and the women represented the Genesis Clan." Oscar handed the journal over to Kendal after opening it to the section Piper had read. "That was the only mention of the group, and my father tried to expand on it without alerting Alejandro. But he didn't know Alejandro was watching him more closely than he thought, so whatever research he did was reported back to him. The sketch in his journal had to have come from someone within the clan."

"That's in the information your father had?" Kendal asked.

"It's in the journal, along with the sketch I showed Piper. I don't know much about the clan, and neither did my father, but the sketch seemed to give him hope that it did exist, and he was right. I'm sorry he died before he learned at least this part of his research was correct, because here you are, and your ancestor obviously fought on the right side of history."

"This sketch is in only one book that I know of, and I trust the person who keeps it, so I'm not sure how your father found it." Kendal glanced at the picture and shook her head. "Do you mind if I keep this for a little while? I'll give it back before we land."

"Sure," Oscar said, and his face seemed to lose some of its tension. "Maybe you'll see you can trust me enough to compare what we each have."

"Baby steps, but we'll get there," Kendal said, holding her hand out for Piper. "We'll be back, so get some sleep."

They stepped into the next compartment of the plane, where Lenore was showing some documents to Molly. "I hate to interrupt," Piper said, and Molly made room for her on the sofa. "Oscar's father kept a journal of the information he thought he'd hidden from Garza, and this was one of the entries."

Lenore stared at it like she couldn't comprehend why it was in this book. "Asra, you have to know I'd never allow this to happen."

"I'm not accusing you of anything," Kendal said, placing her hand on Lenore's cheek. "You know better than that, but is there a copy of my history anywhere but in the archives you're responsible for?"

"No matter what we're given, there's a copy in the main complex. We have moved some to computers, but the elders are fanatical about having a backup that has nothing to do with technology." Lenore rolled her eyes, but Piper knew of Lenore's love for paper, so the argument was weak. "Histories like yours are always popular with the elders who've never held a sword. To share that with anyone outside the clan is punishable by sleep. You know that as well as anyone."

"To let that out is a good way to bring who we are into the light, but someone wasn't worried about that since Sebastian Petchel had this." Kendal tapped the book.

"As soon as we land I'll call Rolla and find out who had access to that archive. The elders who seldom leave the main compound still have to be accountable for whatever they look at. It's the only way we can prevent something like this."

"If that rambling place has any reason to it, I sure didn't figure it out while we were there," Piper said, remembering the vast space that was like an incredibly cool maze. "Most of everything in there is stacks of papers, and no one seemed to be watching anything."

"You may think that, but trust me, if you'd tried to walk out of there with something that wasn't yours, someone would've slapped your hand. I'll find out exactly who did it." Lenore took the journal and studied the picture and explanation that went with it. "Why this one of all the lives you've lived?"

"I wondered the same thing," Piper said. "I've seen the entire set of books about you, and not much happened in this one. At least, not that I can remember. What do you recall, baby? Is there something you didn't put in there?"

"I spent most of my time pushing out to places the clan wanted me to explore. The world was changing, and Ora and her like weren't sitting in one place, so it was important to find the far reaches before their numbers reached a point that would've been a problem." Kendal glanced down at the page. "This was right before Erik Wolver and I moved more toward what's modern-day Cambodia."

"So nothing out of the ordinary?" Lenore asked, as if she understood where she was going with her questions. "Something that maybe you thought wasn't important for the archive but might be important now."

"That was a long time ago, but I'll think about it." Kendal's expression was pensive, and Piper knew she'd started her on another hunt she would keep at until she found what would explain all this. "Did you find anything else?" Kendal pointed to the other documents they had spread out on the small table.

"Aphrodite was right. There weren't many elders alive back then, and people at the time weren't exactly bound by the facts. The few accounts we've found sounded more along the embellishment than anything we can use," Lenore said, and Molly nodded.

"The few archives we have from the clan members who actually witnessed the dragons before they were cleared from the skies don't give any hint as to how they were put to sleep. From what these say, they tried to study them so they could educate the people to stay away from them, but once the knowledge spread that their eggs were gold, no one listened." Molly slid a book toward her. "It was ancient times, but they were beginning to understand the importance of gold and wealth."

"That's interesting, but it won't help us," Kendal said and winced when Piper pinched her. "Good information, though."

"Some of the places in our history were in the area you're talking about," Convel said from her spot in the big leather chairs with Lowe next to her. "Some of the people you keep an eye on moved in that direction. The books I read talked about the explorer nature of the weres and how they were accepted even after the natives found out what they truly were."

"People had more imagination back then and accepted the differences in us all," Kendal said, and Convel finally looked at her without a hateful expression. "In a way we're all hiding now, but still trying to keep the balance."

"What side of the scales are we on?" Lowe asked, making Convel smile.

"I'm sure you've heard the story of that scar." Kendal pointed to Convel's hand. "But I'll tell you now what I told her then. Not everything deserves killing. Have you had any experience with vampires?"

"Not yet," Lowe said, trying to keep eye contact, even though Piper could tell Kendal made her nervous.

"I've been friends with Tala and Lovell for years because they have a soul and they care about those they're responsible for. That can't always be said for vampires. Some retain an essence of their humanity, but I've seen the very worst in the most beautiful face." The way Kendal said it made Piper think Kendal was thinking of her brother.

"I understand that, but where does it leave us?" Lowe asked.

"That you have nothing to fear from me, unless you do something to try to harm my family or the pack. I take my responsibility to your queen as seriously as I do the care of my family." Kendal opened her fist when Piper took her hand. "We don't have to be friends, but we don't have to be enemies."

"Thank you for saying that," Lowe said, and she offered Kendal her hand and smiled when Kendal accepted it. "We don't know why we're here, and we've lost our family."

"You haven't lost anything," Kendal said, and Convel lost her smile. "I might be wrong, but I think what happened was Lovell's way of pushing you to a place where you've been missed."

"You don't know anything about me," Convel said and began to stand, but Lowe kept a grip on her arm. "Tala and Lovell might trust you, but I'm never going to do that."

"Fair enough, but don't get in my way." Kendal stepped away and headed to the very back of the plane, where the nannies were sitting with the children.

"Eventually you'll stop lying about what happened to you and take responsibility for your bad choices," Piper said, straightening her shoulders. "And before you open your mouth and make a bigger fool of yourself, I saw what happened, and I mean every second of it. Your pack might follow you, but they're following a lie."

"You know this because you listened to her side of the story?" Convel said with heat.

"I know because my gift allowed me to see it. You can believe me or not, but I can also tell you exactly when and how you found Lowe and came to love her." She glanced at the smaller woman who seemed so devoted to Convel. "If you need that proof I'll take you back to that night when she first saw you and rolled to her back and submitted."

"How?" Lowe asked.

"Sometimes I don't mean to see something so personal, but I guess whatever or whoever gave me this sight deems it necessary so I can prove that I'm not telling you something so vague you won't believe me." Piper didn't let go of her anger at this immature, infuriating woman. "So give Lowe the same respect and kindness she's shown you by telling her the truth. It won't change the way she sees you, of that I'm sure of."

"You can't know that." Convel seemed to lose all the steam she'd built up.

"My visions aren't only of the past. When it's important I can see far into the future as well." She smiled and glanced in the direction Kendal had walked off in. "It's a wonderful thing, especially when we see those we love still standing right beside us where they belong."

"How do I know you're telling the truth?"

"You don't, but I'm not the one living with the mountain of boulders on my shoulders. The only way to lighten your load is to share it with someone who loves you. You don't have to, but then you'll never really know if the love is real or something you imagine it to be."

She walked to where Kendal stood watching Hali sleep alongside Anastasia. The sight made her wonder if in twenty years, their daughter would be as tall and strong as Kendal. If she was, some lucky person out there would be fortunate to have Hali love them like she did Kendal.

"Can I talk to you?"

"Any time about anything," Kendal said as she put her arm around her waist.

"It's nothing important, and since we're on a plane with a bunch of other people, it can't get too personal," she said and smiled, enjoying the way their bodies fit together perfectly.

"I'm sure we can find a quiet spot if you want a private conversation." Kendal kissed her temple and tugged her closer.

"Come on, trouble," she said, pulling Kendal with her to the big chair next to the double bed. "I realize we don't know much about what we're getting into, but can you tell me what's going to happen when we land?"

"We have another short flight to get closer to where the dig site is, but I have a house close to there, and plenty of security for everyone and the babies. I want to go see what exactly is on the ground where these Fuego people have concentrated so much of their effort. With any luck we'll run into a few of them while we're searching and get our next clue."

"Do you think this is like the sword and we're on a timeline?" She rested her head on Kendal's shoulder and stared at Hali as she stretched before going back to a little ball to sleep. "We'll need so many more answers if that's the case."

"I did do one thing before we left the house, and I wanted to run it by you before we land." The way Kendal said it made her sit up to look at her better.

"What?"

"I sent word to Vadoma through the contact she gave me. It's not easy for them to travel such long distances, so I'm not sure when she'll get here, but she might make an appearance. If she does, I didn't want it to be a surprise."

"What do you think she'll have to do with all this?" She still couldn't accept the fact that Vadoma had held her grandparents with the intent to kill them.

"I'm not sure, but you heard that we need to pool our resources."

"Ha. That bitch—" she said too loud, before snapping her mouth closed.

"I don't disagree with you, but that bitch saved me and Morgaine. At least she thinks she did."

"So now she probably thinks you owe her," she said, not ready to back down. "I don't want to think we're in debt to her."

"If you're really against it, I'll tell her to forget it. This is going to be hard enough without making you uncomfortable."

"Wait," she said, realizing that no matter what they faced, it was better with an army than with their small group. "Don't do that yet, but if she lays a hand on anyone I love, I don't care what you promised her."

The night they'd met the new queen of the vampires, Vadoma had broken into Kendal's English estate and threatened to kill her grandparents. Kendal had killed some of the people she'd brought with her and brought Vadoma out to meet the sun. Before that could happen, Kendal had made a deal with her that helped them win the fight for the Sea Serpent Sword, but in return Kendal had promised she wouldn't hunt Vadoma for years.

"She knows the rules of that game," Kendal said, cupping her cheek. "She comes anywhere near any of us, especially your family or the baby, and I'll kill her."

"Do you promise?" she said, needing Kendal to say it.

"You have my word as well as my heart."

CHAPTER EIGHTEEN

Aishe was almost to the top of the steep mountainside, and the farther she climbed, the more pissed she got. These assholes had blindsided her, but she was also pissed they'd taken her phone. A call to Rawney would put her out of the miserable worrying she must be doing. Waking up in the middle of a thick forest covered in blood with numerous broken bones was somewhat embarrassing, since she'd insisted she was ready for fieldwork on her own.

"A fucking monkey, of all things," she muttered as she saw the edge right above her head.

She was sweating, but the higher she got, the cooler the temperatures grew, so she slowed down and tried to hear any kind of movement or sound from above. The area was quiet, and she'd tried to angle to the right of the platform she saw when she was about five hundred yards below. She didn't remember anything after the monkey startling her, but if she had to wager, that's where she'd taken the trip down the mountain.

The last thing she wanted was to wait until the sun went down, but that's what she was going to do so she could move around the property and try to see what she could. Whoever the Order of Fuego was, they didn't mind taking out anyone they saw as a threat, and she wasn't the only one they'd disposed of that night, since not far from where she'd landed she'd seen the body of a man dressed like the security Alejandro Garza had brought with him.

"Their employee review must be something you don't want to flunk," she said as she inched up so she could just see over the edge.

The place was quiet, with only a few scattered workmen pulling weeds and cutting grass. She didn't see anyone who might've been guarding someone or anyone who appeared to be working in any other than a menial sense. It was midday, though, so whoever lived here might be inside or in an office somewhere nearby. She did a quick survey and saw the shrubs that hid some outbuildings to her left and the trees beyond them.

"As long as there's no monkeys, I should be fine," she said, starting to move along the edge so she could climb up beyond the shrubs. She'd sit in some high branches until dark and then move in. These people certainly wouldn't expect her to rise from the grave they'd dumped her into.

She'd made it into the tree when she heard the helicopter in the distance. It was a big corporate-appearing craft that usually had plenty of space for passengers and could travel longer distances than the average one. Maybe if she spotted a logo on the side or some name she could follow up on, she could figure out not only who but maybe where the hell she was. The people working in the yard all stopped and stared at the ground as if they didn't want to get caught staring at whoever might get off. It was bizarre, and she'd encountered some strange things in her life.

She glanced around for a road out of wherever she was, but the house and the rest of the buildings seemed to be surrounded by vegetation, and she didn't see a vehicle anywhere. "Great," she whispered as she realized that returning to civilization would be harder and longer than she planned.

Only one thing brightened her mood. The people who were staring down at the ground couldn't all live here. If they came and went every day, she doubted that they did so on the beast landing in the big clearing on the side of the main house.

When she saw the smallish man she now knew was Alejandro Garza step off the helicopter and head inside, she decided not to wait. She had to find a way out that didn't include hacking her way through the vegetation that would just get thicker farther down this plateau, so she sat and waited for the best opportunity to come along. She needed him to walk close to where she was, so she held her breath, patient.

"Tell her I'll be home in three days," the man said, sounding agitated. "I don't give a shit," Garza's guard said even more loudly. He stared at the phone after he finished the call and peered up when he must have heard the whooshing noise of her body coming off the branch.

They both hit the ground hard when she landed on him, and she wrapped her arm around his neck, grabbing her own wrist for more leverage. He flailed his arms back, trying to knock her off, but if he did she was going over the side again, and that wasn't happening. His hits were growing softer and slower, so she squeezed even more, and in a few more long minutes, he finally went limp. She was no killer, but she dragged him to the side and pushed him off, not wanting to raise an alarm if he was found.

She very carefully took the back off his satellite phone and glanced inside to make sure Garza wasn't the kind of person who kept more than an eye on his people. Aishe worked for the elders, but she was also trained in electronics, so it was easy for her to spot the small piece that didn't belong. The guard's boss was listening in on his conversations and keeping track of where he was.

She took it out and placed it on the branch of one of the hedges before she accessed the GPS on the device to locate the coordinates of where she was standing. She couldn't possibly memorize all the numbers on the screen, so she texted them to the only number she thought was safe before she headed into the trees. She had to be far enough away before she made the call she was desperate to make.

"When I come back we'll see how well you recover from a bullet to the forehead," she said as she started a slow but steady jog.

The airstrip where the group with Piper and Kendal landed was remote, but a group stood on the tarmac to meet them with enough vehicles to take them all to the house Kendal had arranged. Piper glanced out at the horizon and could tell they were in a higher elevation. The heavy cloud cover hid most of the view, but a few peaks showed through.

"Where are we exactly?" Piper asked.

"About twelve miles from where the ruins are, and six miles from the house. It's remote, but I wanted to be close enough to walk in once we're settled." Kendal held Hali on her shoulder and placed her hand on her back as she descended the stairs. "I'm sure they haven't given up the search, so I want to see who's actually on the ground that's not a grunt." She nodded to the man who stood at the bottom of the steps with an AK-47 strapped to his back.

"Who are these guys?" Piper asked, looping her fingers into the back of Kendal's pants.

"They work for my friend Rueben Margoles. He's the one I called about Aishe, and I trust that they're working for us and not anyone in the Order or in the Clan, for that matter. Someone from the main compound shared with these people who we are so they could find us. That makes me not trust anything that's coming from anyone except Rolla."

"How about everyone else?" she asked as they started down, since their fellow passengers were ready to get off. "We've got a few elders with us."

"I sincerely doubt Bruik or anyone else with us would have put us in any kind of danger. After talking to Oscar, it sounds like his father and the rest of the Order knew we existed but not really what we are." Kendal kissed the side of her head and smiled. "For now, I'd like to keep it that way."

"There's that and the fact that I'd like to keep them from finding out the truth of that dig. Oscar seems to be on the right track."

"About Oscar," Kendal said, stopping before they reached the bottom of the steps.

"I'm not, and I won't let anyone else, share anything with him until we know for sure he is who he is," she said and winked. "I'm not some military genius, but Pops taught me not to be overenthusiastic about giving anyone an edge."

"I'd have to disagree with you on that genius thing. Had my pharaoh known you, I'd have been knocked down the ranks faster than I could ride." Kendal winked back. "Right now all I want to know is what they hope to accomplish by going this route. Dragons sound cool in theory, but having a sky full of them doesn't seem to me like a good idea."

"That's one reason I'm glad Gran is now on the job."

"I'm thrilled that they'll be with us no matter what, but what do you mean?" Kendal's brows came together as if she was confused.

"She's an excellent history professor, so no more of the cryptic shit we have to deal with from all the people who left breadcrumbs, like you said. She's a great historian as well as teacher, so if we need to refer to something a thousand years from now, I promise you she'll have a complete report with plenty of backup research," she said and laughed.

"Welcome, Ms. Richoux," the man said, standing up straighter once they were on the ground. "My name is Miguel Korbe, and Rueben wanted you to know he'll be here in two days. Your family will be safe until then. You have my word."

"Thank you," Kendal said, handing the baby to her when she started to fuss. "I want people posted around the house around the clock. I don't care about the cost."

"No worries. Rueben took care of everything. He said he's worked with you before, so he'll know what you expect."

She listened to the conversation and took a few deep breaths as Hali curled up against her. Something right at the edges of her mind wanted to come into the forefront, but it lingered just out of reach. "Hon," she said to Kendal and regained her balance when Kendal put her arms around her.

"I'll talk to you later," Kendal said to Miguel and led her to the first car. "Molly," Kendal said to her grandparents as they came down next. "You and Mac take the next car, and we'll meet you at the house."

"Everything okay?" Molly asked, sounding concerned, as if she was tuned into Piper's distress.

"It will be," Kendal said with a smile. "We need some privacy and some quiet."

They rode to the house along a winding road that seemed to follow a steady ascending incline that eventually put them in the cloud bank. After about half an hour their driver took a dirt road to the right, and she put her hand on Hali's legs as they endured the ruts that made their SUV rock through the thick mud. Finally, in about three more miles, the beautiful estate came into view.

"If it's not too remote for you, I thought this might be a good place for us when we want to spend some time alone," Kendal said, and she leaned more heavily against her.

"It looks wonderful." And it did. From what she could see, the house overlooked a thick area of trees and seemed to be more than big enough for everyone with them.

"Just breathe, my love, and try to figure it out."

"How do you always know?" She closed her eyes and for some reason started crying. Nothing in her life had made sense until Kendal had come along and really seen her for who she was and what she believed in. "I'm so lucky."

The baby started crying, and the sound only made her cry harder, but Kendal never left her. "Close your eyes, my love, and think about anything but what's going on. Can you do that for me right now?"

Kendal reached over her and released Hali from her car seat and held her until she calmed enough to doze off. "I'm not sure what's wrong with me," she said and leaned against Kendal like she couldn't sit up on her own. "I've never been weepy."

"Do you remember that you had a baby just recently?" Kendal said with no condescension in her tone. "I'm not making light of that fact, but immortal or no, your body can't be completely back to normal."

"Thanks for finding an excuse for me, baby," she said, and kissed Kendal's chin.

"I'm in love with you, so it's not finding an excuse. We're a team now, and I need you to know that I'm going to take care of you first, no matter what's happening in the world." Their nanny came to the door and held her arms out for the baby, and Kendal handed her over. "She should be good for another hour, so call if you need us before then."

"Are we going somewhere?" What Kendal had said about the baby was true, but she didn't want Kendal wasting time worrying about her either.

"For a walk to the backyard," Kendal said, kissing her before getting out and coming around the car and lifting her out. "The rental agent promised something I want to check out."

She put her arms around Kendal's neck and rested her head on her shoulder. She'd never daydreamed of the person she'd end up with, and now she was glad. Kendal had so far exceeded any hidden expectation she'd even thought of having and seemed to always go out of her way to show her how loved she was. It was time to start doing something in return before Kendal felt neglected.

When Kendal walked longer than she'd expected, Piper opened her eyes and noticed they'd gone downhill a little until the house was out of view over the slope. The stand of trees they seemed to be headed to had some kind of structure under it, but they were still too far away to see what it was.

She bit down on Kendal's neck when she saw that a swing wasn't on the large frame but actually a hanging bed secluded in the trees yet still with a great view of the valley in front of them. Kendal gently put her down and took time to pull her shoes off before joining her on the other side.

"Places like this always remind me of the world's agelessness. When you're some place like New York, London, or even New Orleans, in a way, you're surrounded in the fast-paced merry-go-round the world has become, but here life is rooted someplace in the past, and they're not interested in changing anything about it."

"I can see why Rawney's mother chose this place to take care of Aphrodite's children. Time wouldn't touch them," she said, a sense of tiredness almost swamping her. "The only thing they had to fear was men's ambitions."

"Right now I want you to think only about the rows and rows of coffee plants that terrace the mountainside, or let your mind wander. I'll be here right next to you, no matter what you want to do."

She closed her eyes again and was right back there with Rawney's mother and the steps she'd taken to do the goddess's bidding, as well as the reward she'd received for her devotion. This time, though, it was like she was invisible and all her vision concentrated on was the spell and the aftermath when the sisters had lost their lives.

Tomorrow would have to be soon enough, but they needed to walk in that place where all this had started and find something that would give them everything they wanted. For them it was for peace and to find their traitors, and for Aphrodite it was to not have any more of the dragons she'd brought into this world slaughtered for no reason.

"If what I see is true, these people won't go so quietly and meekly and fall in line. They have too much at stake."

"I know, but then, so do we." Kendal held her tighter and smiled. "How would you like to take a walk with me in the morning?"

"Do you want to head to the site?"

"I'm taking only a few people with us, but I'd like to look around and see what's happening."

"Then we'll worry about that in the morning, but right now you should worry about trying to keep your pants on."

"Really?" Kendal said and laughed. "I'm beginning to think you've developed a taste for love outdoors."

"It's more a taste for love with you, and I don't care where we are. So don't make me have to get rough with you."

❖

Piper went back inside to feed the baby and sit with her grandmother once they'd spent a few hours together, so Kendal changed and joined Morgaine and Charlie in the yard to do some drill work. The movements, which came as naturally as breathing, helped clear her mind. She had been on so many of these missions on behalf of the Clan, but something about this one seemed different.

The danger or the unknown didn't bother her, but she was edgy, which came out in the speed of her blade. Once she'd knocked Morgaine's sword out of her hand for the third time, Morgaine made a rude movement with her hand. "Are you trying to show me up or just being overenthusiastic?" Morgaine asked.

"Sorry. I'm not in total control today," she said, opening and closing her free hand.

"Something wrong?" Charlie asked.

"Nothing I can narrow down. Something about all this doesn't seem right, and it may have to do with the gods."

"Knowing they really do exist does make you think differently about devotion, but I can't say I'm sorry. Without Aphrodite and her like, neither of us would have a beautiful child." Morgaine rested her hand on her shoulder and smiled. "When we were young and prayed because that's what the world around us expected of us, we never imagined having those prayers answered so personally."

"I never spent much effort on the gods, but in my time the priests and the pharaohs loved and worshipped plenty of them. I guess I'm making up for it now." She closed her eyes and cocked her head, trying to concentrate on something that seemed to be on the wind. "I'm sure we'll be fine, so let's call it for the day, and we'll start out early in the morning."

Charlie and Morgaine watched her go, but she glanced back only once as she headed down the incline past where she and Piper had spent the morning. The music she heard almost sounded like it was in her head, but from the edge where the slope became much steeper, she saw her.

"Do you doubt me now?" Aphrodite asked as she sat on the bench that appeared to be translucent and didn't glance at her when she stepped closer. "You know that I love not only you but Piper as well. I'd never do anything to bring either of you harm."

"I know that, and please don't take what I said to mean that I doubt you." Since the goddess hadn't asked her to sit, she knelt by her side. "I don't think this life I've lived would have been possible without you and the others like you. The magic that keeps us alive springs from somewhere in your heart."

"You've never been a great believer in the mystical, Asra, so don't go changing something so fundamental about yourself." Aphrodite caressed her cheek. "I wouldn't know what to do with myself if you did."

"My feelings come from somewhere I'm not sure of, and this has never happened to me before." She had no reason to be dishonest, and maybe Aphrodite would have some insight into what came next.

"You've never been truly in love, and you've never had a family before. Not that you have more to lose, but you have more to think about." Aphrodite moved over to make room for her, so she joined her on the bench. "I wish I could take credit for you, Asra, but no one in my family can. Through the years I've kept you in my sights because, while you serve faithfully, you're not like the rest of your kind."

"How so?" Like a quick flash of rapid-fire pictures, all the times Aphrodite had come to her in every lifetime went through her mind.

"They have kept history for the sake of history, but you have truly lived it. You have enjoyed all the days you've been given, and very seldom did you ever feel despair. Your wonder and adventurous soul have been the well from which you've found your strength." Aphrodite's hand was smooth and soft, as if she'd never done anything strenuous in her long life. "Because of that, I know my children will be safe with you."

"Can I ask why dragons, of all things?"

The goddess laughed and kissed her cheek. "Until you come to see one, I can't really answer that question in a way you'll understand." Aphrodite rubbed her hands together, then raised them, palms out. Her hands glowed, and streams of light started to flow out before them. They swirled until they formed a dragon. "I wanted to create something that was a symbol of my love."

The beast was huge and intimidating, but after one glance in its yellow-tinted eye, Kendal knew this was no savage animal. It clearly felt as strongly and loved as much as she did. "I understand why you did it, but you have to know they won't survive now. The world won't take the time to see what you just showed me. They'll destroy them before they realize the truth of them."

"As sad as that is, I do realize what man is capable of. My brother Ares's influence is sometimes hard to overcome."

"Does he have anything to do with this?" She couldn't take her eyes off the dragon as it lazily flapped its wings to stay afloat in front of them. "I know he's as real as you are, so his influence, as you say, can be just as strong in some people."

"Ares has a way of keeping everything to himself, so I can't answer that. If anyone in this world and any other is always trying to manipulate something to his advantage, though, it's him." Aphrodite turned to her and framed her face with her hands. "While Piper owns your heart, remember always, Asra, that you are mine. My claim on you will help you for the fight to come, and I couldn't have asked for a better champion."

"For all that you've given me, my sword will always be yours."

"Remember to keep the sword that Hephaestus made you close. I swear to you I'm not certain what's coming, but like you do, I have a sense of foreboding. He said the blade will keep you as safe as possible."

"Then we begin tomorrow and see what happens," she said before kissing Aphrodite's forehead. "Are your children in pain from the long sleep they've endured?"

Aphrodite smiled, and she truly was a beautiful woman. "Only you would think to ask me that." She moved her hands to Kendal's shoulders and squeezed. "They really are like you in that they're noble of heart but wild creatures that will never conform to someone's will, so they long for freedom. I tried my best to make them understand before I took them from the skies, but their rightful place is there."

"Then you have my pledge that I'll bring them no harm."

"I know. That's why you're my chosen and have been for so long." Aphrodite waved her hand again and the dragon disappeared. "Go back inside and give Piper a kiss for me. I think you've kept her waiting long enough. She's got some things to tell you."

"Will we see you again?"

"You've always had the means to summon me, Asra, so nothing will change that."

She didn't understand that statement at all since she'd never conjured a god. "I'm not sure about that."

"I'm not giving you a cell phone, if that's what you're waiting for," Aphrodite said and laughed. "But think about all the times I've come to you and why. Only now if you want me, you'll have to think up something better than loneliness. Those days are over."

The goddess faded from sight, and Kendal thought of what she meant. All those women in her past who had helped her when she realized she'd never be able to grow old with someone had really been just Aphrodite. She'd cared enough about her to offer comfort when it was needed most, but she was right. Now all she needed was Piper and Hali.

"Thank you," she said into the wind. "But a cell phone couldn't hurt."

CHAPTER NINETEEN

Aishe checked the GPS again and saw that she was ten miles from the house she'd climbed up to, so she headed into the jungle and hunted for a clearing far from the road. The heat was oppressive and she was thirsty, but she really needed to hear Rawney's voice more than anything. She stopped when she heard another helicopter overhead, but it didn't hover or slow. It was, though, headed back in the direction she'd come from.

"Hello," Rawney said, and Aishe leaned against a tree in relief.

"I'm so sorry for worrying you," she said and closed her eyes. "I'll tell you what happened when I see you, but I don't want to be on the phone too long."

"Where are you?"

"I'm not exactly sure, but I need to go a little farther before you send anyone to get me." She told Rawney about the house she'd come from.

"Kendal is ready to get you now."

Kendal's voice replaced Rawney's. "Aishe, can you send me your coordinates?"

"I've already sent a set to Charlie, but don't do anything about those yet. I'm still too close to not be spotted."

"Trust me. I can get someone to you without a problem," Kendal said, and Aishe immediately disconnected the call when she heard something close to her, as if running in her direction.

She dropped to the ground and flattened against the tree. Whatever it was, it was still too far away for her to distinguish whether it was an animal or a person. If it was a person, she hoped it'd be someone who wouldn't recognize her as the woman they'd thrown over the edge with a fatal gunshot wound to the forehead. Seeing her again would mean a gunshot would be the luckiest thing that could happen to her.

The running stopped, but she didn't give in to temptation to glance around to see what she was up against. Some leaves fell from a few trees over, and she looked up to find a group of howler monkeys shaking the branches as if they were trying to either get the attention of something or scare it away. The movement started again, but now it seemed to head to where the monkeys were becoming much more animated.

She stared in shock as the creature shrieked up at the pack of monkeys as it stood on its very short hind legs. It was as tall as a man but with the head and body type of a snake, only exaggeratedly larger. It also had four legs and a row of very sharp-appearing spikes along its back. Nothing in nature came even remotely close to whatever the hell this was.

"Naga," a man yelled from a distance, and the creature turned its head but didn't move from its position. The monkeys had started to jump on the branches, bringing down more and more leaves, but the thing kept shrieking. "Naga," the man yelled again.

The creature finally seemed to pay attention when she heard something that sounded like an electric current. The man came close enough for her to see that he was dressed in what looked like a Kevlar suit and held a tool resembling a cattle prod at the end of a long pole. One quick tap got the creature to drop to all fours and snap its large head a few times in his direction before the guy hit it with the prod again. That shot made it docile enough to follow the man back toward the road, but it kept peering up at the monkeys like it wanted to attack.

"What in the hell was that?" she whispered as she got back to her feet but didn't move from her spot until the jungle returned to some sense of quiet.

"Kendal," she said softly when she relaxed enough to dial again. "Something strange is happening in this area." She told Kendal what she'd seen and tried her best to describe the creature.

"I need you to stay put unless you see something else. Climb, if you can, and it shouldn't take us too long. We're not far from you."

"Whatever that was came from the house where they tried to get rid of me. Maybe I should travel some more to keep—"

"Save it, Aishe, until you're here and safe."

"I'll be waiting."

❖

Kendal went in search of Convel, not believing she was already having to ask for her help, but sending Convel and Lowe would be better than having one of them simply walk in and find Aishe. Convel smiled as she stared at her, so she simply asked and waited for any flack.

"Exactly what do you want me to do?" Convel asked.

"She described something that might give you a problem even in your shift form, so I need you to go in and give her a ride out. I realize what I'm asking is probably demeaning, but I don't want her to be discovered. Whoever owns the house she sent the coordinates for shot her and left her for dead. Finding her now would make them lock her down, and it'll take a war to get her out. I don't want to start from that position."

"Do you think they know we're here?" Lowe asked.

"It sounds like Garza likes to control every situation by having a steady stream of information. He may know we landed, but I tried to get here without raising any flags so that when we head in there tomorrow, no one will be waiting to ambush us." Kendal was starting to like this quiet but very intelligent young woman. With any luck she was the calming factor that would keep her from having to beat Convel into cooperation.

"How close can you get me?" Convel asked.

"How close can you get *us*?" Lowe said and ignored Convel shaking her head.

"About a couple of miles, but let's check the satellite maps so I can be sure. If the place she found is as secluded as this one, I'm sure getting too close will put them on alert."

"Let's go, then. The faster we get her out, the faster we'll know exactly what she saw," Convel said.

Kendal and Morgaine took the Jeep the house had come with, and Convel and Lowe loaded into the back. The road was as bad as the one they'd taken to the house, and it was starting to get dark by the time they arrived at the spot they'd decided on.

"Drive back a few miles and we'll find you," Convel said as she started to remove her clothes.

"If you run into any problems, shift and have Aishe call me. We'll come in and get you out."

"I think we can handle it," Convel said.

"But we appreciate you backing us up," Lowe said with a smile before turning around and removing her shirt.

Kendal stared out at the jungle as they finished undressing and thought about what Aishe had said. She didn't know Rawney's partner well, but the woman wasn't one for exaggeration, and whatever she'd seen had definitely scared her. The sound of their passengers shifting made her glance in the rearview mirror, where she caught sight of them before they dropped out of sight. Just as quickly, two large wolves appeared next to her door, where they looked at her before heading into the dense vegetation.

"What do you think Aishe saw?" Morgaine asked.

"I didn't get a chance to tell anyone before Rawney came to get me about Aishe, but I had a conversation with Aphrodite." She gave Morgaine a rundown of what the goddess had told and shown her. "Any group that has devoted itself to finding something has most probably found some stuff along the way. Whatever Aishe saw has to be something like that."

"You think it's something Aphrodite or some other entity put out here?" Morgaine unholstered the pistol she'd brought with her, since she wanted to be prepared for anything, but their swords were next to them as well.

"I'm not sure, but if I see her again, I'll make sure to ask."

She turned the Jeep around and headed back to the spot Convel had pointed out on the way in. The sharp curve would put them in complete darkness and hidden from anyone coming from the direction of the house. Once she pulled off the road to hide the Jeep from the other direction as well, they got out and headed into the trees.

Kendal leaned against a large mangrove-appearing tree and closed her eyes to acclimate to the darkness. Her thoughts drifted momentarily to Piper, but she did her best to concentrate on her surroundings. She opened her eyes when she heard something in the distance.

"Do you hear that?" Morgaine said, obviously having heard the same thing in the dense cloud cover that seemed to amplify sound.

"I'm not sure where it's coming from, but it's hard to believe it would be the house that Aishe mentioned. We're like ten miles from there."

The drums had a certain beat, but it seemed to be speeding up slowly. She tried to figure out exactly what direction it was coming from, but the jungle had a way of making it seem like it could have been anywhere. She straightened up when she heard something new in the strange noises around them. It seemed too early for it to be Convel and the others, so she drew her sword from the scabbard strapped to her back.

"What?" Morgaine asked in a harsh whisper and raised her weapon.

"Listen," she said, stepping farther from the tree and holding her sword at the ready.

She heard what sounded like footsteps on the leaf-covered ground, and they were rapid. She stepped closer to Morgaine until they were back to back, cutting down the chances that someone would sneak up on them. The shrubs in front of her sounded like they were being shredded, so it wasn't a person headed toward them. She gripped the sword as she waited with just enough light to see about fifty feet in front of her, and her brain froze a little when she saw the creature Aishe had described.

The body was covered in snakeskin, but it was wider like that of a monitor lizard, with the definite diamond-shaped head of a poisonous viper. Its short legs seemed strong, and it moved gracefully and fast, as if it wasn't at all scared of either of them. She waited until it was close enough that she could strike at the head before she moved. Whatever it was had gone after her throat to kill, and she'd had to stab through the severed head once she'd sliced through it. Once it stopped moving she studied the body and found very small, useless wings tucked along the back. It appeared to be a sort of hybrid dragon type of creature that didn't at all resemble the dragon Aphrodite had shown her.

"Okay. What the hell is that?" Morgaine asked, touching it with the tip of her boot.

"It's one or the same thing Aishe saw," she said, pulling her sword free of the head the size of a flat basketball. The fangs would've done some damage had it gotten anywhere near her, but the small bit of venom it managed to spit on her was making her skin tingle.

More running interrupted the drums again, so she pointed toward the trees, and Morgaine took up her position beside her. This time, though, the sound of running came from the two large wolves headed toward them with Aishe on the bigger one's back. Just as fast another creature came out of the darkness, headed toward Lowe, and Kendal took off at a run. She reached them in time to sever the head again and drive her sword through the head to make sure.

Convel crouched down to let Aishe off before moving to Lowe and licking her face. Once she seemed convinced that her lover was fine, she moved to the dead body and started sniffing it. "Go ahead and shift back so you can study it before we go," she said, and Convel moved to the Jeep. It didn't take long before she and Lowe had moved back and crouched down to study the creature.

"Thank you," Lowe said, lowering her head in Kendal's direction.

"Yes, thank you," Convel said, sounding like she meant it.

"I guess there's more than one, so stay vigilant," she said, nodding to Lowe in return.

"Have you ever seen anything like it?" Convel asked.

"No, and unlike you and your pack members, it wasn't a thinking being at all, so I'm not convinced it's any kind of were. Whatever it was, it's known to the people who took Aishe."

"The one I saw was bigger than this," Aishe said, touching the body. "At least it seemed like it was bigger."

"Wait here," she said and moved more into the bush. If every one of these things had a handler, then the guy might not be too far away.

She kept Morgaine in sight and moved slowly, trying not to make too much noise. They hadn't gone far before she saw the glow of something in the distance, but whatever it was, it wasn't very large. Morgaine made a circular motion with her finger, and she put her hand up in acknowledgment.

The light was coming from the end of a pole and appeared to be electric, so she waited until Morgaine was behind the guy before trying to get his attention. She put her hand up and waved it, and the man stopped and seemed to simply stare at her as if he were seeing things.

"Who are you?" he asked in Spanish in a tone that sounded like he was used to being obeyed. "Answer me."

She watched as he raised the prod higher so it was even with her chest and shook her head. "If he zaps me with that, I'm going to kick your ass."

"What?" the man said before he dropped like a sack of wet grain at Morgaine's feet.

She sheathed her sword and bent to pick the guy up so she could drape him across her shoulders. "Let's see what all this is about before we run into any more of their pets tomorrow."

They walked back to the others, and Convel waved her over to where the body of the creature she'd killed had lain. She ended up dropping the guy when she saw the body of what seemed like a young woman, meaning that the head had also now transformed back to its original state. When she saw the head with the wound slightly under the forehead, she realized it was indeed a young woman with the frozen expression of death plastered on her face.

"Doesn't this usually happen instantly?" she asked Convel.

"Usually, but I think the reptile part of the equation is what made it take longer. Sever a snake's head from its body and it still can survive for a little while," Convel said, her eyes still on the head. "Are you sure you don't know anything about this? I've never seen anything like this, and we have quite a few different types of weres in our family."

"We'll have to check any archives we have, but I'm only familiar with your family. The Order of Fuego, though, has kept its secrets well, so there might be some more of this type of thing before we're done."

"This could be a problem," Lowe said.

"Why do you think so?" she asked, wondering what was going through Lowe's mind especially, when Convel nodded.

"It's smaller than us, but in a fight, whatever this is can hurt us."

"You don't know me well yet," she said, putting her hand on both Convel and Lowe's shoulders, "but it'll have to get through me first."

"Let's make a deal," Convel said as she started to cover the head with dead leaves. "It'll have to get through all of us."

"Sounds like the best beginning we can plan," she said, going to the body and doing the same thing. "Because an ass full of that venom is going to ruin our day."

"Do you think someone will miss whatever it was?" Piper asked after they got home and she carried their guest down to the pool.

"I wish I had an answer," Kendal said as they all gathered and she tried to bring the guy to. "Not even Convel has any reference to it, but I'm sure Alejandro Garza and his people have kept that and themselves away from any kind of public notice. We need to know now if anything else like that is waiting for us."

She slapped the guy again, and he finally moaned and opened his eyes. Morgaine had really clocked him, and his collar was caked in blood from the cut on the back of his head. He moaned before startling totally awake. To not waste time, she put a dagger under his chin hard enough to draw blood.

"Who do you work for?" she asked in Spanish, and he closed his eyes and turned his head. She applied more pressure and ignored the blood now trickling down her blade. "Your pet is dead, so pay attention and answer the questions."

His head whipped around, and he glared at her when she finished. "There's no way you killed Sasha."

"If you mean snake girl with four little legs, then she's dead along with her little snake friend. What was she?"

"Kill me, because I'm not telling you anything," he said and started crying.

"I'm not really into torture, but I always make an exception to everything," Morgaine said, hitting him so hard he spat out a large amount of blood. "What was that?" Morgaine pressed the prod quickly to his leg.

"She wasn't an *it*. Sasha was my daughter, a gift from the gods." He covered his face with his hands and started to cry.

"She wasn't born like that?" Kendal asked, surprised that anyone would allow that to happen to their child.

"Senor Garza personally oversaw her transformation, and she was growing stronger," he said. They were having a hard time understanding him through his tears. "Sasha was a soldier of the order, and her sacrifice would be rewarded once the gods return."

Before they could ask him anything else, he grabbed Kendal's wrist and drove the blade into his chest. It was a quick, efficient killing blow that kept him from answering any more questions. "Son of a bitch," she said, pulling him off. When he dropped to the pavement, Convel went through his pockets.

"I wonder if this Alejandro guy conjured her from their writings, or if she was born like Lowe," Convel said when she didn't find anything. "And we also need to know what kind of snake Sasha and the others like her are."

"From the shape of the head, it's a type of viper," Morgaine said.

"Can it kill us?" Lowe moved close to Convel.

"Not us, and not them, but it can slow us down enough to cause problems," Convel said, and Kendal had to agree. "The body color and markings look like those of a python to me, but while they're dangerous, they're not poisonous, so this is something not found in nature. Because your skin tingled, though, it's poisonous."

"Does it make a difference?" Piper asked, her eyes on the dead man.

"My nature is wild, but I'm not an animal," Convel said. "My animal spirit still retains the essence of who I am. That's how it is for all of us. If his daughter made a choice to change, she gave up who she was to become something Garza is using for his own reasons. I doubt Sasha's father would've needed a cattle prod to make her obey if she was like me and Lowe."

"And you don't think this is the one you saw, Aishe?" Kendal asked.

"I didn't want to get any closer, but it was bigger, and its name was Naga. The man called it a few times, and the prod made it finally leave the tree where it had cornered a pack of monkeys."

"If you want to talk inside, we can take care of this," one of the guards said, and she nodded.

They listened to Aishe's story and knew the watchers were a liability going forward. They had accepted their money to keep the dig site safe, but their loyalties now were with Garza and the Order, yet so far Franco Rodriguez hadn't given up on them completely.

"Luckily he really can't tell Garza much even if he wanted to," Lenore said. "It's surprising that he even knows it's the Clan he's working for. Rolla doesn't give out that kind of information no matter what you're doing for us."

"I'm sure that information came from whoever gave Leonardo part of my history. Once we figure this out, we have to find where our leak is," she said, wanting to leave for the dig site before the sun came up.

"If we have to head into every situation from a compromised position, we're going to have a problem."

"Gran found something while you were gone," Piper said, handing over a small leather-bound book. A coiled snake was stamped into the cover, and the book seemed to be written in Italian.

"The Order of Fuego and other organizations like it have spent time and money to break all the spells people like Rawney's mother have left throughout time," Molly said, flipping to the pages that showed something like what they'd seen. "Most of the spells have been supposed to save us all from things that shouldn't exist, but Garza and his like have a need for whatever you saw out there."

"So he started turning some of the followers into monsters?" She flipped through the pages, trying to find something close to what Sasha had turned into.

"Everything has a purpose, I guess, but from what we read, the change is irreversible," Molly said, and she finally found something like what they'd seen.

"This is it, only bigger."

"How do you even go about changing into something like that?" Piper asked, shivering.

"For us, it comes from a bite that isn't fatal, but the transformation feels like it should kill you," Convel said, and Lowe nodded. "For me and my family, it's just who we are."

"But Lowe is like you, even if she had to suffer the change?" Piper asked, and Lowe nodded again.

"When I shift, I still know right from wrong, and I know who I love," Lowe said.

"Well, it's better to find out now that these things are out there, so we have to be extra careful tomorrow. Everyone who's joining us tomorrow has to either arm themselves or travel with a slayer." She glanced at her watch. "We'll meet here at five in the morning."

Everyone left the kitchen and headed to the bedrooms they'd been assigned.

"Why do you think he changed those people?" Piper asked once they were alone.

"Because he needed something to lord over until he gets what he really wants."

"Which is?"

"Control of Aphrodite's children without the cattle prod, but I could be wrong."

"Maybe when I'm actually there I'll get something else," Piper said as she moved to sit in her lap.

"I got to sit and talk to Aphrodite one more time," she said and told Piper about the meeting. "She loves them, and they're like you said, so I wish I could wake them if they'd be safe, but I doubt that's going to happen. I can't think of any place in the world they could live without someone trying to destroy them."

"Then we'll do our best to keep from disturbing them."

"We will, but I won't be surprised if the complete opposite happens. No matter how dedicated people should be to good, evil seems to hold a more powerful sway."

"Don't be a pessimist, baby."

"Don't worry. I'm the poster kid for high hopes."

"Good, because Garza and his followers probably aren't going to find you as cute as I do."

CHAPTER TWENTY

Pauline sat on the first step of the largest pyramid and glanced at the pits she and Oscar had found. The workers had set out torches so they could see as they continued to cut away the vegetation from the other three carved slabs they'd discovered. She hadn't ordered them removed for further investigation because she didn't want to lose anyone else unnecessarily. And she wasn't about to head back underground without Oscar unless she was sure some curse or something as horrific as the snakes wouldn't kill her.

She'd walked the length of the avenue of pyramids and figured at least ten more slabs existed, but she didn't have a clue as to what the hell they were supposed to either hide or hold. It was a waste of time to remove them and then have to burn the bodies of the unlucky workers on the altars. "Señora Pauline," one of the men said, staring at his feet as he talked to her. "Your father called and said to start taking the slabs off."

"We're not doing that until we know how to release the triggers before we send someone down."

The man took a satellite phone and, after dialing, handed it to her. "What are you waiting for?" Alejandro said in a voice that chilled her. "I sent you there to get this done."

"If you're so brave, then come down here, and we'll start popping them open for you. Then you can go down and show us how it's done," she said, tired of being her father's punching bag. "But you aren't going to do that, are you?"

"Listen," Alejandro said in a lower, more controlled tone. "We're running out of time. If the answer is there, find it before you lose the opportunity."

"Each one of the pits is rigged to kill, and we don't have enough men to open them all if we lose as many as we did before."

"I'll send as many as you need, so go ahead and start."

"Are you sure?"

"They know what's at stake. I thought you realized that as well, but perhaps I'm wrong."

"We'll start, so send more men." She hung up and threw the man his phone back, knocking him to the ground with a kick to his chest when he caught it. "Since you feel the need to make points with my father, I'll send you in the pit first." Some of the men shouted as the next stone was removed, so she grabbed him by the collar. "You can use your nice phone to call him and tell him what you see."

She dragged him to the hole and threw him in. It took only a few seconds for him to start screaming, and the rest of the men backed up as if not wanting to go in next. The screaming stopped, replaced by whimpering, and curiosity made her shine her flashlight into the hole. The man was lying on his back covered in blood, his face completely blistered as if someone had sprayed him with acid.

He raised his hand toward her, but she figured he couldn't see anything since his facial features were slowly starting to melt away. Pauline ignored that sight and concentrated on his fist. He was clutching something, and it stayed in his fist as his hand dropped back down. He stopped moving when his mouth fell open.

"Go down and see what's in his hand, even if you need to sever it from his body," she told the man closest to her. He was smart enough to lower a rope and loop it around the man's wrist. Whatever he had gotten into made his hand come off easily once they started pulling.

When she opened the rigid fingers she found a ruby the size of an apricot that appeared flawless. Considering everything had been empty so far, it shocked her to find anything of value. When she held it up and aimed her flashlight at it, it looked like the eye of something, since a pupil-appearing hologram was cut into the center of the stone. It resembled the pupil of a serpent, and when she moved the stone, the pupil seemed to glow.

"What is it?" the man next to her asked.

"I'm not sure, but send someone else down and see if there's another one." He nodded enthusiastically. A few moments later the next man was in as much agony as the first guy, but from the look of it, he hadn't found anything else.

"Open the next slab and keep going until you've searched all of them." She glanced down at the two dead men, had the closest crew lower a ladder, and pointed inside. The next two men went in with no problems, so she followed them down. Like the other chambers, this one was simply a stone room with no writing on any surface. Whatever their purpose, maybe they'd find it eventually in one of the remaining chambers.

"Do you want us to use the radar on the walls and floor?" the man who'd carried out her orders asked.

"Did you find anything in any of the first ones we searched?"

"Not yet. There was nothing under the floor like Oscar thought, but we'll look if you want to be sure."

"Let's open the rest of them first," she said, gripping the stone they'd found. "If there's nothing else, then we'll go back to see if we missed anything."

She pressed the stone into her palm and let out a surprised breath when it cut her. Nothing on it appeared sharp enough to do harm, but when she opened her hand she saw a fairly deep gash at the center of her hand. The blood that had covered the ruby seemed to heat it more than it should've, and as the blood pooled, it grew so hot she almost put it down.

"We found something," she said to Alejandro on her phone as the men placed crowbars under the next slab. The second it moved slightly, another group of large snakes slithered from under the stone and attacked the workers.

"What?" he asked, not bothering to question the screams coming from her end.

"A large ruby with a serpent eye cut into it."

"Bring it to me," Alejandro said, sounding almost giddy.

"Are you sure you want me to leave now?" One of the snakes moved toward her with its mouth open, the fangs easy to see. A bite wouldn't be fatal, she thought, unless those sharp points were able to sink into something like her throat.

"The workers know better than to steal from us."

One of the men stepped in front of her as the snake moved closer, and she put her hand on the man's back. She didn't know much about snakes, but these pythons seemed abnormally large, so she tried to keep the man between her and the one stalking her. It didn't shock her when the man went down and disappeared into the coils of the powerful body after the snake grabbed him by the throat and subdued him.

"I'm coming," she said, realizing the man had given his life to save her. Perhaps her father loved her more than she'd given him credit for, because it was devotion to Alejandro that kept these men working despite the dangers. "And I won't be coming back here."

"I know, but I think we've found everything worthwhile there."

"Do you want them to stop digging?"

Alejandro laughed, and the sound made her close her eyes. "It won't hurt to lose a few more lives in order to make sure. Tell them to keep going."

She nodded and thought it would take years for the screams to disappear from her memories. They'd opened the next chamber, and the yells of agony had started again. The ruby seemed to be the only thing of beauty this place held. The rest was simply pain.

❖

The morning started with rain and lightning dotting the mountains around them, but everyone mounted the horses Kendal had provided and rode into the jungle without complaint. Piper hung on to her arm since she rode in front of her as they made their way through the path the men Rueben sent had cut. Oscar had pointed out another, better way in, but the men working for Alejandro had cleared it, so she wanted to avoid any contact with them if possible.

She slightly clicked her heels against the horse's side as the incline grew steeper, but because the animal's footing was good he made short work of the climb. The thick greenery around them made her wonder what this area had looked like all those years ago when the site was built, but she doubted it had been much different then than it was now. It had taken a lot of perseverance to haul all that stone up these inclines if the weather was always mostly bad.

"All this dripping is getting damn annoying," Piper said as she wiped her face yet again.

"Thank God I gave up armor a long time ago. If not I'd be rusting by now," she said, then quickly put her hand up. She could hear shouting in the distance, so they weren't that far away from the site.

Oscar moved up in the line until he was next to her and pointed to the top of the ridge in front of them. "It's over that, but we have to head down into the valley to actually get to where the pyramids are. We'd stopped working after everything that happened, but Alejandro must have made them start again. That bastard doesn't care who dies for what he wants."

"Did he ever place guards around the place when you were here?" Morgaine asked from behind them. Lenore had decided to come with them as well, and she appeared as pleased as Piper with the weather as she sat behind Morgaine on the large horse.

"Not while we were working here, but I can't say he wouldn't. After he killed my father and I got away from him, I wouldn't doubt that he'd think about it." Oscar removed his hat and wiped his brow. "I'm sure he doesn't want anyone finding something before he does."

"Okay," she said, moving a little ahead of him and dismounting before helping Piper down. Charlie came up and led the riderless horse to the front of the pack. Quite a few things were strapped to its back, and she untied the top pack and started unwrapping. "Wait here for a little while."

"Where are you going?" Piper asked.

"Hunting." She strapped a bow to her back, tied the quiver to her waist, and disappeared into the brush with Charlie closely behind her. Morgaine stayed with them, arming herself with the same set of primitive weapons, but in this case, if they went the easy route with guns, they'd just be inviting more trouble.

Kendal pointed to the left, and Charlie nodded as he carefully made his way, staying in sight. The area seemed clear, but the vegetation was so thick it would be hard to spot anyone until you were right on top of them, and if that was true, they would lose the element of surprise.

A few more yards and she put her fist up, making Charlie stop. The cigarette smoke gave the guy away, and luckily he was staring down at whatever was happening rather than at his surroundings. The gun hanging from his shoulder was a fully automatic weapon not easily found in Costa Rica, so she doubted the guards would have any problem using them since they were already breaking the law.

Charlie stared at her and waited, so she pointed at him and made a fishing-reel motion with her hands, hoping he knew what she meant. It wasn't her style to simply kill someone for doing a job they were hired to do, but if the guy started to shoot first without engaging, that was a different scenario.

Charlie strode out and purposely stepped on a branch to make enough noise to get the man's attention, and the guy immediately raised his weapon and aimed. Before his finger could squeeze the trigger, he dropped to the ground with an arrow through his throat. It wasn't a killing blow, but she wanted to prevent him from calling out.

The man was gurgling when they reached him, and he looked up at them in almost disbelief as he pawed his side for the service revolver in the leather holster. She twisted the arrow enough that he stopped moving and breathing.

"Thanks," Charlie said, pulling the guy under a thick mass of vines. "I didn't want to get shot this morning."

"Let's see how many more there are before we head down to the site."

It took them an hour, but she was confident they'd cleared the ridge of everyone working for Alejandro. Charlie had returned for the others, so she crouched and studied the area below them, staring at the pyramids with the dragon heads at the base of all the steps. Knowing they were trapped in time and stone made her sad in a way, wanting to give the dragons what they probably craved. Every living thing deserved to be free, but in this case, giving in to that desire would only cause their destruction.

"It looks exactly like in my vision," Piper said, pressing up behind her. "What happened?" Piper asked as they both watched the workers standing over four lifeless bodies. They were too far away to see any type of wound, but the men appeared very dead.

"I'm not sure, but we need to clear the site so we can look around. Maybe having Lenore and Rawney here will help Oscar come up with something."

"I'm sure Lenore and Rawney will do that before he can think of anything," Morgaine said when she joined them.

"Sometimes it takes an outsider to jar something loose," she said as Rawney and Aishe walked up.

"Wait a minute," Aishe said through clenched teeth. "That's Franco Rodriguez." She pointed to a man standing off by himself with his arms crossed over his chest. The flat stone in front of him was being covered with wood, and he seemed to be crying since he savagely swiped at his eyes every few minutes.

"The watcher?" Piper asked.

"That's him, and I'm going to kill him for what they did to me," Aishe said, her voice rising to a point someone would probably hear them.

"Wait on that," she said, glancing at Morgaine in case Aishe lost control of her temper. Kendal notched another arrow and stood. "Land some right at the workers' feet, but don't hit any of them," she said to Morgaine and Charlie. "Then follow up with a few to the men already dead. I need these guys to scatter."

"So Franco gets away with what he did?" Aishe said angrily, and Rawney put her hand on her arm.

"I need some information first, and after I get it, you're free to do whatever you think you need to."

Kendal glanced at her to keep her quiet, and thankfully Aishe complied. When she saw that Morgaine and Charlie were ready, she released, and almost instantaneously Franco howled in pain when the arrow sliced through his shoulder. She released another one into the men lying dead on the ground and continued until the scene below them had dissolved into chaos.

Charlie and Morgaine kept up their attack until the men started running and screaming to the vans parked at the very end of the avenue of pyramids. She held everyone off until the area grew quiet again, wanting to see if anyone aside from Franco was still around.

"Try to collect all the arrows as we walk around," Morgaine said, and she agreed they didn't need to leave any sign of their presence.

Oscar didn't seem too fazed by what had happened as he tried to keep his footing when they started their descent. He seemed to be focused on the hole the men had been gathered around and not the tall structures.

"They've opened another four chambers since I was here," Oscar said, walking next to her. "I wonder how many men they lost uncovering empty rooms?"

"What he's looking for isn't in the ground," Piper said, and Oscar seemed to want to shake Piper for more answers.

"How would you know that?" Oscar demanded.

"Not yet, Oscar. You're here to show us what you've found so far and explore what was done in your absence," she said and kept going, holding Piper's hand.

"I'll take Morgaine and Rawney," Piper said as they reached the bottom.

"Take Charlie with you, and shout if you need anything," she said, kissing Piper on the lips. "Don't let them talk you into going in any holes until I'm with you."

"Don't worry so much, baby, and I'm not losing sight of you."

Morgaine and Aishe followed her to where Franco was kneeling and groaning in pain. He stared up at them as if shocked to see anyone not familiar to him, but he shook his head as if showing he didn't intend to cooperate. She was done with patience for the moment, so she grabbed him by the jaw and forced his head up.

"Before you convince yourself that if you hang tough I'm going to leave you to your misery," she said to him in Spanish, making his eyes widen, "that's not what's going to happen here." She grabbed the arrow that had pierced all the way through and pulled enough to make the double pointed tip go back into his shoulder. The obvious intense pain made him cry out and pale.

"I don't know anything. I'm only here because my son died here, and I came for his ashes." He placed his hand on her thigh and tried to push her away, so she twisted the arrow again.

"My name is Kendal Richoux, and I'm an elder with the Genesis Clan. Your family was hired to do a job, and leading a dig and having your family work for the man who financed it wasn't part of that job."

"You're not the person I've dealt with, so how do I know you're telling the truth?" His speech was low and staggered, but she knew it was from the pain more than fear.

"Because you know the contract you signed and what the consequences of breaching that contract mean to your family. Your son is already dead, but it's my right to take the rest of your family. Once I'm done with you and your loyalty to Alejandro Garza, I'm going to kill your wife, daughter, and mother. You'll be erased from our history, along with everyone who came before you, and I'll put one of your gardeners in your place." She squeezed his jaw until he dropped his eyes. "They'll appreciate what you obviously don't."

"What do you want to know?" The question came sooner than she thought, but Morgaine nodded at her threat. The clause actually was in the contract but was seldom applied any more.

"What exactly is Garza looking for?" Morgaine asked.

"His family has information that for a long time was thought to be a legend of some great treasure buried here. It wasn't until his grandfather took it seriously that they started searching in earnest."

"How did he contact you?" she asked, knowing that whoever had given Garza her information also had knowledge of the watchers. It was the only way they found the site at all, since she was convinced someone like Rawney had placed a spell to keep it hidden.

"He came to the house one day and offered me more than the elders had given me, but it wasn't about the money. The Order of Fuego's mission is just. I believed in it enough to send my son to find what's been lost for too long." It was as if Franco had forgotten about the pain and the injury when he started talking about his betrayal. Fanaticism always interested her. True believers got so wrapped up in something they were willing to lose everything, including those they loved.

"How did he get his information about the Genesis Clan and some of our members?" Aishe asked him.

"I didn't tell him anything about that. You were there that night, you heard," he said, gazing at her like he couldn't believe he was actually talking to her. "They shot you in the head…how—" He didn't seem to know how to finish the question.

"He knows and someone told him," Aishe said, taking over and twisting the arrow before jabbing it through again.

"It wasn't me or anyone in my family, I swear."

"Did they find anything?" Morgaine asked.

"Pauline found a large ruby, but the rest of the rooms were empty. Twelve more men died, but I told Alejandro that I'd take charge when she went to give it to him."

"What's he keeping near his home?" Kendal asked, still curious as to the strange snake-appearing weres they'd seen.

"I've never been to his home. He always comes to me."

She nodded, as did Morgaine, so she glanced at Aishe. The anger was still there and she understood it, so she placed her hand on her shoulder and smiled. Whatever Franco's fate was, it was in Aishe's hands.

Oscar was coming out of one of the newly uncovered chambers and shook his head when he saw her. "It's like the others—empty."

"According to Franco they found a substantial gem, and Pauline is on her way to give it to Garza." She walked to the dead men and didn't see any sign of how they'd died. "Did you ever figure out how the men with you were killed?"

"No, and I fought to return them to their families, but Garza refused. They were burned like before on the altars and their ashes scattered over the ridge."

"Aishe, wait," she said as she noticed the large knife in her hand. "Bring him."

The last chamber was only partially open, but the opening inside was visible. "If you believe so much, then go meet your fire god," Aishe said as Franco struggled not to go through the hole. As soon as he fell in, he started screaming, and instantly all of them drew their swords when quite a few large pythons slithered from below the stone.

She wasn't afraid of snakes, but she'd never seen any this aggressive, and she had to decapitate one to get the others to move toward the pyramids. They didn't seem to have any problem reaching the tops and coiling themselves as if they were sentries guarding their posts.

Franco's screams had stopped, so she glanced down, and his blank expression and unblinking eyes immediately showed he was dead. She stuck her head through the opening and searched the closest walls for any type of trigger that would kill so painfully and fast, but saw none.

"I think this is more involved than we thought," Morgaine said.

"Not as involved as quantum physics, so let's start looking for whatever the answer is."

Chapter Twenty-one

Piper walked the length of the avenue of pyramids and started up the stairs, Rawney and Morgaine behind her. It was so different in the light and quiet of day so many centuries after that fire ceremony, but she was compelled to see the spot where the dragons had landed before their surrender.

"Your mother and aunt died here," she said, standing to the right. Lumas and Rowen, she sensed, shared a bond that men who didn't realize the power they were messing with had tragically broken on this spot. "And here is where Drakon and his mate sleep."

"What was the rest of your vision?" Rawney asked, placing her hands on the stone at Piper's feet.

"The old man she'd trained came back like she'd asked and burned them together there," she said, pointing to the altar where the men had been piling wood. "He waited until they were both ash before he took them to where she wanted to be buried."

"Where?" Morgaine asked.

Piper led them back down and touched both dragonheads before glancing toward Kendal. She didn't detect any danger, but she wasn't the one with a bow and sword strapped to her body, and she didn't want to go without Kendal. Both Kendal and Morgaine left Oscar to his search of every chamber now uncovered under Charlie's supervision and joined them. Kendal took her hand and let her lead them into the trees. After taking the trail twice in her mind, Piper didn't need to look around to know she was headed in the right direction. The spot was about a mile from the largest pyramid, which anchored all the others, and didn't have any kind of marker or sign that something was there.

"Where exactly?" Kendal asked, taking the small shovel Rawney had brought with her.

She touched the ground and closed her eyes, fighting momentary shock that the book was still intact. It seemed to almost call out to her. "Here, about three feet down."

They stood back and watched Kendal dig through the soft wet dirt until she was sweating, but eventually she hit something solid and dug around it until she uncovered all four corners. The stone box seemed like a solid square with no lid or door, so Kendal stood back and let her and Rawney study it.

"If it's a carved square, how did they put anything inside?" Rawney asked, her tears starting to fall. No matter the span of time, it was obvious she still missed and loved her mother.

"I'm sure it's not solid, since I saw the old man put their ashes and your family book in here. It must need a key."

"You didn't notice anything in the old man's hand?" Kendal asked, still cleaning the dirt away from the stone. She ran her hand along every edge as if searching for a seam or hinge.

"All I saw was him coming to this spot and placing the urns and book in here. I doubted the book would've lasted this long, but I know it's still in there." She moved closer and placed her hands on the top with her eyes closed. The present melted away, and she opened her eyes to Lumas, sitting on the object that would be her tomb.

"The only key you need is standing next to you," Lumas said, which confused her.

"What do you mean?" she asked, not noticing anything or anywhere a key would go.

"The slayer that came after me is blessed by the gods, and together you will keep the light of truth lit and the darkness at bay. I have every faith in that, but you must start to trust in what you are to her, and that is the other half of her heart and soul. The other slayer must also prove to her mate that they too will be important in the coming fight and that they belong together as much as you and Asra do. You were all chosen for a reason." Lumas stood and placed her hand on the back right corner. "Remember, it must be done together."

Piper opened her eyes and saw Kendal with her head cocked as if in question. "The right back corner. It's where the key goes."

"And the key is?" Kendal asked, moving her hand to where she'd said.

"I'm sure we'll figure it out, but we have to do it together." She ran her hand where Lumas had shown her and discovered that they'd missed the spot, since it was packed with dirt. "Right here."

Kendal crouched down and rubbed her finger over the slot. "What did you just see?" She told Kendal, and as she spoke she stared at the sword strapped to Kendal's back. Kendal didn't move when she reached for it and slid the weapon free.

"Take my hand," she said, and Kendal placed her hand over hers on the hilt. They placed the tip in the slot, and she instinctively knew it would fit. "Lenore," she said, and Lenore freed Morgaine's blade. "The other slot has to be opposite this one."

"On three," Kendal said and counted. Both swords went in to the hilt. It took a few seconds before they heard a distinctive click, and then the front fell open, making Morgaine and Lenore hop back.

Inside they saw two urns hammered out of what seemed like copper and something large wrapped in leaves. Rawney dropped to her knees and reached inside for the urn that had her mother's favorite flower stamped on the front. The other had a wolf, which her aunt always considered her spirit animal. When she placed her hands on it she started crying for the loss of a woman who still had so much to teach her.

"Take the urns and place them in the box we brought to keep them safe," Piper said, and Aishe did as she asked. "Rawney, take your book. It belongs to you now."

They started back to the site, and Kendal clasped her hand again. "Do you think the book will hold the key to what we need to know?" Kendal asked.

"I'm not sure what we need to know or even what questions to ask. Our best bet is to try to find what Alejandro Garza wants, and what the ruby that woman discovered means to all this." Piper squeezed Kendal's hand and glanced around her as they walked. The tomb was the only thing out here, and she knew they had to go back to where the dragons lay sleeping. "Can we go into one of the chambers they uncovered?" she asked Kendal and smiled when her lover nodded. "It has to be one that none of the workers have entered."

"Only if you let me go first," Kendal said, stopping and putting her arms around her. "If anything's in there that's going to hurt, I'd rather get the brunt of it."

"I love you more than you'll ever know."

Oscar was coming up from one of the chambers about a fourth of the way down from the largest pyramid. He shook his head and headed toward her when he noticed Rawney carrying the book and Aishe holding the case with the urns. "Did you find something?" he asked, his hand out as if wanting to take the book from Rawney.

"We did, but we'll talk about that later. Did you see anything different down there?" Piper asked as Kendal took a step forward, stopping Oscar instantly, so she placed her hand on Kendal's back and gently rubbed it.

"It's the same as the others," he said, combing his hair back. "They're all empty and devoid of any markings. I'm surprised Pauline found anything at all, but it was in the fifth one."

"How do you know that?" Kendal said, taking another step forward.

"I discovered a small platform where the ruby must've fit perfectly into the indentation carved in the stone. I swear to you on the souls of my parents, I'm not hiding or keeping anything from you. I just want to know why this is here and for Alejandro to pay with his life for what he's done to my family." He pointed behind him and shrugged. "If you want, I'll show you what I mean."

"I need you to show us the best way to remove one of the capstones so I can look inside," she said, and he shook his head in an overexaggerated way.

"No. Please don't even think that. I've studied each one after we lost some men, and I can't figure out where the trap is and why in the hell it's been set. The rooms are empty except for the one with the stone, so there's no reason for anyone to die over nothing." He seemed to mean what he was saying since he moved closer to her, ignoring the big protective bear standing next to her.

"Let me go down into one you've cleared, and we'll take it from there," Kendal said, walking with Piper to the first one Oscar said they'd opened. She placed the bow and quiver next to the hatch and climbed down the ladder. The trigger was something she'd seen placed in the tombs of the pharaohs and was rather sophisticated for the time period during which it was placed. "Did any of the men who died show any outward sign of injury aside from falling off the ladder on the way in?"

"None, and we looked for anything that might've led us to what happened to them. They went in, screamed, then fell before dying what sounded like a painful death," Oscar said.

"It was something they inhaled," she said, pointing to the very small hole in the dirt. "I'm not sure exactly how it works, but it's a type of motion-sensored thing, and there might be more than one in each chamber. It's a type of deterrent to anyone trying to enter a tomb, for example to steal the treasures inside." She found four more holes and wracked her memory for any information on how they were set.

"How did you know that? We looked for weeks before I decided to send anyone else down, with the same kind of result," Oscar said, moving to the next one and finding the same thing. "Are you an archeologist?"

"I'm more of a student of history, and I've seen the same kind of thing in Egypt. They set them to scare off grave robbers, but after the final trap was sprung, they emptied those tombs fast and without fear."

"So how do we get in without inhaling ancient poisonous gas?" Piper asked.

"Let's get the top off, and I'll think of something." They moved to where the next set of small flags was stuck in the ground after Oscar had said that was how they'd marked the next slab of hieroglyphs that covered each chamber.

"Why not walk the length and see if that's the one you want to go into?" Kendal suggested to her, and she nodded, holding out her hand again. "Take your time. I've got people looking out for any of Alejandro's men in case they come back."

Piper started slowly making her way along and thought of the first time she'd seen this place and of walking this in the opposite direction with Lumas. They'd made their way slowly to the large pyramid, and only now did she realize they'd paused toward the back of the avenue. Lumas hadn't said anything, but her having stopped to greet her was her only clue, so Piper stopped at the same place.

"This one," she said, and Morgaine and Kendal started cleaning the dirt and grass that grew over the slab so Rawney could look at it. It took all of them and the help of the horses to move the stone enough to reach the hatch, and she had everyone stand back until she was sure no more snakes or other surprises were coming out of the hole.

Kendal walked back to where the dead men lay, picked one up, and slung him over her shoulder. They lowered a ladder into the hole, and she slowly slid the man down before pulling him up and then lowering him again. Whatever set the trigger off made a small puff of air, then another when she picked him up and lowered him again.

"It should be fine now," Kendal said, glancing at Oscar and laughing when he took a step back. "And I volunteer to go first, so you can relax." She went in and turned the flame up on the lantern she'd brought with her so Piper could see when she made it down. "I don't think anything's down here," she said when Piper stood next to her.

"Would you sit with me for a little while?" she asked, and Kendal moved to the corner as if wanting the best view of the room. "My mind wanders better when you're next to me."

"Let's hope that doesn't happen all the time," Kendal said, kissing the side of her neck when she made room for her on her lap. "Sometimes I want your total attention."

"I don't think you have to worry about that, but be quiet for now."

She rested her head on Kendal's shoulder and closed her eyes, thinking only of how her life had so dramatically changed in such a short period. For so long she'd worried about nothing but the next contract and getting the job done at Marmande Shipyard, and now she was sitting in an ancient room built to house things neither she nor anyone else would believe ever existed.

"Breathe, my love," Kendal said, and she seemed to float very gently into a past that was as real as Kendal.

Costa Rican Rain Forest, 6130 BC

"Do you want us to carve the walls as well, Lumas?" the old man asked as they stood in the center of the chamber Lumas had told them was as important as the large structures outside.

The workmen had done an excellent job of stacking stones for the walls and finding capstones for the roof with the hole cut out for the hatches. They would all be topped with stones covered in writing that none of the tribe knew the meaning of, but that wasn't important right now. The messages carved in stone weren't for these people. They were for the ones who'd come years from now.

"Yes." She took the animal skin from her bag and gave it to him. "Tell the stone workers to make sure they follow each symbol precisely, and let me know when you're done."

"Why all these rooms?" The old man asked the question with his head bowed, as if almost afraid of either the asking or the answer.

Lumas peered over his head and seemed to meet Piper's eye. "The rooms will seem like a waste if they're ever found, but they hold everything important to the gods that will rest here. Not everyone who will search will find the answers, but they'll wait for the worthy one to reveal themselves."

"It will be done," the old man said and climbed the ladder to carry out her wishes.

"If you found the book and our remains, then you need to find the answer to these rooms," Lumas said, coming to sit next to her. "Once you succeed, you need to leave here and find the truth of what the goddess wanted all along."

"So the truth isn't here?" she said, thinking of all the men who'd died.

"The truth isn't what the Order of Fuego thinks it is, but you need to find it before it's twisted into something that won't be able to be undone."

"Can't you tell me more than that? If I knew more, we could stop whatever these people want to do," she said, taking Lumas's hand.

"The telling isn't for me to give you, Piper, but you have everything you need now. Anything found here won't overcome what and who you have with you. The last page will bring the light into this darkness."

Piper woke to Kendal holding her and shook her head. She stared at the spot where Lumas had sat, and she had seemed so real, Piper expected to see her. "You're right about some of these things we have to do. They're damn aggravating."

"What exactly did she say?" Kendal asked and listened as if she'd have to take a test when she was done. "I think I know why she sent us to the tomb first."

Kendal called Rawney down and asked her to bring her book. "What do you want me to do? I've been skimming the book and can't understand most of it. This was my mother's, but it's not the family book."

"Try the last page," Piper said, understanding what Kendal meant.

Rawney started speaking in what sounded like a meshing of different known languages, but she didn't understand any of it, yet Kendal seemed to be following along. Kendal turned and stared at the blank walls until the veil that seemed to cover them fell away. Whatever the symbols meant was yet another mystery because she didn't recognize even one.

"Do you know what it says?" she asked Rawney and groaned when she shook her head.

"It's the first hieroglyphics used in Egypt," Kendal said, running her fingers along the carvings. "My father taught them to me so I could use them in the field when I needed to send him a message for his eyes only."

"What do they say?" Rawney asked, sounding sad. "It's like she wanted everyone but me to understand her and why she did this."

"Maybe not." Kendal moved back so she could see every line. "To my child," Kendal read, and Rawney took her free hand. "My grave holds more than ash and knowledge, so take everything to where we answered the goddess's call. First, though, go to the golden palace that holds the dragon's heart."

"She didn't happen to put any GPS coordinates, did she?" Piper asked, and Rawney laughed.

"She couldn't take the chance that someone would decipher how to uncover the message before we got here. All we need to figure out is where that is," Kendal said, smiling at her. "You might have to go down into each chamber before we head back to the house," she said to Rawney.

Piper climbed out and waited for Kendal as Rawney entered each chamber already opened, and they worked to unearth the others. Oscar took pictures of every capstone and the writings on the wall Rawney had unearthed. He reluctantly handed his camera to Charlie when he finished but seemed to understand why they mistrusted him.

She followed Kendal to the top of the pyramid, where the pack leader was buried, and they watched the team uncover the last chamber that was marked. Like the first one they'd witnessed, snakes came out and started toward the pyramid they were standing on. Only this time they stopped and clustered together, raising their heads in unison, their bodies twisted together.

"There's nothing else here," Kendal said, taking her hand for the way down.

"How do you know?"

"Because if anything was here, it's not here any longer. We'll have to travel again, but we have to do some more things before we leave."

"No wonder all these things are a big riddle. You're talking, but I don't understand what in the world you're saying, so you're cut from the same cloth," she joked.

"The next place we have to look is a world away, but we need to find everything Lumas left us before we go." The snakes slithered into the jungle before they made it down, and she was just as glad since they weren't her favorite creatures in the world.

"Maybe next time, Lumas could send her messages through cute bunnies."

CHAPTER TWENTY-TWO

Pauline gazed out the helicopter window. Had the ruby they'd found been mentioned in any of the archives Alejandro kept in a large vault in the middle of the house? She stepped out and immediately got back in and had the crew close the door when she saw some of her father's experiments headed toward the chopper.

"What the hell are they doing out of their cage?" she asked the pilot.

"I'm not sure, but let me call the house." He spoke to someone, and a few minutes later Alejandro stepped out and the pilot exited and opened the door for her, even though the creatures were still close by. "He said to meet him out back on the platform."

She took a deep breath and stepped out, trying not to show fear when one ran toward her and stopped to hiss. The creatures weren't new, but she couldn't believe some of the villagers from the settlement less than five miles away had agreed to subject their family members to this hellish existence for the promise of power and money once the gods were set free.

Her insides felt like they were vibrating from fear, but she tried to show no outward sign as she walked past the creature still hissing and now snapping at her while its handler backed it up with a smile, as if pleased with her discomfort. If the decision was hers she'd kill every one of these things her father had created and return to their mission and nothing else.

"Give it to me," Alejandro said, extending his hand to her and opening and closing it as if impatient to see the first tangible thing they'd actually found at the dig.

She reached into her pocket and fisted the ruby before handing it over. The stone seemed flawless and radiated some sort of warmth that wasn't from her own body heat. "It was on a small platform with a perfectly carved indentation to house it."

"That chamber held no markings either?" he asked, holding the stone up to the sun.

"The walls were blank, just like the others. I was surprised this was in there, but we lost another two men opening the chamber. If we can't figure out what's killing them, I doubt even the most devout will continue to work on this project." She stood away from him, not chancing that he'd take his usually bad mood out on her by throwing her down the mountain.

"There's nothing else to find," he said, placing the stone in his pocket and pointing toward the house. "Whoever this Genesis Clan is, they're at the site now, and Franco Rodriguez is dead. I'm sure their next stop is to visit his family, so I sent someone to take care of that before they mention my name."

"How do you know all that?"

"I had men watching over you, and one high up in the trees to make sure nothing went wrong." He sat at his desk and placed the stone in front of him. "They found something away from the site, and my man couldn't see exactly what it was, but they walked right up to it as if they knew it was there."

"You didn't find anything about that in the archives?" She watched him take a box from a drawer that fit the stone perfectly. Oscar was right that her father knew more than he was saying, since he obviously was sure the stone would eventually be found.

"No. If I had, I'd have told you or that idiot Oscar to dig it up. The site is a dead end now, so we have to concentrate on the next phase of our mission." He stood and motioned her to follow him to the large vault, where he placed the stone on a shelf next to a stack of books. Putting it away with no explanation meant he wouldn't share with her what it might mean to their plans. The table at the center of the room had a few books opened on it, but he poured two drinks and pointed to the chair opposite him. "Let's talk about what comes next."

She glanced down at the books and saw the sketches of dragons in one, and a man standing in the flames in the other. Her guess was, Alejandro saw himself as the man who'd defy death in the dragon fire once the time came. "What happened to Franco?"

"My man told me the people that are here to stop us killed him for information about me." He drank some of the liquor he'd poured with a smile, and she wondered what he was thinking about. "He didn't give up much before they dropped him into one of the chambers, effectively killing him, but the one interesting thing was the woman we shot and threw over the mountain side was one of the people questioning him."

"How is that possible?" she asked, and it seemed her life had veered off into some strange place where she didn't know much about her surroundings. It hit her how much she missed her mother and the sense of peace she'd brought to her heart. "Maybe it was someone who looked like her."

"He said he was fairly sure it was her, so it makes me want to know more about this Genesis Clan and what they're about." He held up his glass and gazed at her with an expression that resembled pride, so she tapped her glass to his and took a drink. "Right now, though, I want to celebrate your find and the dedication you've put into this. Of all my children, you've come the farthest in this journey with me."

"Thank you," she said, but the room started to spin a little so she placed her glass on the table, not wanting to spill the rest. "I'm sorry," she said, holding her head and blinking rapidly, trying to make herself focus, but his face was starting to dim around the edges. The last thing she remembered was glancing at the glass and cursing her need for his approval.

Alejandro watched as Pauline slumped forward, her face landing on the table as slack as if she were sleeping, and waited for his second high priest, Javier Valentino. Javier knew as much about the site and the archives as he did, but he seldom allowed anyone to meet him in case the outside world discovered how important his second in command was to him and what he wanted. Since they were raised together from almost birth, Javier knew all his secrets and would take them all to the grave, but he didn't plan to take any chances.

"Are you sure?" Javier said, combing Pauline's hair from her face.

"You've read the passage as many times as I have," he said, throwing Pauline's glass away. "Up to now our plans have gone flawlessly, and she found the stone like you predicted she would after we sent Oscar running."

"Fear's always a great motivator, so we'll wait Oscar out and get him back when he's found something. Right now, though, it's time."

Alejandro took his jacket off, picked Pauline up, and carried her to the building next to the main house.

The building had only one huge room with a replica of the large pyramid where the two demons had killed the gods years before, and it still served as their altar. So much time and so many secrets had been lost since that night their forefathers had made the witches pay for their act of betrayal, but that was getting ready to end. They were so close he could almost touch the beasts that would bend to his will.

A stainless-steel table sat at the center of the altar, and he placed Pauline on it. Javier immediately started to bind her in case the drug wore off before they could start. When his daughter had first told him about the snakes that had come from the ground after they removed the second stone, he couldn't believe what he was hearing, having read it years before. The spirit of the gods had to go somewhere, and they'd been lying dormant until someone released them from their prisons.

The men had run from the abnormally large serpents, but he'd trusted Javier's followers to capture as many as they could find for the ceremony they were about to perform. It'd worked up to now, but not like the accounts the archives had listed, so he figured they needed someone with a true believer's blood.

Javier opened the box next to the table, and one of the large snakes came out and coiled on top of Pauline, as if it knew what was expected of it. Alejandro smiled when he noted the size of it and leaned down and kissed Pauline on the lips to wake her up. Her lips reacted under his, and she opened her eyes and started screaming until he squeezed her face so hard all she could do was whimper, but he could see the wildness in her expression as she looked from him to the snake.

"Stop fighting me," he said as he placed his palm out and the snake rested its head on it. "You know this has to be, and you'll be the first of your kind who'll serve me until we're able to wake the beasts."

"Don't do this," she begged, shaking her head as much as she could.

He let her go, and the snake started to sway to the incantations Javier read from the oldest book they possessed. Javier's voice grew louder, and he made his way around the table, handing Alejandro the ancient blade they'd uncovered in the highlands of Mexico, and he made the necessary cut in Pauline's abdomen. It was the only invitation the serpent needed, entering the incision and slithering inside as Pauline screamed as if in horrific pain, which he imagined must have been real.

Pauline convulsed as the last of the snake disappeared inside her, and she rattled the table enough to move it toward the back of the altar. She stopped only when Javier poured the elixir they'd mixed into her mouth, and she swallowed only when he covered her mouth and nose. He'd seen the transformation before, but he still stood back and watched as her skin started to change and take on the distinctive markings of the python and the head momentarily came out of her mouth.

One of the handlers entered with a prod as she started to fight her bonds, and he and Javier moved behind him. An awful-sounding howl came out of her as she started to change, and after her bones broke and her features melted away, a child of the gods stood before them on the table, larger than any of the others they'd created.

"This is what they were supposed to look like," he told Javier, moving forward with his hand out. Pauline hissed louder, but she didn't move from the table because the handler was prodding her until he pointed to the floor. She got down and moved toward him on the small four legs that held up the thick serpent body that appeared more lizard-like than snake. "You will do my bidding, but first we'll see if you're truly one of the chosen."

He led her to the bottom of the altar and studied her strength before nodding to the handler, who shot her with another drug that made her drop. When she became slack, he placed the large serpent head on his lap and stroked it. A few minutes later the transformation happened again, and she opened her eyes, naked and clearly confused.

"What did you do?" she asked, making no move to cover herself.

"Set you free."

Kendal took only Morgaine when they returned from the dig site to visit Franco Rodriguez's home, but they found every member of the staff and family slaughtered throughout the house. Someone had found a way to keep any more information from them, but they searched anyway, finding very little.

"What do you think they sent in here?" Morgaine asked as she looked down at Franco's wife and daughter lying close to each other, each with horrific-appearing wounds. The pools of blood made an almost unholy halo around them, and it looked like they'd tried to reach each other but had only gotten within an arm's length before they died.

"You saw those things. If it was Garza and he can control whatever those creatures are, then they'll kill for him." She opened a cabinet and found some journals that Franco's family had kept, so she went in search of something to put them in.

She ran into Lowe in the kitchen, or who she thought was Lowe, sniffing the ground. For such a petite woman she was a substantially sized wolf, and she raised her head and growled when Kendal stopped at the door. "Okay. Let's not do anything stupid," she said with her hands up and out in front of her. "You're supposed to be the reasonable one."

"Who are you talking to?" Morgaine asked as she moved closer, stopping when she saw the wolf. "How'd they get here?"

Kendal shook her head and went in search of Convel, finding her in the master bedroom. Unlike her lover, Convel actually appeared amused as she moved to lie on the bed. She used that spot to transform to her human form.

"Don't get pissed right away, but we can find things you can't, no matter how talented you are, so we decided to crash your party. There are five dead in the yard and another six in the house. It looks like they tried to outrun those things we saw close to that fucker's house, but plenty of them were here." Convel stood and walked to the closet to find something to wear. "At least five of those things were here, from what I could tell, but I haven't been on the other side of the house yet, so there might've been even more." She stepped out in a T-shirt and jeans.

"Anything else?" she asked, pissed that Convel hadn't listened to her, but she couldn't complain after she'd done what they'd asked of her. No werewolf wanted to be seen simply as a bloodhound.

"I need to get to Lowe before I can answer," she said, moving to the kitchen. "We're about to get visitors, and I don't want her to freak out."

"Care to tell us who that's going to be?" Morgaine asked, following her.

"You invited her, so don't act surprised that she showed up," Convel said, glancing back and smirking.

Lowe moved toward Convel when she saw her, but she couldn't play twenty questions when the front door opened. If it was the police they'd have to go out the back before they finished searching the house, but she doubted they knew anything about this yet. Convel held on to Lowe when Vadoma stepped inside and kissed Kendal on the mouth.

"Did you miss me?"

"Terribly," she said, trying to keep her sarcasm to a minimum. That she had to include all these people she didn't really care for wasn't going to make this any easier.

"I would've waited for an invitation, but the smell of blood made this place irresistible." Vadoma glanced around, her face twitching. "What in the world happened here? Did you let your pets loose?" Vadoma asked, and Convel had to really hang on to Lowe when she growled louder and moved closer, making Vadoma's true self manifest itself.

"Okay. Let's all calm down and take some deep breaths," Kendal said, putting her hands up. "We'll go over everything when we get back to the house, but for now we need to finish in here before the scary lizard people come back and we have to add to the body count."

"Scary lizard people?" Vadoma said with a smile. "I know you're immortal, but did you get into some bad peyote or something?"

"Trust me. You won't believe it when you see it, but a lot's happening here that's hard to explain." Morgaine cocked her head toward the bedroom so Convel would lead Lowe out.

"Anything you want me to do while we wait for you to finish?" Vadoma said, and Kendal could hear movement outside but figured the queen of the vampires very seldom traveled alone.

"Sit and try to keep your urges under wraps," she said, smiling. "We shouldn't be much longer, so try to think teamwork."

"I'll do that as long as you keep the mutts on a leash," she said, pointing in the direction Convel and Lowe had disappeared in.

"Let's all keep our fangs in check, and this will go as smoothly as we can manage."

ALI VALI

CHAPTER TWENTY-THREE

Lenore and Molly went through the journals Kendal had found
while Morgaine made plans to leave as soon as they could manage
to travel with the eclectic group they'd amassed. Vadoma and the
weres had managed somewhat of a truce when the sun came up and
the vampires retired to the guesthouse farther down the slope. Neither
party, though, appeared thrilled that they'd be working with a usually
sworn enemy.

"Find anything?" Piper asked as she entered with Hali strapped
to her chest.

"It seems like the Rodriguez family visited the site as often as they
could manage in search of any treasure that might've been left behind,"
Molly said, going through Lenore's translations. "They found a few
things but didn't disturb the slabs you all opened while you were there.
The generations before this one seemed to abide by the agreement with
the clan and searched only in the places that were readily accessible."

"Did they catalog their finds?" she asked, bouncing the baby to
keep her calm.

"Kendal and Morgaine must've walked right by them," Lenore
said as she showed her the sketches the journals contained. "Up to now
they've discovered mostly pottery and small statuary, but Franco and
his son found a stash of scrolls in a niche toward the top of one of the
smaller pyramids."

"That they would've noticed," Piper said, flipping through the
book to see if Franco had mentioned what was in them.

"He didn't put anything in there," Lenore said, looking at her as if
Piper should be able to read her mind. "If he didn't hand them over to
Garza, then we need to go back and search. Whatever's in them might
be something we'll need, so *we* need to go and find them."

"We as in you and me?" she said, laughing. "I'm sure our spouses will love that idea."

"Hey, we can be adventurous too," Lenore said, and Molly nodded.

"Planning something?" Kendal asked, joining them with Lowe.

Piper explained what they'd found in the journals, and Kendal seemed to agree with Lenore, which surprised her a little. "We need to go back to the Rodriguez house," she said, telling Kendal what they'd found. "If it came from the site, we need it back."

"Then you all should go and look, but so far no one's claimed the bodies or reported them, so how about we let Rueben's guys go in there and clean up? Once they've cleared the place, you can look as long as you need." Kendal bent and kissed Hali's head as she slumped sleeping against her chest.

"Where are you going to be exactly?"

"We need to search someone else's house, and now that I have reinforcements, it's time to visit Señor Garza. I'll send our other backup with you, so both of us should be fine."

"Would you like to repeat all that so I understand what you're talking about?" She held Kendal's head eye level with hers and kissed her.

"Convel and Lowe will keep an eye out while you and the others look around, and I'll take Vadoma and her group of misfits with me. If there's any trouble, I'm sure I can ring the dinner bell and have them deal with any problems," Kendal said, smiling.

"Tell her if she decides to kiss you again, I'm going to introduce her to a wooden spike with her name carved into it," she said, and she wasn't joking.

"I'll be sure to mention it." Kendal kissed her as if no one else was in the room, and she pinched her side to cool her down before her grandmother got a glimpse of the part of their relationship that should remain private. "Do you think Franco might've turned it over to Garza?"

"From what we read, it sounds like he kept everything he found," Molly said. "If I had to guess, he wanted some insurance so in case things got tight, he'd have something to sell."

"Wait for nightfall, and don't lose the big dogs going with you," Kendal said, taking Piper's hand and leading her out. "That's about an hour away, so promise me you'll be careful."

"You know I will, but where I'm going isn't the dangerous place." She placed the baby in her crib and slumped against Kendal. "This man Garza reminds me of Kenny Delaney when he tried to steal the company from us. He'll do anything to get what he wants."

"Garza's a lot worse, since he has some interesting hobbies if he had anything to do with those things we saw. So I need you to be careful. Granted, nothing can happen to you, but I'll go nuts if someone takes you from me." Kendal tightened her hold and pressed her cheek to the top of Piper's head.

"Concentrate on what you'll be doing, baby, and I'll be fine. Once we get what we're after, we can move on. Which is where exactly?" she asked, enjoying the warmth of Kendal's body.

"Do you remember the way the snakes all clustered together?"

"Considering they give me the shivers, yes."

"It's a golden temple that holds the dragon's heart. That could be anywhere in the world, but the snakes narrowed it down for us. A serpent with multiple heads is well known in Buddhism and is known as the god Naga, so we'll start in Cambodia. I have a feeling the temple isn't golden any longer, but it was at one time."

"After we're done here, maybe we can sit and think for a little while."

"Or fool around, whichever comes first."

Kendal stepped from the trees after watching the house and grounds for over an hour and seeing no movement. The lights were on, but the place was eerily quiet, as were the surroundings. Next to her, Vadoma glanced around and shut her eyes as if trying to sense anything close by.

"There's no one here," Vadoma said before moving toward the house. "Not human anyway."

"Pay attention, then. Whatever those things are, I'm sure they pack a painful bite." She followed her to the back and tried one of the doors.

"Want me to try to pick it?"

Kendal drew her sword, smashed the glass in, and stepped inside. "I want him to know we were here and that I know it's him we're up against. I just can't figure out why he left."

They checked every room, with Morgaine starting on the other side of the house, until they met in the office at the door to a rather large safe. "If we're going to find anything, I'm guessing it's in here," Morgaine said, placing her hand on the metal.

"True, and if I ask nicely, would you open it?" she asked Vadoma, knowing her hearing was a hundred times better than that of anyone else in the house.

"Tell me what this is all about first, and I'll be glad to."

"We went over this already," she said, longing for the days she'd worked alone.

Vadoma shook her head and crossed her arms over her chest. "And knowing you, what you said wasn't all of it."

"There's a place that everyone thought was a Mayan ruin not that far from here, but it's actually the resting place of Aphrodite's dragons. The guy who owns the house wants to bring them back as part of some order his family rules, and the goddess asked us not to let that happen." She shrugged when she finished, knowing her explanation sounded incredibly far-fetched, but the truth wasn't always exactly normal. "Might sound crazy, but that's all of it."

"Everyone be quiet, and I'll try my best to get this open."

"So you believe me?" Kendal asked, not thinking it would be this easy.

Vadoma simply locked eyes with her and smiled. "You're more of a soldier than a storyteller, so I doubt you have the imagination to come up with something like that."

The safe seemed impenetrable, but Vadoma slowly twirled the dial and in about ten minutes pulled the lever that would open the thing if she'd been successful. Before she could fully open the door, it swung out viciously and knocked Vadoma to the ground as two of Garza's creatures immediately pounced on her and went for her throat.

"What in the hell is that?" Vadoma asked an instant later, covered in the creatures' blood, both heads still moving close to her. Both Kendal and Morgaine had drawn their swords quickly and pulled up in time not to slice through Vadoma as well.

"Give it a minute and you'll see something interesting," Morgaine said. "But since you're about as old as Asra, have you ever seen anything like it?"

"No one's ever seen anything like it," Vadoma said, wiping her face, the sudden expression of realization shaping her features. "The blood's human, but it's mixed with venom."

"They change back to their original form, but it takes time," Kendal said, entering the vault. "Whatever they are, they're made by something Garza did, I think, and they're a type of were."

"That's fucked up," Vadoma said as the young girl started to take shape before them, her head several feet away from her body.

"Do you think your people will help us carry all this out of here," she said of all the books and other things still in the vault. "I guess he thought the alarm system was enough to deter any thieves."

"We'll get it all, but we need to check out the rest of this place. No one sends something like that after me without paying a price."

Vadoma appeared angry and somewhat embarrassed, so Kendal pointed to the bathroom. "This should be everything important in the house, but I saw some buildings outside, so wipe all that off and meet me out there."

One building looked like barracks for guards or staff with pens that had hay strewn on the ground, but the other one was a good replica of the pyramid at the dig site. The table on the top had leather restraints that were broken through and a layer of what appeared to be a shed snakeskin. Morgaine touched it and held it up, and both of them were amazed at the size. It was shaped like the snake weres, but this one was much larger than any they'd seen so far.

"He's perfecting his craft," Kendal said, not able to take her eyes off the skin in Morgaine's raised hands. "But I don't get why."

"Sometimes the why of something is as stupid as seeing if you can do it simply to do it," Vadoma said. "You find something like a book or a distant relative, you unleash something that can't be undone, and you end up with what attacked me."

"I can't answer that question, but from what we've seen, the only way to undo this is through death. The first one I killed had a handler who turned out to be her father, so maybe whatever this is, it has to be a female for it to work."

"Or they're willing to sacrifice their daughters but not their sons," Vadoma said with what sounded like compassion when she joined them at the top. "My body might be technically dead, slayer, but I do still have a bit of heart left."

She placed her hand on Vadoma's shoulder and squeezed gently.

"I knew that. If not, I would've killed you the night you came into my house," she said, smiling.

"That's what my cousin Ora never understood about you, and what you don't understand about this man. No everyone should have power, so if we don't find him, he'll kill at will until he gets what he wants. Not everyone fights on the side of right for no reward, so start thinking like him before he leaves you behind like he did tonight. You need to find everyone working for him, like those people who were supposed to be working for you."

"Thanks," she said, thinking it was a sort of compliment.

"Where do you think this thing is?" Morgaine asked, holding the skin up again.

"I think the last of the ones he first created were the two in the vault, but this one seems different, so wherever he went, that thing went with him." She touched the leather restraints and noticed how they'd frayed under considerable pressure.

"That's going to be tough to get through customs if he left the country," Morgaine said.

"Not if it walks out with him on two legs," Vadoma said, and the statement rang true.

❖

Convel sat in the front seat next to the driver who'd picked them all up from the helipad and taken them to the watcher Rodriguez's house, and was now bringing them back for their flight home. It wasn't a very long stay since Piper had almost immediately headed to a statue that had appeared to come from the site. Charlie picked it up and turned it over. Inside were tightly rolled scrolls that appeared to be old animal skins.

She glanced back at Lowe, noticing how animated she looked talking to Piper. They were probably about the same age, and Lowe hadn't had too many good friends among the weres that had traveled with them, so she seemed to be enjoying Piper's company. They needed to discuss this situation before they went anywhere else, and it sounded like Kendal had figured out the next step, so they'd be moving on as soon as they were all back together.

Convel really wanted to talk to Tala and Lovell and ask exactly why they were here at all. Neither she nor Lowe was prepared for this, and before they were placed in a situation she couldn't save them from, she needed all the answers. She hadn't treasured anything or anyone in so long, so nothing was worth losing Lowe. She wanted to complete their obligation, but she'd walk away before she sacrificed the one she loved more than anything in her life.

"When we get back, we need to talk," she said to Lowe when they stopped and everyone started for the helicopter.

"About what?" Lowe slid her palm against hers and waved for Piper to go on. "Are you okay?" Lowe lifted her other hand and caressed her cheek.

"Nothing's wrong. I just want to spend a few minutes alone talking to you before we have to go out again." Lowe nodded and kissed her before tugging her toward their ride.

Piper stopped and waited for them, then asked Lowe to give her a few minutes with Convel. When Lowe seemed reluctant to leave them alone, Convel leaned down and pressed her lips to Lowe's temple and let her go. Asra's mate was more than she seemed, and up to now she'd underestimated her.

"Will you tell her the truth?" Piper asked with no judgment. "I know you think she'll change her mind about you, but she won't. Like me, Lowe knows her mate's not perfect, but you are the other half of her soul. It's not about forgiveness. It's about acceptance."

"Do you think I have a soul?" she asked, wondering what the Clan taught its converts.

"Does it matter what I think?" Piper smiled in a way that made her appear young and beautiful. "But if you really need an answer, then I think you're as human as I am. I might have joined Asra in forever, but I don't think I'm any different than before, and no matter what you have trapped inside, you're not different."

"So you're a seer?" Unlike the were seer Trudy, Piper didn't flaunt her gift.

"That's what they tell me, but I'm not very good at it yet. Some things come easily and clearly, and Lowe's love for you is something even I can almost touch."

"Thank you," she said, lowering her eyes to the ground.

"Give her the chance to prove her love for you. The forever part of it is so much better when you give her your true self," Piper said, placing her hand on her forearm. "Only then do you know that you're loved for all the right reasons."

The trip was quiet, as if everyone aboard was lost in their own thoughts, so Lowe followed Convel to their room when they landed and locked the door when they were both inside. Before she could say anything, Lowe came to her and pressed against her before tugging her head down and kissing her like she was trying to brand her.

"I need you to know something before we go any farther with the slayer and Piper," she said, then went rigid. The shift came before she could undress, and her clothes tore from her body as she growled at the door. Lowe opened it, and she ran to the master bedroom and stood between the three young vampires and the baby bed.

The handsome young man and the two women shifted as well, going from their beautiful façade to the faces of the demons that now lived within them, but she lowered her head and snarled at them. If they took a step toward the slayer's baby, she'd rip their throats out before ripping their hearts from their chests. The nanny was behind her next to the crib, but she would've been no match for Vadoma's filth.

"Move aside, animal," the male said as the women stood a foot behind him.

She didn't move when Asra arrived with her sword with Piper right behind her. The vampires hissed at the slayer but moved back a few steps when Asra, like her, showed no fear. To add to the tableau they were locked in, the baby started crying, sounding totally miserable.

"Convel, watch Hali," Kendal said as Piper stood back.

It didn't take long for Kendal to move and drive her sword through the male, and he disappeared in a cloud of dust. The women shrieked and divided to try to get around Kendal, but her sword struck again and another one died, but the other one got close to Hali before Convel jumped on her and sank her fangs into her throat. She shook her head and the woman clawed at her eyes, scratching her before Kendal was able to turn around and drive her sword through the woman's chest.

Her mouth filled with dust a second later, and she shook her head in disgust. The danger was gone so she shifted, not caring that she was naked, but Piper held out a robe to her and embraced her when she'd tied it off. "Thank you for saving our daughter."

Kendal nodded and offered her a hand. "Thank you. I'm in your debt, but Vadoma will pay for this," Kendal said, turning to leave.

"Wait," Convel said, holding on to Kendal to keep her in the room. "These didn't belong to her. Believe me, I hate to say it, but I recognize the scent. They're not of her creation."

Vadoma came up as if she'd sensed they were talking about her, and her eyes went from them to the smattering of dust on the floor and the sword in Kendal's hand. "What happened?"

"Some of your disciples decided my baby was fair game," Piper said with so much anger that Vadoma took a step back, shaking her head with her hands out in front of her.

"Do you honestly think I'd condone that?" Vadoma stood straighter and seemed to make a decision when she stepped closer. "I was once a mother who had to leave her child after my cousin took my humanity, so I would never allow any follower of mine near a child. You don't have to believe me, but that's the truth."

"Piper, it wasn't her," Convel said, not happy that she had to agree with this abomination. "They were followers of Ora, but they weren't from her or from here. The accents were European, so we need to figure out how they got this close to us without raising any alarms."

Piper nodded, then ran out of the room and down the hall toward Lenore and Morgaine's room. When they all joined her, Lowe was standing near Ana's bed with Morgaine close by with her sword in her hand. The moment Vadoma stepped in, Morgaine raised her weapon and went after her with the obvious intent to kill her until Kendal stopped her advance by raising her own sword and stopping the swing.

"I know you're pissed, but it's not her," Kendal said, the muscles in her jaw clenched to keep Morgaine back. "They were Ora's, and they've probably been out there awhile, but only decided to attack now. That doesn't make any sense, considering we're in here, and they had to know they wouldn't succeed. They would've had a better chance had they waited until we were all away."

"They were fledglings," Convel said, placing her hand on Morgaine's wrists. "I can't explain why they were here, but they were probably some of her last converts."

Lenore placed her hands around Lowe's thick neck and cried into the soft pelt. "Thank you for protecting our child."

"Thank you both," Morgaine said, finally relaxing.

"Asra, we have to leave by morning, and we have to be vigilant tonight for any more attacks," Convel said, moving toward Lowe. "I can't be sure, but I think this is Garza's way of telling you that he's untouchable. He knows you're here, and he's flaunting his power over every one of your enemies and showing how you can't beat him at this game."

"I'm not interested in touching him," Kendal said menacingly. "I'm interested in killing him and whatever kind of freak show he's got under his spell."

"Lock the doors and have Rawney place a protection spell to keep out anyone not welcome until we're gone," she said, taking Lowe back toward their room. "The problem with taunting anyone is you show your hand, and that only makes it easier to chew off."

Convel dropped Kendal's robe and waited for Lowe to shift back once they were alone again, wanting to finish their talk before anything else happened. She held Lowe, enjoying the press of her skin along her length. This woman had reached inside her and made the world much more bearable, and had never let the cruelty that had marred much of her human life extinguish the hope and wonder she seemed to have in abundance.

"They were going to kill those little babies," Lowe said tearfully.

"I don't think that's why they came, but I'm glad we stopped them."

"Why do you think they came?" Lowe leaned back a little to look her in the eye.

"To take them, not kill them. You take what's most precious to someone, and they'll do anything to get it back," she said, knowing she hadn't been that different when she was younger. "I want to finish our talk from earlier."

"Nothing you can tell me will change my mind about being with you," Lowe said, intuitively knowing she was afraid of the conversation.

"I hope that's true, but Piper's right in that you deserve the truth." Lowe took her hand, led her to the bed, and curled around her with her head on her shoulder once they'd lain down. "I met the slayer early in her life in Macedonia," she said, and the faces of those who'd followed her away from the pack and their families came flooding back to her.

"It's okay, baby," Lowe said, rubbing her back. "Just say it."

❖

Macedonia 142 BC, The Korab Mountain Range

Convel sat up in the cave they'd been using as their den and tried to drink some water. The wound on her hand the slayer had put there had festered and left her feverish for days, until she'd used the salve Erik had left. It was actually healing, but it would take time since she'd waited so long to apply it. Two of the males had led the hunts while she recovered, and her lover had stayed behind to care for and protect her.

The pack returned with two calves from the farms below them and dropped them at her feet. Her two best men seemed proud of themselves as they stood naked and bloodied from their easy victory. It was then she knew that part of what the slayer had said was true. She'd led these people not only away from their families, but away from their true nature. Wolves were true hunters, not thieves that brought down farm animals.

"We're leaving as soon as I'm healed," she said, and the celebration and feeding frenzy stopped. "It's time to start hunting again before we forget how."

"I thought we left so we didn't have to scrounge like the rest of the pack," one of the males said. "These people will learn to fear us, and that'll allow us to take whatever we want."

"The slayer found us easily enough, so we need to move on, but more importantly, we need to remember the part of ourselves that makes us unique. Hunting is our right and our heritage."

"No," one of the others said. "Taking from those sheep down there and killing anyone who gets in our way is our heritage." The others nodded and looked back to her.

"Then we stay, but be prepared to fight."

"The slayer can't take all of us," the hunt leader said. "If he comes back we'll leave his throat and eyes for you, Convel, but he's not running me from my home."

She shifted since the healing went much faster in this form and howled loudly, shaking her head when the pack joined in. They were right, this was their home, and no one would take it from them.

CHAPTER TWENTY-FOUR

W hat happened?" Lowe asked when Convel paused in her story.
"I didn't find out until much later that Erik Wolver was
actually Kendal, but she'd done the job she was sent to do. She warned
me, and I chose to ignore her since I had fifty-three in my pack. Erik
couldn't possibly kill us all."

"How long were you there?" Lowe said, still touching her gently.

"About a year, and it started slowly," she said, closing her eyes.
"I'd send out hunting parties, or they'd go out on their own, but a
few wouldn't return. At first I thought it was the ones who'd gotten
homesick and left without warning so we wouldn't think them weak,
but then we started finding the bodies. The heads were severed, and the
wounds were infected with the same silver that had cut me."

"How many?" Lowe said and stopped her hand.

"In a few months only about ten of us remained, and instead of
leaving I stayed to hunt the slayer and make him pay. The last day
we were all together I bragged about how I'd kill the butcher that had
taken so many of us, and I could barely see through my hatred." She
remembered touching her lover but with no tenderness, yet she hadn't
cared. Her spirit had embraced the animal inside her, and it wanted
blood.

"Another five were killed before they begged me to leave like the
slayer had said, but I wanted revenge more than I wanted to keep them
safe. I ordered them to come out with me until we found Wolver again
so we could fight to the death."

"Did you find her?" Lowe asked, placing a kiss on her jaw.

"The slayer wasn't responsible," she said, having to take a deep
breath to keep from sobbing. "The butchers that had killed my friends

were hunters hired by the locals, and they'd put a high enough price on our heads to drive them into their own killing frenzy. So on that last day, they had us surrounded, and my pack fought to stay alive, but I ran. There were too many of them, and they knew about the silver somehow."

"It's okay," Lowe said as she cried.

"The hunters used arrows first, and when they had weakened my pack enough, they used their swords and pikes. I watched and did nothing as they slaughtered my friends and my little sister."

Lowe wrapped her entire body around Convel and held her as she cried, but she didn't leave. It was the first time she'd told anyone what had really happened and how she'd fled from her responsibility instead of leading her pack. Kendal had known the truth, but she'd never called her on it.

"They killed your sister?" Lowe asked, wiping away her tears with the corner of the sheet.

"Felan had come with me, thinking it would be one big adventure, and had tried to talk me into going back every chance she got, but I didn't listen. That day she stood with the pack while I hid, and she's only alive because of the slayer." She remembered Kendal standing between those men and her little sister and killing a couple before the others realized their hunting job was over. "She saved her and brought her back to the pack. I've hated Kendal ever since because she knew the truth about me. I'm nothing but a coward."

"No," Lowe said loudly. "A coward wouldn't have faced her past and the woman who was a part of it, and a coward certainly wouldn't have protected the slayer's child."

"I left them all to die. Don't you understand that part?"

"When I was young, my parents threw me out because I liked girls, so I had to hook to survive. I didn't want to, but I did it to stay alive. What you did was like that, so I'm not going to judge you for it. Everyone has an innate urge to try to cheat death, so don't think it's something to be ashamed of," Lowe said, kissing her. "You saved me, and you love me, so don't ask me to judge you. I love you too much to ever do that."

"She was right," she said about Piper, not forgetting but letting some of the guilt go. "I'm sorry for not telling you sooner."

"This was the perfect time to tell me, so honor those guys who followed you by burying the past but keeping their memory alive. Right now and the future belong to us."

She put her arms around Lowe and rolled her over. "You have to believe me that I'll never leave you. I love you, so I'll try my best to always protect you."

"I know that," Lowe said, running her hands down her back. "I belong to you, but you belong to me too, so we'll protect each other. And when this is done, I want to meet the rest of your family. It's time to go home, baby."

"I promise, but not until we finish this. Right now I can't face those families who lost children because of my immaturity."

"No matter what, the people that are the most important are the ones who forgave you a long time ago without asking anything in return. The rest, you'll have to accept and do your best to live with, but you deserve a home and people who love you."

"Thank you. My mother is going to love you."

Vadoma followed Kendal downstairs to the large office space and ordered the two people with her to wait outside with Charlie. "Some part of you probably doesn't believe Convel, but no matter what you might think of me and my kind, my word still means something to me."

"I believe her," Kendal said, surprising her by the surety of her words. "Our truce brings balance, and if it's broken, the only way to achieve it is for me and my kind to go back to work."

"I'm sure some of the slayers would love that as much as some of my followers would love to take up the war again. That's something we can both agree on, but we don't have time to worry about it now. Ora might be dead, but it's evident that a group within your numbers doesn't accept your rules." Kendal unclipped the scabbard from her back and placed the sword on the desk.

"My cousin shouldn't have lived as long as she did," she said, sitting in a leather wingback chair across from the one Kendal picked. "All those years only fed the craziness, not to mention the cruelty."

"Her death and why I wanted her dead should prove to any followers she had left that I'm more than motivated when provoked, no matter how long it takes." Kendal poured herself what appeared to be whiskey and closed her eyes when she took a sip. "Do you have any idea how any of her killers would've met and followed Garza?"

"Ora made quite a few pacts through the centuries when it helped her in the fight against the Clan elders. Until you contacted me, though, I'd never heard of Alejandro Garza," she said, remembering the taste of liquor and how much she'd enjoyed the wine her family had made. "Why did you contact me about this?"

"I called you to stack my deck, as it were, when it comes to weapons, but it's more than that. You've lived almost as long as I have, so I need your experience with some of the things we've faced so far, but you've never seen anything like them before either. The appearance of Ora's little bitches makes me glad you're here." Kendal drained her glass and twirled her empty glass between her hands. "There's only one problem."

"Only one?" she said and laughed.

"Piper's family has a history with Ora they really didn't realize until recently, and I want to put a stake through any remaining ties to that bitch and what she's done to them. The only way for me to do that is to start killing anyone of your kind who crossed my path in my hunts, but that would mean going back on my word to you." Kendal poured another drink and crossed her legs before looking at her. "I couldn't do that, so I thought you'd be the best way for me to surgically remove both our problems. Only you will know which ones are her creations."

"The truth is I never wanted the title of queen of the vampires, but eventually I came to crave it only so I could control our future. Under Ora we'd eventually all die off when she pushed you and the others to kill us all."

"If any harm comes to those children, I won't be able to change the tide against you," Kendal said, and the honesty was refreshing.

"Between us and your pets they should be fine."

"Good. I need you to stay and hunt your cousin's remaining idiots."

"Where are you going?"

"To find the key to give Aphrodite something she doesn't know she wants."

❖

Pauline opened her eyes and shook her head, wondering how she got on a plane. A glance out the window didn't clue her in since they were over water, but her father was next to her. Alejandro was reading something, holding the large ruby in his hand. She tried her best to find the missing time, but nothing was coming to her.

"Where are we?" she asked and flexed her hands. Her skin felt different.

"We're headed to the next spot on the map my father found in his youth. It'll be a safe place to wait until these people who want to stop us come back," Alejandro said, sounding like he usually did by not committing to anything. "How do you feel?"

"What happened to me?" She shivered as her heart started to race, and she started panting.

"You were sick, so drink this." Alejandro held up a glass with what looked like water.

One taste, though, and she knew that wasn't what it was, but that one sip made the light in the cabin grow dim. In her last seconds of consciousness she wanted to scream when she lifted her hand with great effort and saw the distinct patterns of the pythons that had crawled out of those chambers.

"No," she screamed, but the word was trapped in her head.

CHAPTER TWENTY-FIVE

Charlie got off the plane first with Kendal and glanced around as Piper readied the baby. Morgaine had stayed with Lenore, as she did the same with Anastasia. Had it been any other situation, Kendal would've left the baby with Molly and Mac until they were done, but now the only way to protect her family was to keep them close.

"Where exactly are we going?" Charlie asked.

"After I saw that site," she said as Oscar joined them on the tarmac, "I knew I'd seen something similar."

"Are we in Cambodia?" Oscar asked as a line of vehicles drove their way.

"Yes," she said, not able to figure this guy out. "And we need to get to the site here before Garza. I don't know if *he* figured it out, but there's a missing piece that wasn't at the site you explored, and it's got to be here."

"Baby," Piper said from the top of the steps with Hali's carrier in her hand. "You ready?"

"Let's go." She climbed the steps and took the baby. The airport she'd picked was twenty minutes from the place they were headed, so she strapped Hali into the back of the lead car. "I want to get there before the sun goes down."

"What are we looking for?" Piper said once they started driving.

"You're going to tell me when we get there," she said, glancing back to make sure the others were right behind them. "But the snakes were a big hint."

She drove along a highway that led to the largest tourist destination in the country. Angkor Wat was a large temple complex that had, by historians' findings, at one time been painted mostly white with gold on the tall spires in the main temples. A mass of people was coming out as the sun started to set, and vendors were waiting outside to sell them trinkets and T-shirts to prove they'd been there.

Kendal parked and waved over one of the Buddhist monks walking toward the still-viable temple, giving him a note with a large donation to deliver to his master. She didn't like to go to religious sites uninvited if she didn't have to, and at times the true believers knew their surroundings much better than she would.

As the sun dropped a little lower, the same novice monk came out and waved them to the long bridge built over the moat. At the end of the railing stood two large stone carvings of Naga, the multi-headed serpent. "We're in the right place, but our problem will be to find which one of these holds any meaning since dozens of them are scattered throughout the property," she said as they entered the holy place.

"Asra, you've come back," the old monk said when she pressed her hands together and bowed as a sign of respect. "The last time you were here, I was a novice, and you were searching for something you didn't find."

"I've found everything I need, so rest easy, Niran," she said, smiling when he took her hands. "This is my wife, Piper, and our baby girl, Hali."

"Come sit and tell me what you're searching for this time," Niran said, leading them to a building that had been a library centuries before. "Can I offer you tea?"

"Not this time, but I promise we'll come back to enjoy the peacefulness of your beautiful home when we can. Right now, I'm looking for something that came as a sign from Naga."

"Come, Piper," Niran said, taking Piper's hand and leading her toward the main buildings that were usually full of tourists. The smell of incense and dust was strong in the room that housed the large standing Buddha, at the moment surrounded by monks chanting their evening prayers. "Sit and listen to their devotion. You'll find the chants much like Asra's love for you."

"How do you mean?" Piper asked as Kendal took the baby from her. She barely glanced up, finding this man mesmerizing.

"They speak of tradition, devotion, love, and kindness. Your mate, once she learned to clear her mind, healed her heart. Because she did, when she found you she was ready to give you all those things that make the bond truly last when you find your true other half."

The way Niran spoke in that slow but steady cadence made Piper close her eyes and sway slightly as she listened to the monks. She didn't understand what they were saying, but a sense of timelessness echoed deep in her chest. The longer she listened, the more she faded into the past, and the picture of what this place had been once appeared in her mind's eye. It was beautiful.

"Come, child," Niran said, taking her hand and helping her to her feet. It was the same old man she'd met, but now he appeared like the young man who'd led them in. "Naga protects what's in the earth, so we've repeated his image throughout our temple, but also to hide that which must never be found."

"Not until the right time," she said as he led her to another bridge, only this time the statue on the left came to life, and the snakes looked exactly like the ones they'd seen in Costa Rica. "We don't want anything more than to give back to the goddess what's rightfully hers. To kill them means killing her, and Kendal and I don't want that."

"Then ask Naga, and he'll give you the answer you seek."

She repeated the bow Kendal had done and asked in her mind for the clue they needed. The live snakes slowly shifted back to stone, but unlike the others, the second head to the right of center had an indentation in its mouth. That was the only answer she was going to get as she came back to the present.

"Thank you," she said to Narin as Kendal helped him stand. "We need the bridge right outside."

Narin walked with them and pointed to the snake head Piper had seen in her vision. "I think we need to put something in there, but I'm not sure what," she said.

Piper squinted to get a better look, so Kendal aimed a flashlight at it, and the hole in the stone was identical to the one they'd found in the chamber in Costa Rica.

"Pauline has the stone, so if it's the key we're done," Oscar said, obviously having guessed what fit in the space.

"The stone at the site was a clue, not a key," Kendal said, and Narin nodded. "I promise I'll put it back if I can borrow it."

"You'll have to climb to the top spire to the King's temple, but make sure you know all the consequences of failure before you go," Narin said in the same kind, gentle tone.

"The only way to save them is to give the man against us what he wants and bring them to life. With us, though, it won't be for power or gain."

"I know, but I still have to remind you of what could happen."

They climbed to the tallest spire and headed to the middle of the structure, where another Buddha statue, this one sitting, was surrounded by candles and offerings. Embedded in his forehead was a large stone that had survived the thieves and vandals that had emptied the place of all its treasures.

"That's the key," Kendal said, bowing again before climbing to the head, taking the stone out, and dropping it into her shirt pocket.

They all went back to where Narin sat. "I've waited all my life to see the true purpose of the stone," he said as Kendal climbed again and very carefully placed the stone in the serpent's mouth.

Nothing happened immediately, but as the moon appeared in the sky, the stone started to glow until it illuminated the area around them. Rawney stepped closer and placed her hand on Kendal's bicep, but Kendal's eyes never left the stone. A finger of red came out of the glow slowly, but just as quickly turned into what appeared to be a laser beam that streaked across the yard and landed on one stone lying on the ground in a heap with a lot of others.

The pile of rocks had been part of the library at one time, but the wall they made up seemed to have collapsed years before. Kendal turned her flashlight on again and held Piper's hand as they made their way to the square stone, which looked very similar to the one Lumas and her sister had been buried in, so they opened it the same way.

"What is it?" Oscar asked, standing on his toes to try to see over the crowd.

It was another book, and when Rawney opened it, she started crying as she touched the pages. "This is what she would've given me eventually had we not been robbed of it all those years," Rawney said.

"What is it?" Oscar said, repeating his question.

"It's the translation of our families' book. You have to understand the power before you can understand the language that will allow you to wield it." She pressed the book against her chest and wiped her tears. "I can't believe it's been here all this time."

"It was waiting for the right time," Piper said, sensing the happiness that almost radiated out of Rawney. "Now we can finish."

"Like you said, now we wait until the right time, and then we finish," Kendal said, going back toward the temple so she could put the ruby back.

"Must you always get the last word?" she said, pinching Kendal's side.

"Not always, but later, when we're alone, I'll let you have the last word, I promise," Kendal said, and she pinched harder as the heat swept up her face.

"What? Maybe I want to talk about tugboats," Kendal said and laughed.

"I'll remind you of that later when we're alone and on a twenty-hour flight back."

Pauline woke up again strapped to a bed and instantly panicked. It was like her brain had frozen on the last image she remembered, and pain sliced through her chest and head from the betrayal. Alejandro had actually used the spell the family had found years before but never knew how to accomplish until she and Oscar unearthed the snakes that were waiting like the dragons. Only she was still in her human form and not permanently trapped in the hideous body the other girls had been turned into.

The door opened, but she could only lift her head slightly so she couldn't tell who it was. Her temper instantly flared when she saw Javier Valentino standing over her. The supposed high priest of the order had convinced all the poor villagers to sacrifice their youngest daughters for the good of the gods. All it had been was an experiment to see if the old documents held any merit.

"How do you feel?" Javier asked, his smile widening when she pulled her restraints as far as they'd allow her.

"You bastard," she said as she started to sweat. The reaction made him take a step back. "You talked him into this, didn't you?"

"Because of who you are, you finally broke the barrier we've been hitting with all the others. You're able to transform into the spirit of the dragon, then come back to your true form." He dropped his eyes to her hands and took another step back. "You have to learn to control the urge until it's time, Pauline. Embrace the power we've gifted you with."

"Why?" she said, conflicted by a heat that seemed to be burning in her stomach, but her skin felt cool, almost cold. Whatever was happening was making her nauseous. "Why in the hell did you do this to me?" she screamed, the heat growing worse, and she was able to tear the right restraint off the bed so she could see her hand. It was now a claw covered in snakeskin, and when she began to speak again, nothing but a loud hiss came out.

Javier stared at her, not having seen the transformation since he'd tied her up in the temple to let the dragon spirit loose. When Pauline tore a leg free he headed for the door to lock her in. Alejandro was waiting right outside and seemed as interested in what was happening as he was. It didn't take much longer for Pauline to completely transform and run to the door with a speed and ferocity that made the walls shake when she slammed against it.

"So anger is the best trigger?" Alejandro asked as they both stared at the door, waiting to see if it would hold.

"That's the only one we've found so far, and once she's completely changed she has no memory of anyone in her life, so you're not safe around her." A piercing groan replaced the pounding, and it sounded like what he imagined pain would be defined as.

"She's going to have to learn, because I need her by my side when we welcome the gods back to do our bidding. That," he said, pointing to the room Pauline was trapped in, "is the language of the gods. To have them do what needs to be done once they awaken, I need her to be able to communicate with me and them."

"She has to learn to control it, and that could take more time than we have," he said, jumping when Pauline punched a hole in the door. "We might have to start using the prod. Since she's your daughter, we've used it sparingly up to now. And she's so much stronger and larger than the others that it might not work the same."

"Start immediately," Alejandro said. "Everything in life worth having comes only through pain. Pauline will eventually understand her part in this and how she can be replaced if she doesn't cooperate.

I have more children who would gladly fill her role, but you're right. She's perfect."

"Are you sure?" he asked. "Some of the others died after a few shocks."

"Get started, and report any progress or lack thereof. I'm going to the site to do one more walk-through before we go back."

"Please be careful. I'll send the team in to start her training. To really be successful we need Oscar back. The scripture said there had to be two for the awakening to happen."

"If we can't, I'm sure we can use someone else," Alejandro said, looking at him in a way that made him move closer to the beast trying to claw its way out.

"Let me get started," he said and tried not to show fear. If Oscar wasn't found, Alejandro would awaken the dragon heart in him. "I've been too loyal for too long for that to happen," he said softly as he stood alone in the hallway. "I'm willing to give only so much."

Chapter Twenty-six

The plane carrying the group back from Cambodia to Costa Rica had reached the halfway point, and Kendal walked through the cabin and saw Oscar sleeping with his notes scattered around him. Rawney and Molly had taken a liking to him and the way he explained himself when it came to things he cared deeply about. She could see why he was a sought-after professor, but she didn't fully trust him. The coming days would be like a footrace, she thought, and whoever crossed the finish line first would impact Aphrodite's future. It would end either when the dragons were killed once they were discovered, taking the goddess with them, or they'd be slaves to Alejandro's ambition, or the dragons would get their freedom and their mother would decide their fate.

"What are you thinking so hard about?" Piper said, pressing against her back.

"Timing," she said, and turned around. After so many years of wandering the world alone, she was still awed at times when she looked at Piper's face. This beautiful woman would always be with her, and from the way she followed her into every situation, she'd always be a true partner.

"Any particular timing?" Piper asked as she ran her hands up her arms until they were behind her head.

"You remember our conversation about balance? Something always balances out everything in the world, no matter what it is." She kissed Piper's forehead and put her arms around Piper's waist. "Winning that battle usually comes after whatever is going to happen is unlocked. We know where, and we know what, but we don't know when. That's the most important thing."

"Lumas left enough clues so it's a matter of going through them, but I have a hunch." Piper pulled her head down and bit her bottom lip.

Any more talk about anything but getting Piper somewhere private fled her mind.

"Do you want to tell me before my brains head south?" she asked, backing away just an inch.

"There's a blood moon in two weeks. If a window to awaken them exists, it's then."

"So we've got two weeks?" Piper took her hand and led her to the back of the plane where the door to the small conference room was closed. Papers were scattered over the table's surface, but the most important things they'd found so far were locked away in the case Lenore had put them in. Lenore and Molly smiled and left the space, closing the door behind them. "Ah, am I going to blush later when we leave this room?"

Piper laughed and pushed her down on the sofa at the back. "We're here for research," Piper said as she sat on her lap.

"I would've done better in school if this is the kind of homework you had in mind," she said before Piper kissed her.

"Cool your jets for a minute, baby." Piper pulled the hair at the back of her head, breaking their lips apart. "I need you to crack a few seals before there's any kind of hanky-panky."

"Are you sure?" she asked as she ran her hand up Piper's leg to her thighs.

"Positive, and it's hard enough, so behave." The case of scrolls Piper had found in the Rodriguez house was next to them, so Piper opened it and unrolled the first one she reached for. "I have a feeling they're in the same language as the walls you were able to read." When she finished and saw the same type of symbols Kendal had deciphered before, she smiled. At least someone with them could read them. "We're in luck. It's ancient Egyptian, and I happen to have an ancient Egyptian on hand."

"Very funny." She glanced at the writing that brought back vivid memories of her father. "This one is a sort of blueprint of the site they called Ventanas Al Fuego. It lists all the pyramids they built as well as the chambers that were underground. Lumas and Rowen were there to oversee the construction, but they made one trip away from the site while the villagers were in the middle of building."

"Does it say where they went?" Piper reached for another scroll and handed it to her.

"Not in this one." She opened the second one and skimmed the lines for the subject of it. "We need to put these in some kind of order."

Piper smiled and stood with the case. "Do you mind if Lenore and Gran come back in?"

"You're a tease," she said, sitting at the table and opening another one.

"Teasing is not following through, baby, and believe me, I love the follow-through." Piper opened the door, and Lenore, Molly, Aishe, and Rawney entered, but Piper shook her head when Oscar started to follow them. "Not yet, Oscar."

"Why am I here, then?" he asked, sounding upset and angry.

"You're here because we allowed you to come," Kendal said, backing Piper up. "When we're done, we'll call you in, so go sit until then."

With all the scrolls open, Kendal moved them around until they were in the order they were meant to be, but not necessarily the order in which they were written. "I think Lumas wrote these three first," she said, pointing to the third, sixth, and ninth scrolls. "But she needed to add the information in the other eight."

"What do they say?" Lenore asked. "I know a lot of languages, but this one precedes a lot of us."

"The first three lay out a type of inventory of everything they built. If this is accurate, then everything there has been found." She moved back to the other eight. "These, though, tell the story of the fracture in the villagers. There were the true believers and those who doubted. That divide led to the events of the night your mother died, Rawney."

"Can you read it verbatim?" Molly asked.

She nodded and started on the first scroll.

I have chosen one of the village elders to learn the ways of the goddess. The seer's vision of the god's home is almost finished, so Rowen and I must complete one more task before I teach the ceremony of fire. When the flames call the gods near, both Rowen and I know it will be our end, but we have this fate for the good of the goddess and that of our family.

My family's book will soon find a resting place in time, and that will be the only clue I will add to the plans laid out. The key to anything that will undo what we have worked so hard for will not be found with the sleeping giants, but in a place where the faithful are true. If what the seer told us holds, my child will once again hold the greatest treasure our family has amassed.

To my child, remember that no matter the cost, the life of the goddess must be protected. The heart of everyone she created is part of her, and to let them die is to kill off the love the light needs to flourish. My faith in you is resolute, so by finding these, you will find all you need to finish what I know I cannot.

"That's it?" Rawney asked, touching the symbols she'd just read.

"That's the first one, but this one's written specially for you." Kendal touched the fourth one. "I would've liked to know your mother."

Rawney,

Remember above all else that you were loved. I think often of our last night together and the words we spoke. My and Rowen's travel across the water was hours away, but all I could concentrate on was your face and the future you were getting ready to begin without me there to guide you. When you finally get the chance to read the family book, go back to that night so you can understand the key to unlock the power you'll need to wake sleeping giants.

You are the key to so many things, but now as you prepare for the battle I couldn't finish, remember too your blood. You come from a long line of strong women who will stand with you no matter how much distance and time separate us. Speak the language of our people and ask for what you need. Believe me, you'll be heard.

To the slayer who will be with you, you were but a far-off dream when I was living, but your story will span generations, and your sword will be legendary. Your heart has touched so many, so let go of the pain caused by your sibling, and go forward with the woman who will share your every tomorrow. Keep my child in your sights, and take care of the evil that lurks in the shadows of the dark land where my sister and I will embrace our death.

This land and its people were the perfect place to hold the goddess's children, but as we started to finish their resting place, the doubters started to organize and become a loud voice. They didn't see what we were doing as a privilege, but as a way to gain power. Rowen's hope is that their interest will wane in time, but I know that all who come after them will continue the search. The power is too great to ignore.

Of all the things the Clan will face, these men scare me more than even the children of the night. They will stop at nothing to get what their forefathers sought, but as your gifts grow, so will theirs. Not many would sacrifice their children, but this is just one more thing that will get them closer to the gods that sleep under your feet.

Look to the trees, my daughter, and take care of the bite of the abomination the high priest of fire will bring to life. The beast will need a mate, so do all you can to keep that from happening.

My faith and my love, my child—both will be with you forever.

Piper had closed her eyes and thought of the woman she'd seen in her vision as Kendal read. The words ran over her like warm water, and she tried to absorb them, but the warnings were cementing her in the here and now. She glanced toward the door when the nanny brought Hali in for her feeding. That anyone would sacrifice their child to an existence of whatever those things were was beyond her.

"When we land we'll have to wait for the blood moon," Kendal said as Piper took the baby and simply held her for a minute. "Until then, we need to post some people around the site who won't be found as easily as we located the ones working for Garza. I know you all haven't had a chance to go through all the information we took out of his house, but I'm sure the most important pieces are with him."

"Do you think we're missing anything else?" Lenore asked.

"Until this is done, we won't have all the answers," Kendal said, and Piper nodded. "If the goddess was here guiding us for every step it might be easier, but that's not going to happen."

"She's not strong enough to do that, baby, but if she could, I believe she would've taken care of this herself." She opened her shirt, moved Hali into place, and smiled when she started suckling. "The gods aren't what they once were, but saving the dragons will ensure she doesn't completely disappear."

"Then let's keep an eye on the spot we're all interested in, and we'll follow whatever you and Rawney say when the time comes."

"Rawney, do you remember the last talk you had with Lumas?" she asked as she gently stroked the top of Hali's head. "I'm sure you've gone through your book, but I'm guessing it's still a mystery to you."

"I thought about that, but I'm not sure what she meant. That last night we didn't really have any deep conversations, and all I remember about it were the days that came after. Those lonely moments when all I could do was search for her and my aunt," Rawney said, her hand on the last scroll Kendal had read as if it was her mother's hand she was holding. "I'll have to go back in my memories and see if I can find what she's talking about."

Kendal took the baby to burp her, and they were left alone again. "We're going to have to do that fire ceremony, so I hope Rawney gets all the steps right."

"Why do you think so?" Kendal handed Hali back so she could switch sides.

"Of all the things Lumas could've shown me, it was that one moment in time. The dragons were placed in stone, and her life ended," she said, leaning against Kendal when she sat next to her. "I think it was a window as to how to undo what she did. All we need now is the words to break the spell she cast and the flames that will reignite the dragons."

"Sounds reasonable," Kendal said, putting her arm around her. "The only unknown is what Garza plans to do once we accomplish all that."

"Do you think he can undo the spell himself?" She remembered the large number of papers and books Kendal and the others had brought back with them after breaking into Garza's house. "What if we're too late?"

"The blood moon makes sense." Kendal kissed her temple. "All this weird shit isn't like fixing a tax mistake," she said, and Piper laughed. "It takes every aspect, from the moon to the words said in a certain sequence. The one person who placed the spell left the only way to undo it to her daughter, so he's waiting. Whatever he found comes after we finish the first part for him."

"What if we do nothing at all?"

Kendal shook her head. "The book has been found, so not doing it under our terms leaves us vulnerable to something like what happened with the Sea Serpent Sword. I'm not looking forward to it, but we're going to have to do this."

"The other thing that didn't make any sense is that the beast needs a mate." Hali finished and went to sleep after she burped again. "What do you think about that?"

"That was interesting, and Lumas had to know that Rawney would still be alive this far into the future, and if that's true, then she had to know what could harm her. There's no poison, weapon, or any other thing that can kill us, but there's always something out there that might change that. Your eyes are still green," Kendal said, raising Piper's head to make eye contact with her. "If the elixir had worked like always, they wouldn't be, but you're as immortal as I am."

"So those things we saw, they could kill us?" Piper placed the baby next to her so she could move closer to Kendal.

"Not necessarily death," Kendal said and kissed her. "But remember what happened to Julius right before he was about to unleash the dark side of the Sea Serpent Sword? One bite from Vadoma changed him, even with the elixir. That's how Lowe came to Convel, so that might be what Lumas meant."

"I love you, baby, but try not to turn into something I have to walk on a leash."

"I'll do my best, since skin-shedding seems like a pain in the ass."

Alejandro watched through the glass in the door as Pauline changed after Javier had jabbed her with a low-voltage prod in her human form. The way her body morphed into the messenger of the gods still fascinated him, especially since Pauline could do it over and over again, unlike the first girls they'd tried the incantation on. Once they'd gotten her the mate the archives said was needed, she would start to follow orders.

The loss of all his family's papers had angered him, but the most important of all the history they'd found through the generations had been with him. He was sure the people trying to stop him had found the missing piece his family had never come close to locating, and he was running out of time. Blood moons were rare but did happen every so many years, yet a blood moon that coincided with a total lunar eclipse on the same night the gods had been put to sleep wouldn't happen for another five hundred years. He didn't have that much time, so he'd pushed these people to finish what he wouldn't be able to.

"We've found another way to make the change happen when we need it to," one of his men said as Pauline fought to get out of the leash they'd locked her into. "She still doesn't understand commands, sir."

He stood in the window so Pauline could see him and waited. It took less than a minute for Pauline to zero in on him and pull hard enough to break the restraint and run toward the door. She hit it hard enough to break the glass and almost make it out of the room before the two men inside hit her with both probes hard enough to knock her out. He stepped forward to make sure she was still breathing and watched her transform back to her human form.

"You're the only one she reacts so violently to," Javier said, motioning for the men to put Pauline back in the bed and strap her to the railing. "If you try to match her with someone she won't accept, all this will be for nothing."

"What's your suggestion?" He entered the room and placed his hand on Pauline's forehead. Her skin was cool and slick. If he'd been born with some sense of paternal instinct, perhaps this would've gone smoother. The obligation of the Order, though, came before everything, so family wasn't something he ever bothered with. He'd done his duty by having children.

"I won't accept failure."

"Then we need to find someone who she's already given herself to," Javier said, standing aside as the medics started a fluid line to keep Pauline hydrated. "It has to be someone she's allowed inside."

"We need to figure out how to lure Oscar out. It's time he joins Pauline in the destiny they both must fulfill."

CHAPTER TWENTY-SEVEN

S o we still don't have the key to unlock the writing?" Oscar asked as the group gathered in the dining room after they'd landed to review what they had so far. "I thought the book we found would've been what we needed."

"The language they used on those slabs has so many interpretations that it could take years to decipher," Rawney said as she stared randomly at the pages in the second book.

"This place still doesn't make sense. It's typical Mayan design but with languages that don't belong here, not even now."

"So you've got no clue as to what Garza is looking for?" Kendal asked as she walked Hali around the room trying to get her to go to sleep. "What did he tell you about the dig site?" They had to have some idea of how close Garza was to the end game.

"You have to know Alejandro," Oscar said, staring at the pictures they'd pinned to the dining-room wall of the carved stone slabs. "He thinks he's some kind of royalty because of the Order of Fuego, and only he can have all the pieces of the puzzle they've found. He's powerful but also delusional."

Piper nodded as she stood and glanced back at Kendal. "I can't look at this stuff anymore, so maybe a fresh start in a few hours might help."

Vadoma followed them out and pointed to the office. "Can I talk to you two a moment?"

When they returned they found that Vadoma had upped her numbers significantly, but most of her followers never came close to the house. They seemed to be patrolling for something specific, and Kendal's guards took over during the day. She'd rarely seen fear in the face of someone who evoked so much fear herself, but Vadoma appeared frightened.

"Did something happen while we were gone?" Kendal asked, glancing down at Hali's sweet face now relaxed in sleep.

"We kept our eye on that place like you asked," Vadoma said, stopping when the nanny came in for the baby. "The older ones with me were even able to stay during the day since the site is so shrouded in shadow."

"Did you find something?" Piper asked.

"Not found something, saw something. Last night a big group of people came and loaded one of the altars with logs and performed some sort of ceremony that attracted some of the largest snakes I've ever seen. They were chanting and dancing, but I didn't recognize the language." Vadoma combed her hair back and exhaled. "They brought ten young girls with them, and when the fire reached its peak, these girls started to sway, and the guy in charge screamed something, and the snakes came for them."

"What do you mean, came for them?" Piper said, standing next to Kendal.

"They sacrificed them to the snakes, who dragged the girls off in their coils. Whatever those things were drained all ten of them of blood, and when the snakes were done, they returned to the ground." Vadoma's voice was low and seemed to have a trace of disgust. "You might not like what I am, but I don't hunt innocent children. What the hell is all this?"

"We've been alive long enough to know how some men gain power, and they'll do what it takes to wake the darkness that'll give it to them." She put her arm around Piper's shoulders and sat on the sofa. "Alejandro Garza isn't any different from any of the others we've seen in our lives."

"This is different, though," Vadoma said and sat close to them. "This is like the sword I helped you with, only the power seems greater somehow."

"Greater than Ares unleashing the power of the sword?" Piper asked, sounding curious.

"The world has become a more civilized place, Piper, but in the beginning those with knowledge tapped into things that created me,

Asra, and so many other creatures. Some of us are still here." Vadoma pointed to herself and to Kendal. "In time, man lost the quest that only magic could unleash, so it went dormant. The problem is, it didn't die, and in all this time it's grown stronger. What I saw last night means, like the sword, in the wrong hands that kind of power can change a balance all of us together might not be able to stop."

"She's right," Convel said, coming in with Lowe. "We need to work together, because even with our gifts, whatever's buried there, aside from what you're looking for, can hurt every single one of us."

"You think something else is buried there?" Piper asked.

"Those things aren't the work of the goddess, and since Lumas was gone, maybe something came after what she did. But whatever that was, only Garza knows," Convel said. "I don't know what happened with the sword, but I'm convinced there's more there than we know. Even a goddess can't see everything, especially if she's not looking."

"True," she said.

"What do you mean?" Piper asked.

"Aphrodite tasked Lumas and Rowen to come here to put the dragons somewhere safe, so once that was done, no one had any reason to think of this place again," she said, and the others agreed. "If she wasn't paying attention, someone or something might've balanced the power structure here so that it holds more than the noble creatures she made."

"Now imagine that power taking over the dragons, if you're able to wake them," Convel said. "By the time we unite to keep the balance we have, it'll be too late."

"So do we let them lie?" Piper asked.

"We wake them and give them back to their mother. Only the goddess can put them out of the reach of men like Garza," Convel said.

"Then Rawney has to remember," she said, not happy they had so little time left.

"Those snakes you saw," Piper said to Vadoma. "Do you think they're like you?"

"Vampires, you mean?"

Piper nodded.

"They certainly appeared to be, but I'm a bit better looking."

❖

Javier put on the robes that were an exact copy of the ones first worn by the priest of the order and started slowly saying the words of the spell he needed. His confidence had grown after their fire ceremony, during which the spirits had answered him. It took an hour but finally the stillness was broken by more than his voice when a car door slammed in the distance.

"He's here, master," one of his assistants said.

"Come." He closed the book of the order and smiled. "Your mate awaits you."

Oscar appeared dazed and sleep-walking, but he moved closer and lay down on the stone altar Alejandro had built outside close to the edge of his yard. One of the guards placed a strong leash around Oscar's neck and nodded to Javier.

He flipped to the right page and started the passages that would deliver what Alejandro wanted. After he finished, Oscar's clothes started to tear as his transformation began, and when it was done, he was even larger than Pauline in size, but that wasn't the only difference. His head was hooded like a cobra's, and he was much more aggressive.

A loud noise came from the house, and he smiled when he realized it was Pauline. She'd obviously transformed when Oscar did, so they were ready.

"Bring him. It's time to finish."

Kendal and Piper were alone in their room with the balcony doors open after the house had gone quiet, so it was easy to hear the sudden screech that pierced the night air. It sounded painful and mournful, but also joyful when another higher-pitched sound answered whatever it was. Kendal got up and stared into the night as all the animals around them became agitated.

The same noise happened again, and again it was answered, but this time it seemed to fill the air around them with a kind of energy that made the part of Piper that craved Kendal come to life. It reminded her of the first time they'd touched the Sea Serpent Sword together, making her skin hot and her sex wet.

"Baby," she said as Kendal turned around and gave her an almost predatory look. The intensity made her take her pants off and move closer to Kendal. All Kendal did was hold on to the door when she knelt and unbuckled her pants. "I need to taste you."

She didn't have to wait to see if Kendal was interested, since she was wet, hard, and ready for her touch. Kendal grabbed the back of her head and pressed her face between her legs, needing this as much as she wanted to do it, and the muscles in her thighs tightened as she came much too fast for both of them.

"Fuck," Kendal said as she reached down and picked her up. In a few quick steps she had her on the bed and ripped her shirt open as if she couldn't wait to touch every inch of her skin, but not as much as she needed her to. Without another word, Kendal put her mouth on her clit and slammed two fingers inside, making her hips shoot up.

"Oh…oh my God," she said as Kendal took her fingers almost all the way out and slammed them in again. "Shit," she said, grabbing two fistfuls of Kendal's thick hair and pressing her closer. It was like she might rattle apart if she didn't come. "Don't stop, baby," she said, so out of breath she had to suck in some air. "Ah," she screamed at the end and, like Kendal, came way too fast.

That didn't matter, though, because they were both ready to go again as soon as Kendal crawled up and kissed her, and she put her hand between her legs. "If I get pregnant again," she said and smiled when she slid her fingers along Kendal's hard clit, "I don't give a damn. All I need right now is for you to make me come, but let's slow it down a little."

It took two more times before the lustful haze that had come over them lifted. "I don't know what the hell that was, but good Lord," Kendal said, rolling over onto her back and taking her with her.

"If it has to do with all this, then we finally got some good out of it, and it sounds like we're not the only ones," she said and laughed when the very distinctive sounds of lovemaking echoed around the house. "Come on. We don't want them to think you're a slacker."

Kendal moved quickly and bit down on one of her nipples, making her squeal before she began to moan. "You mentioned something about slacking?"

CHAPTER TWENTY-EIGHT

A week later Kendal waited at the small airport close to the house while the private plane she owned but seldom used came to a stop. She'd debated whether to include Hillary in what came next, but the planner part of her personality thought it'd be wise to have someone, while incredibly annoying, who loved Piper watching out for her in case this was harder and more impossible than she thought.

"I got all the information on Alejandro Garza you asked for," Hill said, handing her a folder as the crew took care of her luggage. "Thanks for calling for me, though I'm surprised you did."

"I'm a firm believer in everyone getting a second chance." She skimmed the pages. "Just remember that you should've explored any chance with Piper years ago. She's settled now, and if you keep pushing—"

"You'll kick my ass."

She laughed and shook her head. "My wife is more than capable of that on her own, but I do think she'll cut you out of her life if you can't accept her happiness. Do you really want to lose a friend you truly love?"

"No, I don't, and I promise I'll do what I can to keep her safe through whatever this is." Hill climbed into the passenger side of the Jeep and couldn't quite maintain eye contact. "And whatever this is seems to be as strange as what happened in London. I'm not sure I didn't dream all that up, but I'm scared for her."

"Hill, not everything in life is easy to explain, but with a little imagination, you can reach a place where all the stories and fables you've heard throughout your life have some merit to them." The road was worse after the torrential rain that morning, so she took it slow. "All those things you saw usually stay hidden in the shadows, unless you're unlucky enough to run into one of them, and then people like me try to keep the balance."

"So you're a vampire hunter like in the movies?" Hill said and nervously laughed.

"Something like that, when I'm not buying businesses and starting a family. If you can't wrap your head around that, I'll still hire you, but you can stick to the normal side of my business."

"Hopefully, one day you'll tell me everything I need to know to do this job effectively, but I'm not going anywhere. I'm sure you'll be able to take care of Piper and Hali, but it won't hurt to have a backup." She glanced back at the box that had been delivered to Oakgrove before she'd left. "There was no return address, but that arrived for you before I took off late last night."

Hill followed her to the office and greeted Piper before handing over all her mail from the shipyard and the house. The baby was lying on a blanket under an activity toy Molly had gotten her and seemed fascinated by all the multicolored things hanging down from it. Everything seemed so normal, but hell was coming, so she took the time to enjoy these moments.

She used her pocketknife to rip open the large box, inside finding what appeared to be the equivalent of modern-day armor with dragons stamped into the breastplates.

Warrior,
    For your upcoming battles, and so you know you're not alone.

She handed the note to Piper and kissed her before heading out to do sword drills. After that strange night, they'd been searching for Oscar for days, since he'd effectively disappeared without any of her or Vadoma's people noticing anything. It was like he was at his desk one second and gone the next. She'd broken a sweat after a few minutes and stopped when she noticed Rolla and Bruik watching her.

"Has Piper had any more visions?" Rolla asked after he embraced her.

"Not since we retrieved the book for Rawney. She's sensing that something will happen in two days when the blood moon is in eclipse." She sheathed the sword and followed them to the large deck out back, where one of the servants had placed a pitcher of wine on the table. "Rawney hasn't figured out how to unlock the book, so all this might be for nothing."

"Can Garza finish this?" Rolla asked, and she and Bruik shook their heads.

"Given the way the spell was cast, he needs Lumas's words to undo it. She was smart in that you need Rawney to make it work, and even she can't remember what she needs," she said, surprised that Rolla had come at all. He was the kind of leader who liked to read about these kinds of things once they were done. "The only thing that worries me is Oscar Petchel. We didn't share a lot with him, but he knows enough to hurt us if he's still working for Garza."

"With so little time, will Rawney come through?" Rolla poured them all a glass and sat back as if enjoying the view.

"Piper plans to sit with her later today and see if she can go back with her. What she needs to understand about the book is trapped in one moment in her distant past, which was followed by extreme grief." She watched Morgaine and Charlie head out to spar, and Piper followed, holding Rawney's hand. "Let's see if some quiet and Piper's soothing presence knocks something loose."

She left Rolla to Bruik and followed Piper and Rawney down to the spot they'd enjoyed when they first arrived. "Mind if I join you?"

"I'm glad you're here," Rawney said as they sat so they all faced each other, close enough to hold hands. "My mother mentioned you in that scroll, so I think you belong here."

"I thought the same thing," Piper said. "When I first remembered the gift that the elixir brought out of the depths of my mind, I didn't know how to process what was happening to me." Piper spoke as if she were floating away. "Bruik told me that it was something to embrace, and to do it justice, I had to let go of what tethers me to the here and now."

"I want to go back," Rawney said, and Kendal shook her head, not wanting anything to interfere with Piper's concentration.

"I know you do, so take my hand and let's go. Your mother's waiting."

❖

Romanian Countryside, 6148 BC

"How?" Rawney asked as they entered the campsite circled by wagons, a roaring fire at the center, and music from different spots. Everything was happening around Piper and Rawney, but it was like everyone stared right through them.

"It's never the same," Piper said, not letting go of her hand. "Sometimes they call me back and know I'm there, and sometimes I go back to see what I need to move forward."

"Over there." Rawney pointed to the good-sized tent and walked quickly, as if wanting to see her mother in more than just her memories.

"But when, Mama?" A much-younger Rawney asked the question as she ran her fingers over the thick leather that bound their family book. "I'm almost of age."

"You'll know the right time, so for now we made you this," Lumas said, holding the book Rawney still had in her possession. "It has almost everything in it, and the rest of what you need will come much later."

"Don't you trust me?" Rawney asked, and her aunt Rowen shook her by the shoulders before kissing her forehead.

"Don't be in such a rush, child. You'll wield the family power just fine until the time is right, so quit your complaining and listen to your mother," Rowen said.

Lumas stood next to a large pot and stirred the stew she'd worked on all afternoon, seeming to enjoy the conversation among the three of them. "Come before the rest of the family gets here." She sat on the cushions piled on the rug and patted her lap so Rawney would put her head down. Once she did, Lumas started running her fingers through her hair. "Do you promise you'll always remember tonight?"

"I always remember all the nights with you, Mama."

"Tonight you got your book, but you have to remember that the key to everything is your family. Remember well the women who worked to put all that in those pages." Lumas lifted one of her hands and kissed it. "You'll have so much more time than we did to add to yours, but you'll need the family to read mine and Rowen's. We've shared one since we were so close in age, and ours is almost complete."

"What are you talking about? You have plenty of time to add to yours and mine."

Rowen scooped out a bowl of stew and added something from the pouch at her side before handing it to Rawney. "Eat, child, so you can enjoy the rest of the night."

Rawney ate until the bowl was empty, and it fell from her hand not long after. When she woke, the rest of the women in her family had arrived, and she had no memory of what had happened during her conversation with her mother and her aunt.

"You're ready now, child," Rowen said as she turned and looked right at Rawney and Piper.

"The blood moon comes only to hide its face," Lumas said and took Rawney's free hand. "It's the window you need to awaken what we had to put to slumber."

"Oh, Mama, I've missed you so much," Rawney said, trying to speak through her tears.

"We have faithfully watched over you, and I'm proud it was you who carried out our work. I love you, and I hope you've forgiven us both for leaving you and taking part of your memory with us." Lumas reached up and dried her tears. "I had to make sure the awakening didn't happen until you were ready to face what must be."

"Face what?" Kendal asked, and her voice surprised both Rawney and Piper.

"You've fought bravely and well for so long, slayer, but this enemy is blessed by the gods as well. He wants the power of the dragons, and if he can get them to do his bidding, he'll tip the balance you work so hard to maintain. What lives in the shadows must remain in the shadows."

"And these beasts he's created?" Piper asked.

"The bite won't kill you, but the poison will run savagely through you enough that it will take weeks to heal. By then, it will be too late, and only the power of the book will give the goddess back what she so desires." Lumas let Rawney go for a moment and placed her hands on Kendal's chest. "You serve the goddess as well as we have, so wield your sword with all the strength you possess, and protect what's not only precious to you, but to me as well."

"Your child is safe with me."

"I know, so go back and remember your promises." Lumas turned to Rawney. "We'll be with you through this, and when it's done, we'll see each other again."

"When?" Rawney asked clutching her mother's hand.

"You'll understand eventually, but for now you must go. It's never a good thing to dwell too long in the past."

❖

"Are you sure?" Kendal asked as she finished putting on the armor Aphrodite had sent. Piper's had the same design as hers, but the others were all stamped with dragons on the chest, while not the same one. "She's had two days to figure it out."

"Again, sweetheart, cryptic clues aren't always the easiest to decipher when you're under a lot of pressure." Piper raised her arms so Kendal could finish dressing her and sighed. "I feel a little ridiculous in this."

"If a big creepy snake with feet comes running at you, this will come in handy," she said as she finished the straps. "Just remember to stick to me and keep the fangs away from this cute face."

"Trust me. I'm not losing sight of you."

They went downstairs holding hands a few hours before sunset and nodded toward Convel and Lowe, who were waiting for them at the landing. "There's something weird in the air," Convel said.

"Like what?" she asked, knowing Convel's senses were stronger than any of theirs, even in her human form.

"Remember the other night?" Lowe asked, and all of them nodded quickly, not needing to expand on the question. "Something like that, only intensified. Whatever happened to cause that reaction the other night has only grown stronger in the last couple of days. It's like a call to that wild part we all have, no matter if you're a were or not."

"That's exactly right," Rawney said as she motioned them down. "A blood moon can mean so many things, but this time it seems to be drawing out a more animalistic nature in everything around here. I think it's a call to the dragons to awaken."

"Have you figured out what your mother meant?" Kendal asked, and Piper elbowed her in the ribs.

"Not yet, but I have faith," Rawney said with a smile as Aishe nodded. "My mother has never let me down."

"Let's hope that holds tonight," Vadoma said from the center of the room, as if staying away from the windows. "We've found more of

Ora's sycophants close to the house and eliminated them, so I've told my people to stay close to you. If things get frenzied, try not to kill any of them."

"How will we tell them apart?" Piper asked.

"They'll be the ones not trying to kill you," Vadoma said drolly. "I'm with the fleabags, though. Something's off about this place."

"Call me a fleabag one more time," Convel said.

"Calm down. We're all on the same side." Vadoma smiled wide enough to show off her fangs. "Those things we saw, they're like a hybrid of both of us—a were but also a vampire. If this guy makes enough of them, there won't be enough humans to go around, especially if they're non-thinking weres with an unstoppable thirst."

"If you see any of them, go for the head," Kendal said, strapping her sword to her back. "Unlike Vadoma and her people, beheading will kill them, but do your best not to get bitten. It will slow you down enough to take you out of the fight for weeks."

"So what's your plan?" Aishe asked, wearing the same colorful outfit as Rawney.

"From what Vadoma's people said, the altars are already loaded with wood for the fire ceremony, so when the moon is almost at its peak, we're going to light them." She put on the gloves and opened and closed her hands to seat them correctly. "If you can decipher the book, Piper and I will wait with you on the main pyramid, because I'm guessing the first to wake up will be Drakon and Peto."

"And then?" Rawney asked.

"And then we'll see," she said as the herd of horses was brought around.

"I hate surprises," Piper said as Convel and Lowe transformed to head out first.

"Tonight's not going to be a lot of fun, then."

Hill was waiting for them in the office and didn't say anything as they entered, appearing, she figured, like mythical creatures from a long-ago past. "Do you need me to do anything?" Hill asked, her eyes growing wider by the second.

"I want you to stay here with Mac and Molly to keep an eye on the baby. There are people here who'd like to harm her because she's mine and Piper's, so if they manage to get in the house, use this," Kendal said, holding a sword out to her. "Aim for the chest, and don't get freaked out by what happens if you manage to hit your target. I'm counting on you to keep Hali safe."

"You can trust me," Hill said, holding the scabbard with two hands.

"You can trust all of us to do everything to keep Hali safe," Mac said and hugged both of them, followed by Molly. "My family has suffered enough because of the bastards. I won't allow it to happen again."

"Piper, please, don't leave Kendal's side," Molly said.

"Not in this or any lifetime, Gran. We love you, but it's time to go."

CHAPTER TWENTY-NINE

The small cauldron of fire illuminated the bugs flying around it, but it also highlighted Kendal's tall form in her armor. The almost-black material tinged with maroon fit her well and made it easy for Piper to imagine her in all the lifetimes she'd lived as a soldier. Kendal was like a knight in shining armor who always stood up for what was right. Piper sensed they were surrounded not only by friends, but those who meant them harm, so she moved closer to Kendal and took her hand.

"You know, building tugs was never this intriguing," she said, and Kendal chuckled. "You think Hali and my grandparents are okay?"

"I never thought I'd say this, but I trust Vadoma's people to protect them. And if they make it through that line of defense, they'll run into something equally terrifying."

"Are you going to share?"

"Tala sent some more of her soldiers down but kept quiet about it until we just left. Not to mention your grandparents and Hill are there as well. I think Mac is dying to try out that sword I left with him, but hopefully he'll just get to practice the moves I showed him." Kendal glanced at Rawney and Aishe as they both stood with their eyes closed but their lips moving. "Five more minutes, and then we have to start."

"Did you bring what I asked for?" Piper asked, and Kendal nodded.

"Rawney," Kendal said, and the witch opened her eyes. "We're almost ready, but you have to know about one more vision Piper had."

"What? Tell me if it's something that could help me remember."

Charlie climbed the steps of the pyramid with the two urns they'd found with the first book. "Like Drakon, they've waited long enough."

"No. It's all I have left of them," Rawney said, her eyes filling with tears.

"Remember what she said when we went back. She and Rowen

will be with you always, so these are meaningless. The truth is in the ashes of the past, Rawney, but they also hold power over us now."

Kendal moved to the cauldron and lit the first arrow, which she shot into the farthest woodpile, lighting it. She kept at it until all seven of them were burning, and Charlie moved back down as the flames rose higher. He looked toward Piper, who held up her hand, remembering the night she'd come here with Lumas. She turned and glanced at the moon tinted in a warm red glow. Seeing the eclipse begin just at the bottom edge, she pointed to Charlie and screamed, "Now."

Charlie dumped both urns into the spot that had created the ashes so long ago, and the flames turned from gold to a deep red before the forms of Lumas, Rowen, and a few other women she didn't recognize floated above them. The sight of them seemed to trigger something in Rawney's mind, because she opened the book they'd found with the ashes.

"In the name of all the women in my line, Lumas, Rowen," Rawney said, naming all the women she'd been taught in her childhood as the founders of their family and the wielders of the power of their family book. That was the spell that broke the chain in her mind that had kept her from understanding the words on the pages. Her heritage and her inheritance were finally all hers.

Piper remembered the language that followed as the same Lumas had used but still didn't understand it. After three pages, the moon had disappeared completely, and the ground beneath them started to rumble. Kendal hung on to her. "Draw your sword, baby. They're coming," she said, and Kendal instantly did as she asked.

She couldn't see them yet, but she knew they were there and waiting, like they had the night Lumas and Rowen had stood here. In those first moments of freedom, the Order of Fuego had to pounce on their opportunity to finish what Lumas had stolen from them. It was her only explanation for being there at the precise moment they were cemented in stone.

Rawney lifted her hands and screamed "a trezi" three times.

"Awaken," Kendal said as she stood in front of Piper with her sword at the ready.

"Behind you, love," she said, grabbing the Sea Serpent Sword Kendal had given her.

Four of the creatures made it easily up the back of the pyramid, their mouths open as if ready to strike. Kendal moved quickly toward the closest one and sliced through the neck like she was returning a backhand in tennis. The next one hissed and made a strange noise as the head fell down the steep slope of stone. "Just hold it out in front of you to keep them away," Kendal yelled as she repeated the motion. One was trying to get to Rawney, so Piper came down hard, surprised the head came right off.

"Don't think about it," Kendal said as if reading her mind.

The hideous thing trying to hurt Rawney was actually a young woman who'd had no choice in her creation, and she'd just killed her. She'd never been a violent person, so murder had never crossed her mind, but that wasn't what this was, so Piper nodded as the pyramid started to really shake. The heads at the bottom of the steps broke away from the structure, and as they soared higher, new bodies seemed to materialize out of the fire's smoke.

The flap of Drakon's wings fanned the flames, and he roared as if embracing his freedom, the smaller dragon at his side answering his call. Like in her vision, he rose and came to rest on the top of the pyramid and lowered his head to Piper. She took her attention off Kendal for a moment to stare into Drakon's face, finding what she assumed to be gratitude, but from the corner of her eye, she saw Kendal fly off the platform, hit by the large reptile body that had dodged her sword.

In Kendal's place stood a smallish man with what appeared to be a cobra with feet, and its size was frightening. Whatever it was seemed to be protecting the man, who also held a book, and another man coming up behind him. Below them, everyone with them was fighting off the large number of creatures and snakes that had come from the jungle, so she was alone with Rawney and Aishe.

"From the time of my grandfathers, we have looked over you," the man she guessed was Alejandro Garza said loudly, and Drakon turned from her and straightened to his full height. His mouth opened, and it looked like he was about to rain fire down on Garza, but he paused. "You belong to me and the fire that burns in me." He said the rest in another strange language, and the large dragon stopped and turned, now listening to the grunting noises coming from the thing next to Garza. Piper turned when she heard something behind her and stepped closer to Rawney and Aishe when she saw the two large snakes slithering up the steps.

Drakon roared again, and Peto took to the air while the other pyramids started to come to life as well. Piper stepped back when suddenly the empty chambers along the avenue of pyramids burst open with dozens of dragons who also flew toward the skies to circle the area. Drakon growled, and one of the snakes slithered closer, seeming to grow as it coiled around the dragon's body and bit right into the middle of his abdomen.

"Kill them all," Garza yelled, and Drakon shot a stream of fire down the structure toward where Kendal and her attacker had fallen.

"No," Piper yelled, and Drakon turned toward her next. His mouth opened and Garza laughed, but the big head came down again to stare at her. "You know me," she said as the snake continued to bite, making the wound larger for some reason, and she suddenly realized what it was trying to do when it reared back and tried to shove its head in the wound. "Rawney, finish," she said over the chaos.

"Kill her," Garza screamed again, and the creature next to him made more noise. Whatever it was made Drakon shake his head. "Obey me or die," Garza said, picking up the sword Kendal had dropped in her fall. The large dragon didn't seem to move as Garza moved closer, seemingly intent on driving the sword into his chest as the snake started to disappear inside.

"Rawney," Piper said, wanting to stop this. If Drakon died, she doubted Aphrodite would survive.

As the sword went up, Morgaine stopped it, and sparks flew from the blades. The man with Garza ran up to help, and the creature must've mistaken it as an attack on his master and sank his fangs into the man's throat and didn't let go until every drop of blood seemed to drain from his body. While it was engaged in the feeding, Piper stabbed it through the chest and stepped back in case it disengaged and came after her.

She moved toward the stairs but didn't take her eyes off the creature, even though she could hear something or someone running up the steps behind her. The thing made another noise that was almost a howl and then started to change in what seemed like a painful process. When it was done, Oscar Petchel lay before her, clutching the wound in his chest.

Kendal passed her and headed toward Garza as if to get her sword back, even though her side was bleeding. He lifted the weapon and held it out in front of him, but she kicked it out of his hand and punched the middle of his face. "Obey me," he yelled again, but the dragons continued to circle.

Drakon seemed to listen and was starting to turn to attack Kendal, so she turned and sheathed her sword to face the dragon unarmed. Piper realized what she was doing, so she tried her best to keep his attention on her as Kendal started jerking on the snake's thick body to pull it out.

"If it gets all the way in, I think whatever power Garza has will take hold," Kendal yelled as she started to make progress. "If he controls the pack leader, he controls them all."

Alejandro picked up his book and glanced down at it as Kendal continued her tug-of-war, then started speaking in the foreign language. He spoke faster as Kendal neared the head, finally drawing her sword. The passage he said again sounded like he was repeating himself, so he ran toward Kendal as she raised her sword to behead the night god he and his family had worshipped. The snakes needed the dragon bodies to gain the power they needed to control humanity.

"No," he said as Kendal's sword came down and severed the thick, powerful body from the head.

Kendal pulled it out completely and threw it off the platform, ignoring Alejandro as the other snake made ready to take the dead one's place. "Kendal," Piper said loudly as Alejandro got close with a dagger in his hand. Kendal moved aside at the last minute when the thing that had knocked her off the platform came running up and sank its fangs into Garza.

The expression on his face was one of shock and anger, and the last thing he uttered was "Pauline."

The fight raged on for a while longer, but eventually the bodies of dead girls littered the ground, along with the fathers who'd sacrificed them to Garza's dark god. Pauline had been the only one who'd shifted back to human form and held the wounded Oscar to her chest. Kendal wasn't sure how many of Ora's minions were left, but Convel and Lowe had considerably thinned their numbers as Vadoma fought with them against Garza's forces.

What awed her was the dragons now sitting on the pyramids

around them and the avenue below them. Lumas's spell had made use of the chambers, but their purpose wasn't revealed until Rawney set them free.

Morgaine, Lenore, and Charlie joined them on the main pyramid, and Kendal held her sword up. "To a victory well fought," she said, and Morgaine slammed her sword against hers, followed by Charlie. The three of them together sounded like a loud bell had been rung, and the dragons lowered their heads as Aphrodite appeared.

"Thank you all for giving me back a piece of myself," Aphrodite said, caressing Drakon's head when he bowed to her. "They will be safe with me from this day forward." She snapped her fingers, and all but Drakon disappeared. "I should've taken them all those years ago, but I allowed myself to be convinced they'd be better off here."

"I can see now why they've been revered through time," Kendal said, holding her hand up, and Drakon pressed his nose against it. "They're beautiful."

"They're like you, my dragon warrior," Aphrodite said and smiled. "Noble of heart and loving of their families. I created them to show man that no matter what the outward appearance, love comes in all forms if you only let it flourish."

"What were those things?" Morgaine asked, pointing to the body of the large snake Kendal had pulled from Drakon's abdomen.

"That's what Garza's ancestors created with the help of some dark force. It might've been Ares or some other entity that exists to try to plunge the world into darkness of its own making." Aphrodite glanced out at the carnage below them. "This kind of thing is their idea of heaven, and Garza tried to up their power by taking over my dragons' bodies like he did with all those girls."

"I'm glad we stopped him, so keep them safe," Piper said, accepting Aphrodite's hug.

"I will," the goddess said, turning toward Rawney. "And you, I have no words to thank you. More than most, your family has sacrificed for me, and I don't want you to think I don't appreciate it."

"My mother and aunt did what they thought was right, and I'd like to believe I would do the same thing had you asked me."

"I know you would, so that kind of loyalty should be rewarded. Lumas knew what would happen the night she died here, but also what would come of the night her child undid her work." Aphrodite clapped her hands together loudly and looked down to the fire. "Come."

They all watched in awe as Lumas and Rowen stepped from the flames and started up the stairs. "Mama," Rawney said, and ran to meet her halfway.

"Rolla knows my wishes, so enjoy the life you'll have together. It's been too long, but your family is lost to you no more." Aphrodite smiled at the touching reunion, then turned to Pauline and Oscar. "Oscar, you've come to this place by force, so I remove the curse that Alejandro placed upon you," she said, placing her hand on his forehead and reaching down his body. When she closed her eyes, a large wound appeared on his abdomen, and the goddess reached in and pulled out a snake, much like Kendal had done with Drakon.

Oscar yelled in agony and slumped against Pauline when Aphrodite was done, and after she touched his head his injuries disappeared. "Thank you," he said, moving to kneel and kiss her feet. "Thank you," he repeated, crying now as if relieved he'd be freed.

"You, though," Aphrodite said to Pauline.

"I was raised to continue my father's work, but the bastard betrayed me despite my loyalty," Pauline said as she stood, and Oscar moved farther away from her. "I didn't know anything else."

"You knew he killed your mother, yet you stayed with him," Piper said, and Oscar nodded.

"How do you know that?" Pauline asked.

"That's not important since it's true," Aphrodite said. "Asra, I'll leave her fate to you."

"Wait, that's not fair," Pauline said, suddenly trying to hide her nudity.

"I'm not a killer, but you need to leave here and never come back. If you ever think of anything to do with the Order of Fuego, you'll end up like your father," Kendal said.

Aphrodite touched Pauline's forehead as well, which made her drop to her knees. "I want nothing from this night to keep you from that promise, so forget about what your father did to you." It didn't take long for Aphrodite to pull the snake out as she'd done with Oscar, but this time she left the scar as a reminder of her warning.

"You continue to prove to me how well I've chosen." Aphrodite kissed Kendal's cheek first, then Piper's. "Go home to your child and your family. This isn't the end of your battles, but I promise peace for a while." She touched Kendal's arm and healed the gash she'd received when she'd fallen. "You have my gratitude, and that of my family, for stopping the worst from happening."

"I'll enjoy the peace, but remember that I'm happy to serve you. Thank you, though, for everything," Kendal said, opening her arms to Piper.

"You can thank me by taking your wife on a honeymoon," she said as Drakon lowered his head again so Aphrodite could climb aboard. "Remember, I am the goddess of love despite the last few things that have come back to haunt me."

"Don't worry. We won't forget," Piper said and waved as they rose. "If I have to worship something else aside from Kendal's body, it might as well be you."

"I'm riding a fire-breathing dragon, sweet pea," Aphrodite said and laughed. "You might want to keep the sarcasm to a minimum."

CHAPTER THIRTY

I can't believe it took us a year to plan this," Piper said as Kendal drove through the Greek countryside in the convertible Piper had fallen in love with at the airport. "But it's been a nice year."

"It sure has, and it didn't take me this long because we had other things to do," Kendal said, downshifting as they entered the small town. "It's just that neither of us wanted to leave Hali before now, but I'm sure she's fine with her grandparents and numerous godparents, including the two wolves who are our neighbors now. Not to mention the occasional vampire sitter."

"That's only because Vadoma is so afraid of anything happening to her it's making her nuts. She figures it's easier to keep an eye on Hali than it is to take a stake through the heart."

"I'm not upset about that, since she put a big warning label to every vampire in the world when it comes to Hali and Ana, so that's one less thing to worry about."

Piper nodded as she glanced around as if enjoying the beautiful views. "It's nice that Convel went home and reunited with her family. If I'm right, Hali and Ana might have some new playmates soon."

"You know I love babies," Kendal said as she parked and took the flowers and basket of fruit from the trunk, then held her hand out to Piper. "But right now I have a surprise for you."

They had to climb a bit, but after a few hundred yards the ruins started to come into view. "Tell me nothing dangerous is buried here."

"It's actually a temple built for the worship of Aphrodite," Kendal said, entering the ancient building and laying the flowers and fruit on the altar. "I remember when this place was full of worshippers. They were so devoted and rightfully so." She took Piper's hand when they both knelt and bowed their heads, enjoying the solitude and quiet.

When they raised their heads, the fruit Kendal had put down had disappeared, and a box sat in its place. Piper stood and walked closer, smiling at the dragon carved into the top. When she opened it she saw four orbs inside with a note.

You asked, and you should receive that reward when you're ready.

She handed the note to Kendal, who glanced at it. "Is that what I think it is?" The orbs in the box were like the one that had been trapped in the Sea Serpent Sword that had resulted in Hali's birth. Aphrodite had blessed them with four more children if they chose to use them.

"You think you're ready for more diapers, warrior?" Piper asked, and she heard someone laughing behind her.

"Of all the things you've ever blessed me with, children will be the most precious," Kendal said, smiling as she dropped back to her knees. "I'll be forever your dedicated follower because of so many things, but Piper and Hali are the most important."

"I know, and for every one of those you use, another of my children will come into the world. It's the one way to keep them safe and for the pieces of my heart I've given freely to flourish in the love I've always had for them."

"Will they mind losing their wings?" Piper said, standing with her hand on Kendal's shoulder.

"There's more than one way to take flight, and having the love of parents who'll give you everything is the best way to do that." Aphrodite placed her hands on their heads and whispered a prayer. "For now, though, enjoy the love you've found and the honeymoon that's been too long in coming."

"Thanks for these," Piper said, holding the box.

"You belong to her, but both of you will always belong to me and be under my protection."

"Don't worry. I'll love her as long as there are tomorrows for us."

"Then Lenore will have plenty of books to add to the archives," Aphrodite said and waved before she disappeared in a puff of smoke.

"Take me home, baby," she said to Kendal.

"Home to New Orleans?"

"Home will always be here," she said, placing her hand over

Kendal's heart. "But right now I'm interested in celebrating what you make me feel in places a little south of that."

"You have a one-track mind," Kendal said, picking her up and carrying her out. "And that's something to give thanks for."

"You bring out the hedonist in me, and I love you for that and so much more."

"I love you too, and I'm looking forward to emptying that box."

The box warmed in Piper's hand, but she forgot everything as Kendal kissed her. The goddess was right that they had many more battles to fight, but the story they'd be most remembered for was the love they shared. That was a tale she didn't want to end.

With Kendal at her side, it never would.

About the Author

Ali Vali is the author of the long-running Cain Casey Devil series and the Genesis Clan Forces series, as well as numerous standalone romances including two Lambda Literary Award finalists, *Calling the Dead* and *Love Match*, and her 2017 release, *Beauty and the Boss*. Ali also has a novella in the collection *Girls with Guns*.

Originally from Cuba, Ali has retained much of her family's traditions and language and uses them frequently in her stories. Having her father read her stories and poetry before bed every night as a child infused her with a love of reading, which she carries till today. Ali currently lives outside New Orleans, Louisiana, and she has discovered that living in Louisiana provides plenty of material to draw from in creating her novels and short stories.